We Must Not
Think of Ourselves

We Must Not Think of Ourselves

a novel

LAUREN GRODSTEIN

ALGONQUIN BOOKS
OF CHAPEL HILL 2023

Published by
ALGONQUIN BOOKS OF CHAPEL HILL
Post Office Box 2225
Chapel Hill, North Carolina 27515-2225

an imprint of Workman Publishing
a division of Hachette Book Group, Inc.
1290 Avenue of the Americas,
New York, NY 10104

Printed in the United States of America.
Design by Steve Godwin.

The publisher is not responsible for websites (or their content)
that are not owned by the publisher.

This is a work of fiction. While, as in all fiction, the literary perceptions and
insights are based on experience, all names, characters, places, and incidents
either are products of the author's imagination or are used ficticiously.

Library of Congress Cataloging-in-Publication Data
Names: Grodstein, Lauren, author.
Title: We must not think of ourselves : a novel / Lauren Grodstein.
Description: First edition. | Chapel Hill, North Carolina :
Algonquin Books of Chapel Hill, 2023. |
Identifiers: LCCN 2023005844 | ISBN 9781643752341 (hardcover) |
ISBN 9781643755298 (ebook)
Subjects: LCSH: Jews—Poland—Warsaw—Fiction. | Getto warszawskie
(Warsaw, Poland)—Fiction. | LCGFT: Novels.
Classification: LCC PS3607.R63 W4 2023 | DDC 813/.6—dc23/eng/20230210
LC record available at https://lccn.loc.gov/2023005844

10 9 8 7 6 5 4 3 2 1
First Edition

For Penelope Lian, my daughter, who crossed oceans

I would love to live to see the moment in which the great treasure will be dug up and shriek to the world proclaiming the truth . . . But no, we shall certainly never live to see it, and therefore do I write my last will. May the treasure fall into good hands, may it last into better times, may it alarm and alert the world to what happened and was played out in the twentieth century . . . We may now die in peace. We fulfilled our mission. May history attest for us.

—DAWID GRABER, AUGUST 1942, WARSAW, POLAND

ONE

====

The man came to my classroom on December 14, 1940, at 16:40 I wrote down the time and date immediately, because he asked me to write down everything immediately, and there was no reason not to comply. "All the details," he said, "even if they seem insignificant. I don't want you to decide what's significant. I want you to record. You are a camera and a Dictaphone, both."

He was tall, with brown curly hair that seemed clean, newly cut. He had heavy brows, hooded eyes, and a sharp nose, and all in all was handsome in a rather somber way. He spoke educated Polish with an eastern accent. His name was Emanuel Ringelblum.

"I've heard of you," I said. He was the one who was organizing relief agencies, soup kitchens.

He smiled, briefly, and his face briefly warmed. "I've heard of you too. You were a teacher of foreign languages at Centralny. Now you're teaching English here."

"That's right."

He put a hand in his pocket, took a glance around my meager classroom. "I have an archival project I'd like you to be part of, if you're interested." He paused as if to consider his words. "It's important work. I've asked several people I know—professors, writers—to take notes on what they witness during their time here, to write down everything that's happened, from the time we wake up to when we go to sleep."

"And we do this . . . why?" I asked. Very few of us here needed more to do.

"It is up to us to write our own history," he said. "Deny the Germans the last word."

A dry chuckle escaped me. "It's hard to deny the Germans anything, Pan Ringelblum."

"Perhaps," he said. "Or perhaps after the war, we can tell the world the truth about what happened."

It was quite cold in the basement; in the few weeks I'd been teaching, I had twice ended class early for cold. Ringelblum didn't seem to notice.

"Our task is to pay attention," he continued. "To listen to the stories. We want all political backgrounds, all religious attitudes. The illiterate and the elite. Every ideology. Interview everyone. Learn about their lives. I need the best minds here to help." He paused, as if trying to decide whether to add something. "Will you join us?"

I was flattered. "I will."

"I'm glad," he said, and reached into his bag to hand me a small white notebook. "Write about what it's like to teach here. Your students, their parents, their friends. Whatever you observe," he said. "There is no privacy here."

Of course, I knew that.

"Ask them questions about how they lived before this. Write down what they remember. And your own life. With your family before they left. With your wife while she was still alive. Your day-to-day activities, in and out of the classroom. I can offer you a small stipend. I'm not sure how long I'll be able to do that, however."

I wanted to ask how he knew about me, how he knew who I was and what I did, but he didn't really invite questions. He had that authority about him.

"If they find the notebook, you could be killed," he said.

"They won't find it."

He nodded, told me that we would meet on Saturdays at the library at 3/5 Tłomackie Street. "You're not religious, are you?"

Before all this, I had barely remembered I was a Jew. I told him as much.

"Well, they won't let you forget now," he said.

"Surely not," I said.

"Our group is called Oneg Shabbat," he said. "'The joy of the Sabbath.'"

"Yes, I'm familiar with the term."

He left the room a few minutes before five. I leaned against the overturned barrel—my classroom had no chairs—and wrote down what he'd said, all the details. The perfect Polish. The hooded eyes. I then wrote down a few scraggly details about myself—my name, my height, and what I imagined was my weight—and then immediately scratched out my height and weight, self-conscious. I had never been a diary keeper. I had never thought myself such an interesting subject. I almost tore the page out and started again, but then I thought: *What if someone found my discarded notes?* And I also thought: *It is not my job to decide what's significant.*

So I kept going.

Name: Adam Paskow
Date: December 14, 1940
Age: 42
Height: 180 cm
Weight: 75 kg

I suppose I'll start by telling you who we were.

Several of us had been printers. A few had been dentists. About the number you might expect had been rabbis. Some of us, however, had practiced more unusual work: Lieberman, for instance, had been an ornithologist and, for a while, kept a stuffed hummingbird next to his mattress as a reminder of his former life. My old neighbor Kalwitz had been a calligrapher. His brother-in-law Weiss had monitored the trolley system. I myself had been an English teacher, and in fact I remain an English teacher, the only one I know who's still at it. My vocation is so useless that I'm not surprised to be the only one, and often I'm surprised I'm still alive.

I teach in the basement under the bomb-crushed cinema on Miła Street. Our class meets after my shift at the Aid Society, before curfew, before our jagged hours of sleep. I have six students sometimes, sometimes four, rarely none at all. Szifra Joseph comes regularly, but I knew her before the war, when she was my student at the Centralny Lyceum. Just last week, Szifra read a few pages of "Moby Dick" without stumbling. (Laugh all you want at Lieberman's hummingbird, but I was the fool who'd brought with me not only "Moby Dick" but also "As You Like It," "King Lear," and "The Adventures of Huckleberry Finn.")

Szifra is 15 and in a better world might have been an actress—she's beautiful and very dramatic—but here she's practicing English in a basement while her little brothers scavenge for food and her mother slowly goes crazy fabricating brushes in a sweatshop forty meters away. Her family had been wealthy once. Szifra spoke to me of a house in the suburbs, several Polish maids. Her father had owned a clothing factory in Praga, but after the invasion some petty commandant forced him to hand over the keys along with a receipt claiming that the factory had been relinquished as a gift. Two days after that humiliation, her father shot himself in the mouth with the pistol he'd brought home from his service to the Polish army. (Szifra said this to me in well-pronounced English, which I complimented lavishly.)

As for me, I have never owned much of my own—such is the lot of a public school teacher—but I enjoyed my life for many years and even now consider myself lucky, all things considered. First, I have no family with me: my brother went in for Palestine several years ago, and now lives with his wife and six children on a cabbage farm outside Jerusalem. My mother joined him there in '38, after the political situation here had become even more tenuous. She had suggested—begged, really—that I come with her. I was already a widower—there was nothing stopping me— but I was thoroughly uninterested in Zionism. We had never practiced Judaism before, and I thought myself too old to try believing something new, or to take advantage of an accident of birth to claim some brown patch of desert as my home. Besides, I liked my job. I liked my life. Pleasant reminders of my wife were everywhere, and I wanted to be close to her grave.

For almost a decade, Kasia and I had lived in the Mokotów District, near the river, in an apartment she had secured with her father's money. Our home was cozy, filled with books and Oriental rugs. Kasia was a stickler about nice bedclothes, so we had fine linen sheets and down blankets, things I never would have bothered with were I to have lived on my own. She wore glasses, curled her short hair. She collected German teddy bears for the children we would never have. She was the fourth and favorite daughter of a government bigwig with some distant ties to nobility, a father who indulged her even after her mother openly mused about disowning her for becoming involved with a Jew.

"But honestly, Anna," her father said to his wife, shortly after our first meeting, "what kind of Jew is this? He has blue eyes! His hair is light! He looks like a Pole. He probably isn't even really Jewish. He's probably a Pole, somewhere in those genes. Look at those eyes! And besides, our Kasia loves him."

"Also," I pointed out, trying to be helpful, "my father died fighting the Russians."

"You see, Anna? His father was a brave soldier. Maybe not even a Jew at all."

(This was not true—we were Jewish to our bones—but what was the point of arguing? I believed in God even less than I believed in the devil.)

I had met Kasia in university, where we were both studying English literature—again, her parents were indulgent, and my mother was too grief-stricken from my father's loss (why did he enlist? what did he have to prove?) to care much anymore what I did. It had been Kasia's plan to move to London after she graduated and work as a translator for the British government. It had been my plan to be an English teacher at one of the Jewish public schools, or, if I could swing it, at a Polish school (better pay, nicer classrooms). It had been nobody's plan to end up seated next to each other at a lecture on Shakespeare's comedies by a visiting scholar from City College Manchester, nor to get a coffee afterward, nor to keep talking until the trolleys stopped running. She was lovely, although that's not the first thing I noticed about her. I noticed first her fine sense of humor, her quick laugh, her honesty when it came to decoding Shakespeare. "I read the Polish translations first," she said. "Do you?"

I did not, but I told her that I did, not wanting to seem like a show-off.

"I have a much easier time," she said, "with the Romantics. Or with Blake." She loved Blake. She quoted "London," even though it was a sad poem and not a particular advertisement for moving there after graduation.

"Do you really think you'll leave?" I asked. It was midnight and we had met only five hours before, but already I was making plans.

"I suppose I wouldn't," she said, "if I had something keeping me here." She coughed a little into her empty coffee cup.

We stood to put on our coats. She was tall—maybe a centimeter taller than I was—with short blond hair and gray eyes. She had a bump on her nose from a football accident; when she was a child, she said, she used to play football in the backyard with her father.

"Which way are you walking?" I asked. I lived in a student hostel near the university. She lived with her family in Wilanów. Both were in the same direction, so after a bit of awkward fumbling with our coats we walked together into the night.

Kasia and I married May 20, 1930, at the registry office of the courthouse, the same one I pass now when I walk to the Aid Society. (There's some sort of tunnel in the basement that you can sneak through to the Aryan side if you're insane enough to try. Some of the children get out that way and come back in, their coats full of carrots and bread.)

We were never able to have children. These days, that seems like a bit of luck. She was plagued by migraines, and, during our seventh year of marriage, in the midst of a particularly bad spell, she fell down the stairs of the Sprawy Zagraniczne building, where she worked. She broke her leg, several ribs, and the orbital bone around her eye, but the most grievous injury was to her brain. According to her doctors, hidden somewhere in her skull was a massive hemorrhage; her brain swelled and kept swelling, and in twelve days she was dead.

And yet: we had a funeral attended by dozens of people, and she was buried in a cemetery, and I know where her tombstone is.

This, too, is luck.

But, as I say, I know I've been fortunate, even in circumstances I might have once found impossible to see as fortunate. It has been this understanding as much as anything else that keeps me alive, that I feel certain will continue to keep me alive. Sala Wiskoff, who sleeps two meters from me, separated only by a curtain of old sheets, says that she's trying to take a lesson from my attitude. She's trying to recalibrate her sense of what luck looks like. But it's not as easy for her: she has two children who spend their days smuggling and stealing, and a husband who won't stop crying for his dead mother. We share our small apartment with the Lescovec family, and she and Pani Lescovec still bicker over the use of the tiny kitchen, even though there's not much food to prepare. Pani Lescovec usually starts the bickering, and Sala can't help herself, battling over who can use the teapot even when there's no tea.

"But sometimes there's tea," I point out.

"Sometimes."

"We have a toilet that flushes."

"Every once in a while."

"We're alive."

"For the moment."

Other parts of the ghetto, especially the larger section across Chłodna Street, are far worse off—starving children are begging in the streets. On this side, most of us have secured jobs with the Jewish council or the Jewish police, or, like me, at the Aid Society, and there's a café on Sienna Street that usually has food, and doctors living on each of the two floors above us, so that even though sometimes gendarmes drive through the streets shooting people at random, and even though Pan Lescovec had been clubbed so hard in the ear he'd lost most of his hearing, and even though living here is undoubtedly the worst thing that has happened to most of us, we know it could be worse, and that it might be, at some point. But for now, it isn't.

And while I wait to fall asleep at night, when sleep refuses to come, I look out the window and remember Warsaw, the bustling, lunatic city where I once lived with my wife.

TWO

====

In the minutes before the students arrived, I read over what I'd just written for Ringelblum's archive. It sounded sentimental, I knew, but everyone here had become almost liquid with sentimentality, and I, unfortunately, was not immune. You should have seen the lot of us: crying on the streets, standing on corners holding framed pictures of the people or homes we'd left behind. Begging the Polish guards to smuggle us or our children out and getting smacked across the face for our trouble, then going home and crying about our bruised cheeks. It was all a bit much, if you asked me, although the other responses—strange bursts of levity, wild dreams of revenge—those didn't seem particularly reasonable either. The truth is, it was hard to know what to think or how to behave, and I spent an awful lot of time either staring into space or digging myself into the deep hole of memory.

Work helped, of course. Work has always helped people keep their minds off the inevitable passing of days, and it certainly helped me after Kasia's accident and in the weeks and months after her death. I poured myself into it, tutoring in my off hours, taking on some of her unfinished translation work and staying up all night to finish her assignments for nobody in particular.

And here in the ghetto, three times a week, I still went to work, teaching my students the fundamentals and flourishes of the English language.

Just before five, I hid Ringelblum's notebook in the satchel I carried everywhere, even when I had nothing to carry. (You never knew when you might find a surprise grosz on the street, or a rogue piece of bread.) When I turned around, three of my students were standing in the middle of the room, quietly; children had learned to be unnaturally quiet here. Roman, Charlotte, Filip. Charlotte and Roman were fractious siblings, while eleven-year-old Filip was the youngest Lescovec boy, and therefore my flatmate, although I rarely saw him in the apartment. According to his mother, Filip had taken to spending most of his time on the roof of our building, even in frigid December. "He'd rather risk freezing to death than spend any more time with us," she said sniffily.

"What's that?" asked Charlotte, pointing at my satchel.

"In English."

"What's that?" she asked. "In the floor."

"*On* the floor."

"In the floor."

"No, idiot," said Roman, who had become crueler and crueler to his sister over the past few weeks. "'In' is *in*," he said, opening his mouth and inserting a finger to demonstrate. "'On' is . . ." he looked around, but he could find nothing to put on anything else. Our room was barren and small, illuminated by a few naked lightbulbs. The walls were damp, crumbling plaster. The floor was pocked concrete. At the Polish school where I'd taught (my position secured by Kasia's father), the hallway floors had been marble and the fountains bubbled fresh water all day long. The students had sat *in* bentwood seats. They had written *on* broad slate chalkboards.

"In, in," Charlotte said.

"*On.*" I tried again. "It's a different sound. Listen carefully. *On.*"

"On," she said.

"Very good," I said.

"Idiot," said her brother.

"Enough," I said. "Now we speak English."

"What is *in* your bag?" Charlotte said, in English, which compelled me to answer her.

"A book."

"You have a book?"

One of my many complaints (how often my lessons devolved into complaints) was that I had no schoolbooks with which to teach them, nor even paper for them to take notes.

"It's just a diary. Eyn togbuch."

"From where?"

But I was saved from Charlotte's interrogation by the arrival of Szifra Joseph, the class's star, radiant even in our diminished conditions, smiling flirtatiously, as though there were someone worth flirting with in the room. She swept her camel-colored coat off her shoulders and onto the floor, then sat down on the coat, leaning back on her palms, crossing her legs at the ankle. This was the signal for everyone else to sit, which they did, although only Szifra dared damage her coat by draping it on the floor.

"Well," Szifra started, "you *would not believe*—"

"English."

She shifted naturally. "You would not *believe*"—and here she mimicked, in her speech, the style of the Hollywood movies she used to love watching; she clipped her words like Joan Crawford—"what just *happened* to me on the *street.*"

Silence. Roman and Charlotte tried not to look impressed by her theatrics, while Filip watched a mouse scuttle across the room. I wasn't sure any of them understood what she was saying.

"Don't you want to know?"

"What happened to you on the street, Szifra?"

"Well," she said, halting a bit as she found the English words. "A gendarme told me to hurry back home, that it wasn't a good idea for me to be on this side of the gates. He said it was filthy here and I was certain to get typhus."

"So?" said Filip.

"So it seemed like he was really concerned about me and my safety, and I couldn't figure out why he was so concerned. And then I realized . . ." Szifra blinked at us, waiting for one of us to say it so she didn't have to.

"He thought you were Polish," Roman finally said, but he said it dully, refusing to be impressed. His English comprehension was better than I'd guessed.

Szifra was blushing. Or, if not blushing, she was at least looking somewhat bashful. "You know, I can't help it if I have good looks," she said. Which did not mean, precisely, that she knew she was beautiful, although certainly she did, but rather that she knew she didn't look Jewish, and that her looks were therefore "good." Blond hair, blue eyes, trim waist, tall. Well-dressed. Curled hair and elegant makeup. There weren't many Jews like her around, but there were a few, and they were often privileged with small kindnesses from the Germans and resented by everyone else.

"How did you respond?" I asked her.

"I said . . . Well, at first I didn't say anything, you know? But he kept talking to me in German—"

"You speak German?" Charlotte asked. Unlike her brother, she couldn't hide her admiration.

"I speak enough. I mean, a few phrases. Anyway, I tried to just walk away, because, of course, you don't want any trouble, but then he followed me and said, 'Really, miss, you mustn't be here.' So I turned around, and he didn't have that usual Nazi face, you know. He wasn't drunk or anything."

"And then?" Charlotte said, hanging on every word.

"Well, then . . . Darn, how do you say this in English? I said, 'Sir, I am Jewish,' and showed him my armband, and he looked very embarrassed, and suddenly I was scared"—and here she lapsed into Yiddish, speaking too quickly for me to stop her—"because you know that if you embarrass one of them they can take it out on you. They'll shoot you in the street, even. But this one, he really did look like he was nice. And he was just a boy, maybe eighteen or nineteen. He said, 'Forgive me.'"

"A Nazi asked you to forgive him?" Charlotte was stunned.

Szifra drew herself up. "He did. Yes, he did."

"So what happened next?"

"Well, quickly I went from scared to mad, because I thought, 'Forgive you? This is what I'm supposed to forgive you for? You steal my home and our property, and my father kills himself, but the thing I'm supposed to be mad about is that you mistook me for a gentile? For one of *you?'* Please. I mean, honestly. Please." She shrugged her shoulders in exaggerated exasperation.

"Incredible," Charlotte said.

"Stupid," Roman said.

"Hmm . . . ," I said, and paused as the mouse darted back across our floor, skirting the fur collar of Szifra's coat. "But that's not what you said to him."

"Well, of course not. I said, 'Sir, if you please,' in German, and then I looked down and away, to be submissive, and then one of his superiors barked something at him, and he got scared and hurried away."

We all waited for something else.

"So that's your whole story?" said Filip, my quietest student.

"What else do you want?" Szifra said. "Honestly, I was just so *mortified* by all of it. I mean, mistaken for one of *them*," she said, although she was glowing. And, truly, what could be more flattering than to be so clean and lovely and blond as to not look like one of us?

"You should have asked him for bread," Roman said.

"English."

"Bread. You should . . . demand bread. He will give you bread. He thinks you are . . . pretty."

"Please," Szifra said, trying not to smile. "I'm not risking my life to ask some idiot gendarme for bread."

"He will give you some."

"I still have money, Roman. When you have money, you can *buy* bread. You don't have to beg."

Roman shrugged. "Maybe one day you might," he said. "Have to beg."

"One day? Why one day? What are you—what are you now, telling the future?"

I could have interrupted, but it was my policy never to interrupt when they were speaking English.

"Just that one day you might not having any more money."

"Oh, puh-leeze," Szifra said, falling back dramatically on her camel coat; I wondered where she had learned that "puh-leeze." We all watched her until she sat back up and wiped off her shoulders. I remembered Szifra behaving the same way back when I taught her at the Lyceum, and her fellow students responding similarly, annoyed and admiring in equal measure. Had any fifteen-year-old girl ever been so sure of herself? Or so able to put on a show of self-assurance?

"Listen," Szifra said, in Yiddish, a tone of confidentiality, "only fools here run out of bread."

It occurred to me that I really should get started. Was anyone else coming? It was getting so cold; I imagined I'd have fewer and fewer pupils as the winter grew darker. "Listen, students, why don't we—"

"Anyway," she said, "we'll all be getting out of here in a month or two."

"Horsecrap," said Filip.

"We really just don't know what will happen next," I said, although it was possible that Szifra was right. (I wanted it to be possible.)

"It's true," Szifra said. "The British will fight back, the Germans will leave, we'll go home."

This was the chorus of the optimistic class. The British, maybe the Americans. Two months, three, then home.

"Horsecrap," Filip repeated.

Szifra gave him a monstrous look. "I actually don't care what you think," she said. "Because I know what I know."

No one dared respond.

We had been meeting here three times a week for a little more than a month, but already we had sorted ourselves: those whose glasses were half-full, whose glasses were half-empty, whose cups would always runneth over.

"Perhaps, Pan Paskow, we should start?" Charlotte, in English.

"Yes, yes—of course." I fumbled, wishing for the millionth time I had an English primer, a proper lesson plan. "Today we're learning a poem by William Blake. There is some good vocabulary in there. It's easy to memorize."

Last Thursday, they had learned Rosetti's "A Birthday," and Wednesday, Hopkins's "Spring and Fall." Today, I recited a Blake poem about joy, for it was my policy to teach mostly happy poems. Or happy-enough. My assembly stumbled a bit over, "a clothing for the soul divine," in both pronunciation and meaning, but fairly soon we were reciting it together, time and again, automated, yes, but with feeling. Even Filip, who could be tentative, spoke loudly.

> "'Man was made for Joy and Woe
> And when this we rightly know
> Thro' the World we safely go.'"

(I no longer believe this is so.)

HERE, IN THE ghetto, I was teaching my students poetry to help them practice their pronunciation; without novels or short stories or grammar primers, poems were the only texts I had. I had memorized hundreds over the years. I also liked teaching poems because I believed poetry was where the English language really soared. It was utilitarian most of the time but somehow able to turn its simple grammar and plundered vocabulary into the finest poetry written: Shakespearean sonnets and Keatsian odes, and Chaucer and Eliot and Pound. I knew and loved them all for different reasons. When I wanted wisdom, I found Dickinson; sorrow, Yeats; company in my grief, Wordsworth.

(The only other language, in my humble opinion, that used poetry to rise above its station was German. My German was far worse than my English, but I knew a little bit, and I was a fan, like many Poles, of Goethe and Rilke. Still, I was unsure that a language that could order children to be mowed down by gunfire was still a sane one to use for poetry, and anyway, when comparing the two, I found English more pleasing to the ear.)

At the Lyceum, my students had been almost entirely Polish—Jewish students were limited by a strict quota system, as were Ukrainians and Lithuanians—but every so often, to be subversive, I'd teach them poetry by Emma Lazarus. After I'd taped a large poster of the Statue of Liberty on my blackboard, we'd recite together the famous words: "Give me your tired, your poor, your huddled masses," etc. I'll confess it struck me as stickily sweet, but the image of Lady Liberty was nice and it allowed the class to consider ideas of welcome and immigration, so different from the nationalist propaganda inculcated into Poles. At the end of the class, I'd mention, as casually as possible, that Lazarus was a Jewish woman whose most famous book was called *Songs of a Semite*. I wanted my students to be impressed, but, generally speaking, they'd just roll their eyes, feeling suddenly superior to a woman whose poems had been published across the globe.

THREE

===

After class, Filip and I walked home together, pausing at the café on Nowolipki Street to see if there was any food on offer. (There was: cabbage and carrot-top soup, kasha, roasted beets.) We stayed close to the walls, since the gendarmes were noticeably nastier on this side of Chłodna Street and neither one of us felt like interaction. It was already dark out and bitterly cold.

"Will you go up on the roof tonight?"

Filip nodded.

"Doesn't the cold bother you?"

He nodded again.

"It's the only way you can be alone?"

He looked down at his feet. A thin boy with a pale sprinkle of freckles across his nose, he favored his father, himself a thin pale man with owlish eyes.

"It can be hard to always be surrounded by people," I said to Filip. "I'm kind of an introvert myself."

"What is an introvert?"

"Someone who feels better by himself than in big crowds."

Filip shrugged. "Crowds are okay," he said. "I used to like being around other people."

As we crossed Żelazna Street, I noticed, with a start, that Merenstayn's confectionery was somehow still open. Merenstayn's! Could it be? I hurried Filip over to the brightly lit window. My parents had taken me to Merenstayn's when I was a child, but I had almost forgotten that the place existed, and had certainly forgotten that it was here, on Żelazna Street, within the bounds of the ghetto. But now that it was in front of me, I could remember the store as though I'd been there the day before: jars upon jars of cinnamon balls, peppermint sticks, small wrapped chocolates imported from Austria. Phosphates mixed behind the counter. In a freezer case, vats of ice cream that Pani Merenstayn churned in a giant electric contraption that rattled in the back of the store. Merenstayn's was where I'd had my first taste of ice cream, in fact—strawberry with bits of fruit swirled in. I was seven years old and hadn't known something so delicious could exist.

"Do you know Merenstayn's, Filip?"

He gave me a rare grin. What child of Warsaw didn't know this spot?

To be a candy store in the middle of a ghetto was to be a paradox in the middle of a nightmare, but that didn't change the fact that it was here. I ushered Filip inside; the interior was smaller than I remembered (what isn't?) but the walls were still decorated gaily (bright-colored cartoons of children eating popsicles and lollipops) and candy jars lining the shelves (emptier now, but not entirely empty). There was no ice cream maker churning; how could there be when cream and sugar were almost impossible to come by? But there were small wrapped chocolates in boxes by the register, and canisters of sucking candies on the countertops.

"Can I help you?"

Materializing as if from nowhere: a gnomelike man in a white apron, a crown of white hair around a bald spot, a face as soft and pliant as a rotting peach. Sparkling blue eyes. I was in a dream; I couldn't speak.

"Do you have any gumballs?" Filip asked.

"Sure, I do," said Pan Merenstayn, pointing at one of the jars toward the rear of the store. "Serve yourself."

The world felt underwater. I watched as Filip crossed the store, picked up a small cellophane bag, placed two large pink gumballs in it, considered for a moment, and then added a third. He approached the counter, gingerly removed a zloty from his pocket, and received a few groszy as change and a pat on the head from Pan Merenstayn.

"Are you still making candy in the store?" I asked.

"Of course," he said. "Where else would I make it?"

"But how?"

"How?"

"Where do you find the ingredients? How do you . . . How are you able to find sugar in the midst of all—"

"Just because I'm not allowed outside the walls doesn't mean my suppliers aren't allowed in," Pan Merenstayn said with a small laugh. "As long as I can pay, I can get what I need to keep the store open. For how long, of course, is another matter."

"I came here as a child," I said.

"Half of Warsaw came here when they were children," Pan Merenstayn said. "Don't you want to buy something?"

I wanted to buy all of it—the store, the jars, the sweets, my childhood, Pan Merenstayn himself—and wrap it up somewhere and keep it safe. But I shook my head dumbly.

"Take a peppermint, at least," he said. "It's good for you. The oils keep the mind sharp."

"I shouldn't."

"Go on," he said. "Consider it a gift."

Gifts were hard to come by here. I took a candy from a jar.

"Listen, don't tell everyone—I don't want a riot—but it's possible I'm getting some Mozart chocolates from Salzburg next week. If my suppliers are being honest with me."

"Are they usually honest?"

Pan Merenstayn shrugged. "They used to be."

"What's a 'Mozart chocolate'?" Filip asked.

"Oh, it's so good you wouldn't believe how good," Pan Merenstayn said. "A little candied hazelnut covered in chocolate, wrapped up in gold, with a picture of Mozart's face on it. You know Mozart? *The Magic Flute?*"

Filip shook his head.

"Oh, that's too bad. That's a shame. If I were allowed to turn on the record player . . ." And here Pan Merenstayn gave me a look to see if he should go ahead and do it. But I couldn't let him: It would all be too much, the candy, the promise of hazelnuts, the sound of Mozart. We could not have that much joy at once; we needed to parcel it out.

"The gendarmes are out," I said. "It's getting near curfew."

"Ah," Pan Merenstayn said. "A shame. But I suppose you're right."

"Thank you for these," said Filip, a boy with manners.

"Of course," said Pan Merenstayn. "Chocolate next week. Don't tell your friends! I don't want a crowd!" And then he winked.

We walked out of the store and back into the real world, Filip chewing on a gumball, me sucking slowly on my peppermint, oily and sweet and faintly bitter. Around us, the night closed in, but I felt warmed. I thought: *I will go to Merenstayn's whenever I have a few groszy in my pocket.* I thought: *It is a miracle that it is here. One of the nicest parts of my childhood returned to me. I will go next week for a Mozart, and I will whistle* The Magic Flute *to my students, and I will hand out gumballs.*

But somehow, lost in the maze of the ghetto, I never found Merenstayn's again, or maybe it had never been there in the first place, and I was already living in a dream.

FOUR

What were we doing here, anyway?

Believe me, it's not like we had a choice.

It was hard to believe that it had been only a single year since the Nazis had invaded, on the first day of September, under the pretext (they desired a pretext for some reason) that a Polish farmer had sabotaged a radio station and broadcast a few lines of anti-German propaganda.

Did this really happen? It seemed unlikely to me—Poles are not known for provocation—but I suppose it might have.

Yet, even if—*if*—such a provocation did occur, did it justify the invasion of our nation, our *sovereign* nation, by ten thousand German troops overnight? The bombardment by twelve hundred airplanes, the shelling of our schools, and the wholesale destruction of our marketplaces? The terrorizing of children, the stabbing of old men on the streets, the rape of our young women, and the public hanging of our soldiers? On my street one early morning, I found a boy no older than fifteen cowering and bleeding as two Nazis took turns stomping on his head with their metal-soled boots. As though I saw nothing, I quickly walked away.

The truth is, our country had been independent for only twenty-one years, since the end of the last big war, and we were poor and disorganized. I knew from my wife's work in the government that whatever armaments we produced we sold to other, wealthier countries in exchange for promises of security. Because we were not stupid, we knew that the Nazis were dangerous—they were, after all, our next-door neighbors—but none of us expected them to actually invade. I remember speaking about it with my father-in-law: "Hitler knows better than to start something with us. Britain and France are our allies. We've signed treaties." He ground out a cigar. "That's a risk that even Herr Hitler cannot take."

But what Kasia's father hadn't taken into account was that Britain had signed a nonaggression pact with Hitler, and therefore, it turned out, its agreement with distant impoverished Poland wasn't worth the ink used to sign it. As for the French, they decided that coming to our aid really wasn't, in the end, an efficient use of their money or manpower. Therefore, while the British and French made their excuses, the Germans mowed us over.

"What do you want here, Pole?" asked a trim blond Nazi three weeks after the invasion as I attempted to enter the butcher shop on Puławska Street.

Because I hadn't learned to shut my mouth yet, I said: "I'm just here to buy a few chops. Please let me pass."

The soldier smiled, said, "Of course," and then, as I prepared to pass, punched me roundly in the stomach.

"A few chops." He laughed as I doubled over on the shop's doorstep. "Don't tell me what to do, you fucking Pole."

They held a victory parade down the streets of heartbroken Warsaw after our brave soldiers surrendered, and Hitler himself appeared to view the destruction created in his name. We watched from our smashed-in windows, agape.

A few weeks after, the Nazis divided us again, only twenty-one years since we had been made whole. The western half of our country was taken by the Nazis; they gave the eastern half to the Soviets in honor of their new alliance.

Here in the western half, the Nazis moved a general, Hans Frank, into Wawel Castle in Kraków, which had been the home of the kings of Poland for more than five hundred years, which housed the relics of Saint Stanislaus, the Sigismund Chapel, and the national treasury. They moved their functionaries into our finest houses, evicting their owners and leaving them homeless. They took over our businesses. They moved their citizens into our villages and towns. We'd looked away, told ourselves it would be temporary.

They called Poles "hewers of wood and drawers of water" for the Reich.

We Jews who had been made aware of Nazis' behavior in their native country (and that was by no means all of us—many provincial Polish Jews had never heard of Warsaw, much less Berlin) had felt sympathy for the Jews over there, but never thought the Nazis would bring their anti-Semitic barbarism across the border. Why would they? What happened in Germany was a German problem, not a Polish one. If Germans wanted to punish their Jews, their Jews would have to either fight or leave. Jews in Poland had faced those two choices for generations.

But now the Germans were here. Those Jews with some foresight began streaming out to wherever would take them; for instance, the chemistry teacher at the Lyceum, by proving some distant ties to an American rabbi, was able to get himself to Chicago. There was Palestine, of course, and Australia, and on the trolley I overheard the story of an entire sztetl packing up and moving, en masse, to some frigid town in northern Quebec.

But those of us who stayed—and most of us stayed—had good enough reasons. We had our lives and our livelihoods, and couldn't envision starting over somewhere as frostbitten as Canada or depraved as Australia.

Meanwhile, the fist closed slowly around us.

First, we could no longer withdraw our money from the banks.

Next, we could no longer own radios or go to movie theaters.

Then, Jews could no longer teach in Polish schools. (And thus began my own exile from the life that I had known before.)

We had to declare our property. We could no longer travel by train. Synagogues were closed.

We could no longer mail letters abroad.

We could no longer visit the parks. We could not sit on public benches. We could not see Polish doctors. We could ride only special Jewish trolleys. We could no longer employ Polish maids.

We had to wear yellow stars on armbands over our clothing, and I found this rule, strangely, the most humiliating of all; I stopped leaving my flat unless I absolutely had to.

And then, finally, in the logical culmination of all that had already happened, we were forced to abandon our houses and move to a new district, one and a half square miles of densely packed apartments and businesses in the old Jewish section in the middle of Warsaw. The few Catholics who lived in that district had to leave.

The Nazis put up signs all over Warsaw claiming that we needed to be relocated because we carried disease. For the health of everyone, Jews had to separate from the "clean" Polish and German populations. According to the German posters on my very street, I was infectious, louse-ridden, filthy. An animal, really.

We were given ten days to pack the small amount we were allowed to bring and abandon everything else. And what apartments were we to find? And how were we to conduct our businesses or send our children to school from this entirely new location? Some of us lived in homes that had been passed down from our great-great-grandfathers. Were we really supposed to give them up? What were the trolley connections in our new location? How would we find our new grocers and tailors and dentists?

Back then, we did not know that we needn't worry about the answers to these questions. Our new district was to be gated. Once we were in, we were to be locked in, like animals.

We referred to our new home as the ghetto.

After a chaotic few days, the gates were locked, on November 16, 1940, at two in the afternoon. They were locked, but we did not believe they were locked. Even after they had taken our jobs, our money, our schools. Even after they had taken our homes. Locked in, guarded, put under curfew, our movements proscribed, our daily calories proscribed. "They cannot do this to us!" shrieked a woman standing on the street below my window. "We are not animals!"

But, ma'am . . . , I wanted to shout down to her, although I'm not much for shouting. *Ma'am, people are merely another species of animal. We just don't like to be reminded of it.*

Name: Filip Lescovec
Date: December 14, 1940,
10:10 p.m.
Age: 11 years, 6 months
Height: 140 cm?
Weight: 30 kg?

Filip Lescovec, age 11, plans on being a construction worker when he grows up, for he very much enjoys building things, as evidenced by the strange small shed he's built on top of our apartment building at 53 Sienna Street. The shed is made of plywood and brick and scraps of lumber he's found among the damaged buildings of our tattered district, and he has filled it with blankets and odd toys, also of his own creation. He showed me a sort of hybrid truck/dinosaur he'd carved out of a large stick. Although I would not have known what it was if I had found it on the street, he pointed out the various features that made it both animal and machine: the scales, the wheels, the pedals and so forth. I asked if it was a truckosaurus, and he gave me such a pitiable look that I was afraid he would no longer consent to be interviewed. "It doesn't have that sort of name," he said. "I'm not a child."

But it seems to me that Filip is, indeed, a child, at least as far as his physiognomy suggests. My time teaching schoolchildren has shown me there are many ways to be 11, 12, 13, as I have seen boys sprouting pimples and faint mustache hairs at 11 and girls who at 15 or 16 could still be mistaken for their own younger sisters. Filip himself is small, slim-shouldered, even bundled into the sweaters that clearly have been handed down from Lescovec child to Lescovec child. He squinted in the candlelight by which we conducted our interview, but when I asked him if he needed glasses he told me that he didn't, that he had had his eyes examined before the invasion and was found to have perfect vision.

As for our interview: there was not enough room in Filip's structure for me to join him in its relative warmth, but it was a still night and I was able to stay warm enough in my gloves and hat to sit with him for a good fifty minutes. Some of that time we spent quietly, as I admired Filip's many carvings (where he had found a decent-quality knife, I do not know, as Jews had been stripped of all items that could be used as weapons), but eventually he began to speak of his life before the war and what he made of his life now. We discussed many subjects, including his feelings about his older brothers (neutral, leaning positive when they find him scraps of bread or candy), his parents (generally tolerable), and his schooling (he missed learning things, which is why he attended English class; also it had been drilled into him that English would one day prove "useful," and he had no reason to doubt that).

A.P. And what did you like about your old school?
F.L. Oh, the usual, I guess. My friends.

(Filip had attended the Akademia Polish school, as did many children of the Jewish intelligentsia. Like many Jewish children, he also attended cheder on the weekends, which he found unforgivably dull. He spent most of his time there drawing variations of dinosaurs on wheels and getting boxed in the ears by the rabbi.)

A.P. When did you first learn about dinosaurs?
F.L. My father took me on a trip to London three years ago. We went to the Natural History Museum. I had never seen

anything like them in my life, and I decided to learn about them. Did you know that if the dinosaurs hadn't died out there never would have been human life as we know it?

A.P. I did not.

F.L. That's because mammals couldn't start to evolve into humans until there was room for them to grow, and there wasn't any room to grow until the dinosaurs disappeared. So if that hadn't happened, dinosaurs would have continued to evolve. Maybe they even would have developed reason, like mammals did. *They* would have been the ones to build the buildings and the airplanes and the cars and everything.

A.P. Don't tell the rabbis.

F.L. When do I talk to rabbis?

A.P. (Laughing) So is this what you're carving? Rational dinosaurs?

F.L. Sometimes. Some of them are rational. Some of them are just interesting. (Filip reaches into his shelter to find more of the dinosaurs, some as small as a finger, all crudely carved but clearly meaningful in their way to their creator.) Before the library closed, I used to get out books about dinosaurs and draw copies of them. That's before I started to carve.

A.P. I used to love the library myself. There was an English-language library on Mokotów Street that I had to stop visiting last summer.

F.L. Yeah.

A.P. I really miss it. The librarian stopped me from walking in one day, and it was quite embarrassing to both of us.

(At this point, Filip displays the general disinterest children feel when adults start to talk about their own problems, so I continue to examine his creations until the cold begins to pierce my gloves.)

F.L. For me, it was football.

A.P. Football?

F.L. Yeah. It's not like I was that good, even, but there was a team in my neighborhood. We were part of a youth league.

A.P. What position?

F.L. Right forward, generally. Neither of my brothers played— they were more interested in school than in sports, and my mother couldn't figure out why I wanted to play so badly. For a while she kept saying, "No. Jewish boys don't need to play football." But I pointed out that she sent me to a Polish school, so maybe she could let me do a few *other* Polish things too.

A.P. Ah. (Having rarely heard Filip string this many sentences together, I fear interrupting his talk.)

F.L. So, anyway, after a whole year of begging, she finally lets me sign up, and I make the team, and at first everyone said, "Hey, who's this Yid on the team?" But then I start getting goals. Like there was this one game we had against the team from Praga. They were these big, huge kids, twice our size, and we were down 2–1 in the final minutes, and then their guard knocked me over, so I got a penalty kick, and it got in just under the net—

A.P. Hey! I thought you said you weren't that good.

F.L.

A.P. I'm sorry. Please go on.

F.L. But then right after the invasion, even before the new rules, they kicked me off the team. The coach said they wanted to be cautious in light of the new government.

A.P. Oh, Filip. I'm sorry.

F.L. My mother said she wasn't surprised. That I shouldn't have expected more from them, that they weren't my friends, even if I thought they were my friends.

A.P. Oh, oh. I am sorry.

F.L. So that's when I started carving. I mean, I had always made up animals and things, but my dad saw how much I missed football, so he got me this Swiss Army knife. I don't know why he thought it would make me feel better.

A.P. But it did?

F.L. I guess. Yeah. I mean, I started carving animals then, and that became interesting to me. My bedroom at home is full of them. I kept thinking my eema would yell at me and make me throw them away, but she never did.

A.P. Well . . .

F.L. I guess she felt sorry for me.

A.P. Or she was impressed with all that you had dreamed up.

F.L. I don't know. It's hard to know with her sometimes.

(The night is hushed, but in the distance, on the other side of the ghetto walls, we can see the Ferris wheel in the amusement park circle round and round, its lights hypnotizing in the dark.)

A.P. Does your mother visit you up here? Or your brothers?

F.L. My mother doesn't. And my brothers have their own spaces on the rooftop.

A.P. They do?

F.L. Sure. There are kids on the roofs all over the ghetto. This is where we go. The sewers sometimes, but mostly the roofs.

(Here, I turn from my interviewee and hold my candle out into the darkness, but all it can illuminate are the few centimeters of Warsaw night that surrounded it. Still, if I close my eyes, I can imagine them, the thin Jewish children of our ghetto, in their individual plywood shelters, spreading out on the rooftops into an infinity of peculiar freedom.)

A.P. Thank you for inviting me up here, Filip.

F.L. I didn't. You just came.

FIVE

====

Several months after the invasion, Kasia's father visited me, unannounced, at the flat in Mokotów. He presented himself with his hat in his hands, but the humility was a performance. He had been my benefactor for so long that we were automatic with our performances for one another: he generous and powerful, me grateful and lonely.

"You holding up?"

I was. The bombing had missed our block of flats, and, after an initial panic, most of the neighborhood had returned to a strained sense of normalcy. I'd been placed on leave from school, but I had a few private students whose parents were still paying me, and honestly I hadn't truly required my small salary in many years. I had the flat. I had Kasia's jewelry sewn into the bottom of a faded woolen blanket. I had the unspent money we'd put aside for a larger house one day, and for children.

"You don't look worse for wear, anyway," he said, looking me over. "Your mother okay?"

"She's in Palestine," I said.

"Ah, that's right," he said, although I was sure he hadn't forgotten. "You're going to join her?"

"The borders are closed."

"We could probably grease some palms."

"Henryk, what would I do in Palestine?"

"What are you going to do here?"

"I've been reading."

Henryk snorted. I noticed he hadn't shaved in at least a few days; a thin film of silvery stubble covered his cheeks. Otherwise, he looked the same as ever: shiny white hair pulled across his balding pate, wide belly, eyes as blue as the Baltic.

"You want some tea?"

"You didn't answer my question."

"I'll wait for the Allies, I suppose," I said. "What else is there to do?"

He sighed, heavily. "I'll have some tea, then," he said, and followed me into the kitchen.

During our marriage, Kasia had cooked endless stews and sausages in our sunny yellow kitchen, on the small gas stove with the cranky burners, but now I used the kitchen mainly to store bread and soup I bought from the shop on Bzowa Street. I had never cared particularly about what I ate, having grown up without much variety: eggs, potatoes, boiled chicken when my mother received her widow's check. Challah on Friday nights for a little while, until she started to forget, and it caused her too much sorrow when I reminded her.

"What are you doing for money, if I may ask? The school had to fire you, I presume."

"I'm really fine."

Henryk poked around the small kitchen. He was a tall man with broad shoulders, bolstered by power, and though life had handed him more than his share of tragedy (he had already outlived two of his daughters, his wife confined to the bedroom with shattered nerves), he still radiated a certain amount of strength. For years, he had been able to pull levers for himself and the people he cared about. But the grounds of his chalet had been badly damaged on the first day of the September campaign, and the day after that he'd turned seventy. Henryk had lived through war after war, dissolution, reunification, and now the Germans, but it seemed the Germans could prove the deadly blow. His blue eyes, which in the past had been icy even during his most beneficent moments, were now rimmed with red.

"It will get bad for you here, Adam," he said. "I know it's already bad, but it's going to get worse. They've destroyed all the Jewish businesses in Germany. We used to do banking with a Jewish firm over there. Our guy was shot in the street, evidently for disrespecting an officer."

"Fortunately, I'm not a German Jewish banker."

"This is no time for jokes." He had a grim look on his face. "I very much urge you not to underestimate the circumstances you find yourself in. You like to be this easygoing guy, you like to act like everything will be okay, but I just don't believe it will all be okay this time."

"Well, what would you recommend I do?"

Henryk shook his head at my innocence or lack of imagination. There was a small photograph of Kasia on the wall above the sink; he blinked at it as though he had never seen it before. "When was this taken?"

"We took a trip to Vienna before her accident."

"Ah," he said. "Vienna." He peered closer. In the photo, a snapshot I had taken with our first Leica, Kasia was in front of the Hofburg palace, crinkling her nose in the sun. She'd worn a checked yellow shirt, a red sun hat. "Wasn't she beautiful?"

"You know I thought so," I said. I didn't like getting maudlin with Henryk, but sometimes he wanted to enjoy grieving with me, giving himself over to the impossibility of it. At the cemetery, I had to keep him from throwing himself into the hole in the ground, in the ceaseless rain, in his beautiful suit.

"She could have married anyone, Adam."

"Let me make you your tea."

"I didn't have to give you my blessing."

I put some water in the kettle, struck a match to the burner. For a week after the invasion, we had neither gas nor electricity, but then, thanks to German efficiency, things began to work again.

"I never had to be so nice to you," he said.

"That's true."

"So I think you should listen to me now. Consider what will happen next."

What would happen next? I didn't know. Henryk didn't know. I had done what the authorities said, sewn a Jewish star on an armband. There had been photographs in the *Gazeta* of rabbis with their beards cut off, made to dance for German soldiers as the soldiers smoked or threw bottles. I'd put down the newspaper and put the image of the rabbis out of my head as though I had never seen them in the first place.

"I can get you baptismal papers," Henryk said. "A Polish kennkarte."

"That would be good," I said, careful not to believe too much of what he said. He liked to make promises.

"You're circumcised?"

"Yes."

"Then keep your pants up." Henryk took his mug of tea, blew on it, put it down without taking a sip. He paced around the kitchen again, then back out into the living room. Gruby, our enormous arthritic cat, was asleep on the couch next to the spot where I liked to read. "This thing is still alive?" he said, patting Gruby on the head, but still did not sit. Into the dining room, pacing, pacing, me following a step behind. Henryk was a good seven centimeters taller than I was, outweighed me by at least twenty kilos, and following him around the house I felt like one of those fish that nervously darts behind a shark's ear.

I kept a small box on the credenza in the dining room that I never used—not the credenza, not the dining room—and I had forgotten what was in the box (anything at all?), so when Henryk opened it and peered inside I was momentarily struck by terror that there would be something shameful (although what? what had I done these past years?). And then he put the lid down and opened the drawers of the credenza, inspecting the bits of silver and china we had earned for our wedding.

"Do you need to borrow our china, Henryk?" I said nervously.

"You're having a party?" Was the china worth anything, really? It was ugly floral stuff from somewhere in the provinces.

He straightened, brushed imaginary dust off his pants. "There were necklaces," he said. "And a ring."

I started.

"The ring was my mother's. You know the one I mean. And the necklace I gave Kasia for your wedding."

I gave him as blank a look as I could muster, although of course I knew what he meant. The ring was a large emerald, a valuable piece of jewelry. Kasia had never worn it. It was sewn into the silk lining of the wool blanket that was folded up in our closet, along with a pair of gold earrings and the necklace she had worn on our wedding day.

"I don't—"

"You want a kennkarte, Adam?"

"It's not that I don't appreciate—"

"I think it would be a good idea for you to have it."

But how could a Polish kennkarte help? In the network of gossips and spies I lived among, false papers would never do me any good. My Polish neighbors all knew who I was: the Jew who had somehow married into the Duda family, Pan Yid, who had managed to find a job in the Polish schools. If I pretended to be Catholic, they would turn me in to the Germans for a kilo of flour. I could never pretend to be something I wasn't and stay in my house, in my neighborhood. Which meant that if I accepted a Polish kennkarte, I'd have to flee.

And if I had to flee, I knew in my bones I would never have a home again.

"It's not going to get better for you here."

I had always thought of Kasia's jewelry as something of a safety net. It had never occurred to us that her father would come after it—with all his money, with all his power, why would he want a few errant necklaces and a ring? Even the emerald, so precious to us, probably wasn't worth that much to him. He had a summer house on the Baltic Sea. His wife wore fur coats nine months out of twelve. He drove a Reo with a retract-able top, something no one else in Warsaw could brag of.

How unbearable it must have become for him if suddenly he needed his daughter's ring.

"What has happened, Henryk?"

"I have been good to you since the day we met." He rubbed an eye with an enormous fist, like an overgrown child. I had known this man for twenty years. He had behaved, time and again, like the father I didn't have: sometimes disapproving, sometimes indulgent, always certain to remind me of my place. He had loved me the most when his daughter died, because he knew that I had been who she loved most, and I was the closest he would ever get to her again. Which is why he never cut me off. If he was fond of me on my own terms, I have no idea.

"I'll get you the ring," I said.

He nodded, put a hand in a pocket. "I appreciate that."

I retreated to our bedroom, rummaged through the closet until I found the pale wool blanket that served as our treasury. Using an old pair of Kasia's sewing scissors, I loosened the stitch on the bottom of the blanket and removed the ring. It was actually smaller than I had remem-bered, the green a bit dusty. I blew on it, wiped it on my shirt.

"I hope it comes in handy."

He pocketed it swiftly. "There was also a necklace—you remember? A pearl necklace. With diamonds? My gift to Kasia on her wedding day."

"It's been a long time, Henryk."

"You know what I'm talking about, though."

"Perhaps it's in the vault in the bank. I'll look." I said this reflexively, even though I knew where it was, in the blanket lining next to the space where the emerald had been.

Henryk looked at me with narrowed eyes. "You wouldn't hide it from me, Adam."

"Of course not."

"It was a gift from me to my daughter," he said.

"It must be in the vault."

"Jews aren't allowed to keep precious goods in bank vaults anymore."

"Then I'll have to retrieve it," I said. My heart pounded—I never kept things from Henryk. But something about his very desperation told me the necklace was too valuable to hand over.

"I'd like that," he said. We both were quiet then, sizing each other up. Why wasn't he telling the truth? Why wasn't I?

"Henryk, what is going on that you need all of this . . . ?" What to call it? Money? Resources? But then I saw his face and felt guilty that I had asked.

Henryk gathered himself. "Obviously, our current political position requires delicate handling, Adam. I have many people to protect. Many people who rely on me for help."

I blinked at him.

"And of course you're one of them."

"Henryk, I'm grateful, but I don't need your protection," I said.

"Ah, but you do," he said. "More than you could possibly know."

So when he returned to my flat a few days after the Nazis announced resettlement—days I'd spent pacing around my apartment, trying to figure out how serious this was (I knew it was serious) and what I should pack (we weren't supposed to take much) and where I would go—I knew Henryk had arrived to save me. And I also knew this was not necessarily because he wanted to save me but because he wanted to prove to me he still could.

"You give me this apartment," he said, "and I'll give you a place in the Jewish district. It'll be a trade. Then, when this is over, we'll trade back."

"I don't know, Henryk."

"Well, you'll need to find *somewhere* to live in the district. You can't stay here."

To be honest, it was still an idea of mine to just stay put, see if I could keep under the radar, which of course was ridiculous—again, all my neighbors knew who I was, and half of them would have loved to get their slippery hands on my flat. But I didn't have any contacts in the Jewish quarter, so I didn't know how to secure a decent place there, and pride had kept me from calling Henryk to help, even though I was certain he'd been waiting for the call.

"It's a very nice apartment on Sienna Street. A lovely street. Only one bedroom, but there's a maid's room too, should you have company visit. And hot water. Oh, and what else? Maybe a balcony? I think they said there was a balcony."

"Whose place is it?"

"An old couple, Germans, actually, living in Poland from a long time back. They're going to go home, see what they can make of things in Berlin. I know them through work. You should be packing, by the way. When are you going to start packing?"

"I don't want to pack."

"Adam, don't be a baby. Things are difficult, I know, but you have to face facts."

"I'm facing facts, Henryk."

"Isn't that what you told me after Kasia fell?" Henryk said. "We had to face facts?"

"I said, I'm facing facts."

"I have the keys now," he said. He was sitting on my couch, stroking Gruby. "Who's going to take care of the cat?"

"How do you have keys?"

"The couple gave me an extra pair."

"And who's going to live here, then?"

"People I know through work. They need a place to live."

"Henryk, the government's been dissolved." I had never understood 100 percent what Henryk did for a living, but I knew it involved the government, and influence, and deals that weren't covered in the newspaper unless he wanted them to be. "Who needs my flat?"

"Colleagues," he said. "Do you want this apartment in the Jewish quarter or not?"

"I don't want to leave."

"That wasn't the question, Adam," he said. "Relocation starts this Saturday. Do you have another place to go?"

I shook my head, then put out my hand. He gave me the keys. I went to the drawer where I kept my own spare pair and handed them over. "Please ask them to take care of the place," I said. "Your colleagues who are moving in. Tell them the water in the bathroom is tricky—you have to press the faucet really hard to turn it. And the door to the bedroom sticks—they might think they're locked in when they're not. And ask them to please remember to clean the icebox. I don't want it to start to stink."

"What do you think, I'd give your apartment to animals?"

I shrugged.

"Adam, come on now. We just have to get through this period. This dreadful waiting. It'll be over, you'll move back home. Or maybe they'll open the border and you can join your family and never step foot in this miserable country again."

The cat nuzzled up against Henryk's chubby fingers, in ecstasy from all the petting. "Henryk, who is going to live in my apartment?"

"Good people," Henryk said. "Very fine people. Don't worry. And you'll love your new place. It's a wonderful place."

I HAD BEEN to the old Jewish district before, of course—it was where the kosher bakeries were, the butchers, the places we would occasionally shop or see friends when I was a boy. But I had never seen it in such disarray, so much screeching and pushing, so much crowding, so many suitcases. I had an old map of the area, which I needed to find my way, but as I squinted at it a small child snatched it from my hands and vanished into the crowd.

Therefore, it took me longer than I would have wished to arrive at the address on Sienna Street that Saturday with my wheelbarrow of possessions, but still, after a few missed turns I found the building and hauled everything up five flights—the elevator had stopped working during the invasion, and nobody knew when or if it would ever be repaired. Relieved to find that the key did indeed work (I didn't realize I wasn't certain it would until I tried it), I wheeled in my belongings and set about inspecting the place (the large bedroom, the small but functional kitchen, the beautiful and heavy wooden furniture) and thought, *Okay. I'll be okay here.*

I took a breath. Put my shirts and pants in the drawers, spread my sheets—Kasia's sheets—across the broad oak bed. The smells in the apartment (dust, mildew) suggested to me that it had been vacant for much longer than Henryk had suggested. In the icebox, a shriveled head of cabbage, and behind the oven, the pitter-patter of mouse feet. German people? Trying their luck back in Berlin?

I sat down at the small table in the corner of the kitchen and tried to figure out how I would make this foreign place feel like it was mine. I knew I was supposed to register with the Judenrat on Chłodna Street, and that perhaps they would find me a job; I also knew that I would need every groszy I had smuggled in here (Kasia's clothes, Kasia's earrings, Kasia's necklace). But I didn't know how long I would stay or how comfortable to feel or what to expect, or how I could be so homesick when I was less than five kilometers from my home.

I was interrupted from my musings by a shriek—a shriek I would grow to know over time, Pani Lescovec's shriek of amusement or horror or fear or delight. "Who are you, and what are you doing in my house?"

"Excuse me?"

She repeated, in the sort of frantic Yiddish I associated with grandmothers: "Who are you, and what are you doing in my house?" Pani Lescovec stood surrounded by her husband, three boys, and about a dozen bags. It turned out they, too, had been promised this apartment—by a genial acquaintance of Pan Lescovec's, a government lawyer they knew, who had told them the place had been empty for months and that it was theirs for the taking if they would agree to give up their comfortable home in the old city. "Yes, yes, Henryk Duda. Yes, he was the acquaintance." When I showed Pani Lescovec my key, she shrieked again: "No, no, it can't be!"

And, of course, this domestic comedy grew only funnier when the Wiskoffs appeared, winded and red-faced, having climbed the stairs under the weight of even more suitcases than the Lescovecs had brought.

"What the hell is this?" Emil Wiskoff said, standing at the doorway, assessing the company in his apartment.

"We live here," said Pani Lescovec.

"*We* live here," said Emil, and soon enough it became clear that Henryk had snookered all of us out of our own places, for reasons we couldn't begin to fathom (who was he putting up? why did he need our money? our apartments?), and that he had made various promises we couldn't imagine were true: he'd find us papers, he'd arrange a passage out of the ghetto, he'd take care of our former apartments as if they were his own. Most important, we knew there was nothing we could do about it, and, after a certain amount of bitter debate, we concluded the best way forward was to try to live our lives peaceably in this small space until a better situation presented itself.

The Wiskoff and Lescovec boys, five in all, were already running around the flat the way boys do, and in about five minutes they'd found the stairwell to the rooftop and were racing up and down, while the adults divvied up the closets and the bureaus, and I claimed my small alcove in the living room. I screwed hooks into the soft plaster ceiling and hung up a drape for privacy. I removed the cushions from the sofa and laid them out for a bed. I covered the bed with Kasia's linen sheets. I placed my books and clothes on the window seat and stowed the sad wheelbarrow in the corner of the living room, where I hoped it wouldn't get in the way. Then I retreated to my alcove, surrounded myself with Kasia's old things, and tried not to panic as I listened to the new ladies of the house scream at each other in the kitchen over who was claiming more cupboard space.

I put Kasia's jewels, the pearl-and-diamond necklace, the small gold earrings, under a loose floorboard.

I was one of ten people in this apartment, and I had never felt more hideously alone. I sat on a cushion, cross-legged, and tried to read, but the words swam in front of me.

"Duda's just a shyster, that's all he is," said Sala Wiskoff, sticking her head into my alcove.

"I'm sorry," I said, "but if we're going to live here peaceably, I need you not to just show up in my limited living space."

"Yes, yes, of course," Sala said—did I even know her name yet? "I'm sorry. I didn't mean—"

"It's okay," I said, worried I sounded rude. "You can come in."

So she did, parting the curtain. There was nowhere to sit, so she sat down on the floor next to me. Our knees touched: our first small intimacy.

"How do you know Henryk Duda?"

"He's my father-in-law."

Sala raised her eyebrows. "Where's your wife?"

"She's dead."

"Oh no. Oh, I'm sorry." She paused, and looked around my strange little room. If I were her, I would have left, unable to handle such a confidence from a stranger. But Sala didn't leave.

"Do you think he's a collaborator?"

"Duda?" I considered it. "I thought the Nazis didn't want to collaborate with Poles."

"Well, Duda's not just any Pole," she said. "That's what I think, anyway. He's a collaborator. Or worse, a profiteer."

I shrugged. "He was my benefactor."

"Some benefactor," she said. "What happened to your wife?"

"She fell. Damaged her brain."

"Ah," Sala said. She brought her knees up to her chest. "I'm sorry to hear that. Was it recent?"

"Three years ago," I said.

She nodded, thoughtfully. "My mother-in-law died today."

"What do you mean today?"

"I mean she was hit in the head by a Nazi guard during the reloca-tion. My husband is walking the streets outside, weeping."

"Christ," I said.

"I know." She looked at me with her dark-brown eyes. "I know."

I decided then that I felt comfortable in her strange presence. It calmed me, or at least made me feel less alone.

"I didn't like her very much," she added. "Which is not a thing you should say of the dead."

"You can say whatever you want," I said. "All the rules are different now."

"She was a terrible snob."

"Some people are."

"But also uneducated."

"As are many snobs."

She sighed. "She was my children's grandmother."

"That doesn't mean you have to like her."

She smiled, revealing one grayish tooth. "Thanks for the permission."

"My pleasure."

I found to my surprise that I was smiling back at her. I didn't think I had smiled for many days.

"Emil and I will be sleeping on the other side of this curtain," she said. "We'll do our best not to bother you."

"I'll do the same," I said.

"Oh, that's all right," she said. "I'm a mother. You can bother me as much as you'd like."

And once again I had expected her to get up and leave, but once again she'd stayed put, sitting with me in my small space, and although I hadn't been this close to another person in years, found I really didn't mind.

SIX

===

At one in the morning, I scribbled down the notes from my interview with Filip, self-consciously, even though I was alone in the kitchen: Was this what I was supposed to do? Had I asked the right questions? I still hadn't heard the boy descend from the roof, and his mother and father were bickering in the bedroom they had commandeered. Should they go upstairs and drag him down? Was he going to freeze to death? They thought they were being quiet, but in fact they were hissing quite loudly and it took everything I had not to pound on the door.

The apartment we shared was quirky in the way of many Warsovian apartments that had originally been designed for one family with servants and had been slowly sealed off and fragmented. The main bedroom served as a dormitory of sorts for the five boys: three Lescovec, two Wiskoff. Pan and Pani Lescovec took the narrow maid's room off the kitchen, and Emil and Sala Wiskoff shared the large living room with me, separated by my curtain of sheets. This was a relatively impoverished situation for our part of the ghetto, where many families had stayed in their original apartments and refused to take in boarders, even for pay. But we had heard that in the larger ghetto across Chłodna Street there were families twelve to a room, and that much of the plumbing on that side had backed up to the point that there was basically no sewage

system whatsoever, and no coal for heat either. (We got our coal by bribing the Polish guards on Sienna Street, twenty zloty for a week's supply.)

I looked up when I heard someone sit down at the table across from
me. "God, I wish they would shut up," Sala Wiskoff said, but she was
smiling; she was one of those women who smiled to hide her irritation.
She was wearing her nightclothes, a dressing gown pulled over herself
for modesty, and was holding a half-empty mug of tea. Although we
had been in this apartment for only a few weeks, we had taken to late-
night conversations; our strange living situation allowed us a familiarity
neither one of us would have imagined in any other circumstance. Also,
neither one of us could sleep particularly well; Sala's husband, meanwhile, slept like the dead.

"Filip told me that lots of kids hang out on the roofs all day," I said.
"Did you know that?"

"My kids are in the sewers," she said. "I'd feel safer if they were on
the roof."

"What are they doing down there?"

"Trading, stealing. I don't know. I told them they don't have to, we
have resources for now, but they want to join the resistance, playact at
being soldiers."

"Is there a resistance to join?"

Sala shrugged. She had dark hair threaded with silver, dark circles
under her eyes. She was maybe thirty-two or -three, younger than I
was, but the years seemed to weigh on her more heavily, or the ghetto
weighed on her more heavily, the way it did on all the mothers.

"What are you writing?" she asked.

"Oh, just . . . I'm just keeping a journal." I covered it reflexively with
my arm.

"What for?"

"To keep one day separate from the next, I guess."

She sighed. "I know what day it is by how gray my hair has gotten.
You can't buy a box of dye around here for love or money."

"You dye your hair?"

"Of course." She laughed. "I started going gray early, and as the wife of an important man, I couldn't go around looking like a hag. Besides," she said, "I used to be much more vain. If you had told me two years ago I'd be sitting in my nightgown talking to a man I barely know without even a dab of lipstick—"

"Which would have bothered you more, the lipstick or the nightgown?"

Sala shook her head. "I could never have imagined it. Never in a million years." She traced the grain in the wood table with her fingernail. It was a substantial table. We also had bureaus, armoires, an enormous teak desk in the living room, all useful in case we ran out of bribe money for the Polish guards and needed wood for heat.

"You know we had been talking about emigrating?"

"I didn't," I said.

"Palestine," she said. "Emil has connections. He wanted to go—or at least he said he wanted to go, because he knew that I didn't. If I'd said I wanted to go, he would have started to have second thoughts. Neither of us really wanted to leave, even though we both knew we should probably leave."

"What was keeping you?"

"Oh, I don't know. Silly things, in retrospect." She looked up from the table. "I guess I just loved my life. I had parties, social obligations. I was the head of the fundraising arm at the boys' school. And we had such a beautiful house. God, when I think of our house, I'm sure the new people already pawned all my furniture . . . Besides, what was I going to do in Palestine? This is where my family is. Was. I couldn't picture it."

"Me neither."

"We should have gone."

For years after my brother left, he'd sent me picture postcards featuring some novel aspect of desert life: a camel, an irrigation line, a date palm. Since we were boys, Szimon—now Shimon—had felt more attuned to his Judaism, or perhaps, more put out by it, which was almost the same feeling. He was three years younger than I was, and smaller and darker. He had never done particularly well in school nor fostered many outside interests, although he was a keen football player and could drink more beer in one sitting than anyone I'd ever met. This was why it was surprising to me when he'd come to our apartment one night and announced he was leaving.

"You're a fool if you stay," he slurred on our doorstep; he didn't come into the flat, because he was certain Kasia didn't like him.

"This is where my life is."

"There is no life here," he said. "You want to stay in a country that doesn't even treat you like a citizen?"

But I had always, for some reason, felt like a Polish citizen; my father's grievous patriotism had rubbed off on me.

"You know, you'll never be one," he said. "It's amazing to me that you don't know that."

"I'm not sure what you mean."

"You married the Polish girl, got the job at the Polish school, but your name is still Paskow, is it not? And nobody will ever think that's a Polish name. Jewish blood runs in your veins, whether you like it or not."

"Blood doesn't have a religion."

"Jewish blood does, brother."

"I'll miss you, Szimon," I said.

He recoiled at the lie.

I wasn't sure what I had expected to happen to him in Palestine— probably that he'd get stabbed in a brawl with a bunch of angry Turks— but instead he found a wife and a cabbage farm and a charismatic rabbi and some date palms, and a house made out of cypress wood and tin.

He had invited me to his wedding. I suppose it would have been pos- sible to go—there were boats, and we had money for travel—but Kasia had her migraines and, I'll be honest, if I was going to travel anywhere, we still both wanted to see London.

Should I have gone to Palestine? Was I really willing to concede that a good life in Poland would no longer be possible for me, a Jew? (*But look at his blue eyes, Anna. His father died fighting the Soviets.*)

"I almost got papers," I blurted to Sala. "From Duda."

"He promised us papers too," she said. "I didn't really believe him. Besides, nobody in their right mind would believe I'm Catholic. Or Emil, even, although he has green eyes. But you . . . you might have had more luck."

"Perhaps—"

"How did you end up so blond, anyway?"

"Would you call this blond? I always think of it as light brown."

"Well, whatever it is, you could probably pass." She reached out and tousled my hair. "*My* face, meanwhile . . . I have a face like the Zionist flag."

I chuckled. "You're much nicer-looking than the Zionist flag."

"You flirt," she said.

It was true; sometimes I did flirt. I stood to search the small icebox for a snack, but all I had in my section were a few wrapped slices of bread, and parsnips I'd purchased from some children on the street.

"I have biscuits," Sala said. "I hid them in the bin behind the pots."

"Biscuits!"

"Don't let the kids know. I'm hoarding."

I opened the bin and found a small pile of vanilla-scented biscuits. I took one and stuffed it in my mouth while I was still standing.

"Have another."

"It's okay," I said, but I did in fact take another, and ate it more slowly, sitting back down across from Sala while she sipped her tea. "Where did these come from?"

"I found a little sugar for sale on the street," she said. "Gave it to Ristak, the baker on Nowolipki. He has flour and, I suppose, some margarine."

"God bless Ristak," I said.

"No, he's a pig. Charged me three zloty."

"Even after you gave him sugar?"

She nodded, yawned. I didn't know how Sala kept her eyes open. She usually stayed awake even after I went to bed, and in the morning she was up scrubbing the kitchen or the bathroom before anyone else had brushed his teeth.

"Do you have regrets?" I asked, after a while. "About staying?"

"How could I not?"

"Does Emil?"

"After what happened to his mother. Of course."

"I'm sorry—that was a cruel question."

"No, it's natural."

Emil's mother had been killed in front of the entire family for the crime of not taking off her wedding ring fast enough. She was trying— she'd said she was trying—but she had worn it for fifty years, and her finger had swollen around it, and the Nazi was screaming so loudly. And she had parkinsonian tremors, and it hadn't taken much to kill her, really. Two blows across the head.

Sala shrugged. We were quiet for a while, listening to the Lescovecs still whispering madly in the maid's room next door. "I wonder if we really are just waiting here to die."

"Come on, Sala, they can't kill all of us."

"Can't they?"

"What would be the gain in that? It's illogical. And the Nazis pride themselves on being logical. Don't they?"

"What's illogical about killing people you despise?"

"It's a waste of human resources."

"What on earth is a 'human resource'?"

"You know, our capacities. Our brains. Our muscles. They could have us fight for them or work in their factories. Build their bombs. Fight on their front lines." It occurred to me I sounded a little desperate.

Sala pinched the bridge of her nose. "So you'd rather see us enslaved?"

"My father was a soldier. He didn't consider it slavery."

"Adam, don't be ridiculous. Your father was an enlisted soldier, not a prisoner of war."

"Not according to my mother," I said, trying to be funny. (But, truly, what would be the point of killing all of us? And how on earth could they pull such a thing off? And would the world really . . . let them?)

She sighed. "It's been funny watching Pani Lescovec trying to be so protective of her children. She wants to know where they are all the time. She thinks she can still keep bad things from happening to them."

"That's natural for a mother, isn't it?"

"I don't know," she said. "For me, it's like . . . it's like once we saw Reva killed because she couldn't get that stupid ring off fast enough, once our boys saw their grandmother beaten to death in front of their eyes . . . We were on the stoop, you know, the front step of our old building. We were trying to move as fast as we could. We had all our belongings, as much as we could handle, those stupid carts, because they'd taken away our car. And there's poor Reva. She's trying to make it down the stairs, that idiotic ring glinting, and we're all just waiting for her, thinking, 'Come on, bubbe, let's go, let's get a move on,' and she won't let the boys hold her hand even though, for heaven's sake, they could have carried her—she hardly weighed anything. And this Nazi comes up, and he starts screaming about the law to turn in anything of value, and we didn't even know what he was talking about. We're just thinking, 'Please, sir, what else do you want? You've taken our home—what do we have of value?' and he's screaming, '*Der Ring, der Ring,*' and, I swear to God, for a minute I thought he was speaking in code. And then I realize what's happening, and it's like slow motion and time speeding up all at once. Emil is screaming at the Nazi to stop, the boys are desperately trying to get that ring off, and the Nazi just hits her. Twice."

"Oh, Sala."

She shrugged again, a sort of *What can you do?* Then she looked back down at the table. "And then he leaned down and took the ring off my husband's mother's dead body and put it in his pocket and walked down the street, as if nothing of consequence had happened."

"Sala."

She looked away for a minute, rested her chin on her palm.

"There were Nazis everywhere. Emil tried to revive his mother, but then a soldier grabbed Rafel by the neck and told us to move or we'd never see our son again. And so we moved. As fast as we could. The soldier let Rafel go, thank God."

"Thank God."

"We had no choice but to leave Reva's body in the street. Emil wanted to go back right away to bury her. He didn't know that once we walked into the ghetto, we weren't going to walk back out."

She took her hair out of its usual knot, released it for a moment, and then tied it back up.

"They say the soul of a Jew who hasn't received a proper burial will never be at rest," she said. "I don't know if that's true, but it's certainly true for those of us the dead Jew leaves behind."

"I imagine that's so."

"We've got to get out of here, Adam," she said.

"We'll get out of here."

"I don't believe you," she said.

"Believe me," I said, and, although she was a married woman and in my heart I was a married man, I reached out and squeezed her hand, and she held on to it for much longer than either one of us would have thought appropriate in any other circumstances, or even these.

SEVEN

===

I rang the bell at 3/5 Tłomackie Street almost nauseated by nerves. I had not been in a library in almost a year and, as I walked toward the building, I felt more and more certain I was being set up. It would be an excellent German plan, wouldn't it? To ask Jews across the ghetto to take notes, and then they'd round us up, steal our notebooks, find out if there were any rebellions afoot, and shoot us casually against the library wall. Or perhaps in the synagogue next door, our ruined bodies spread across the ruined bima. Very cinematic, very Nazi.

But my terrified imaginings were interrupted by a woman in a neat blue dress, who opened the door, nodded at me, and led me up the stairs to a small room whose warmth felt almost miraculous—I hadn't realized how cold I'd been, for how long, until I entered a room with a woodburning fire. I looked at the woman quizzically; she gestured for me to sit down.

There were about two dozen people scattered about on leather couches and velvet settees, and it was like I had entered a movie set, this whole thing was a movie—where was I? I turned around, quickly, still half expecting to see Germans, and was almost ready to accept my fate for the comfort of a real fire in a fireplace, a soft velvet couch to sit on. *Fine, kill me, shoot me in the back. Just let me sit here in this room for ten minutes before I go.*

"Pan Paskow, I'm glad you could join us." It was Ringelblum, the man who had found me in my classroom a week ago, still authoritative but less intimidating in these comfortable circumstances. "You've met my wife, Yehudit." The woman in the blue dress. "And this is Uri, my son," he said, gesturing to a boy of about ten sitting in the corner with a book. A boy with a book! In a corner! As if this world were almost normal, as if he could tune out everything and immerse himself in a book.

The others went about the room, introducing themselves, and it turned out that I'd heard of many of them before: a watercolor painter of some renown, an esteemed historian from the University of Warsaw, the rabbi in charge of the Tłomackie Street synagogue, next door. Someone passed around a plate of dried apricots. "Courtesy of our friends in the Joint Distribution Committee," Ringelblum said. They were sweet and tart, and soft against my teeth; after I ate one, I stuck one in my pocket for later.

(How did the Joint Distribution Committee get apricots here? And was it really so much easier to get dried apricots in than a trainload of Jews out?)

"You know," whispered the woman sitting next to me, "there's a secret restaurant on the corner of Gęsia Street that's serving roast goose in wine sauce. And they have chocolate. I copied down the menu for the archive." She gestured to her white notebook.

"Where on earth do they—?"

"From actual *Germans*. They're drinking German wine. I can't even imagine how much they bribe."

I kept my face impassive. I had heard that such things went on—some of our neighbors on Sienna Street looked rather rosy, despite the circumstances, and I had heard music and dancing from some of the courtyards on certain sunny afternoons. But I tried not to hear the music, tried not to imagine how they got away with what they got away with. And what nerves would it take to swallow roast goose in a corner restaurant?

Starving children would press their faces against the windows like the walking dead.

The woman was clear-skinned and smelled nice, and I had to stamp out my own embarrassment at what I probably looked and smelled like. We had soap in the apartment, but it was a sort of gritty composite made in the sink by Pani Lescovec and sold to me for fifty groszy a bar. It smelled mostly like candle wax, and I used it everywhere: my toes, my groin, my hair.

"Shabbat Shalom, everyone," said Ringelblum, which was evidently the cue that the meeting was starting. Everyone repeated "Shabbat Shalom," except for me, out of practice.

"I hope you all are in good health and spirits, all things considered," Ringelblum said, and everyone acknowledged they were, even me—even as I was planning how I could get another apricot and whether or not I had the guts to visit the roast goose café, and with what money. Could I start charging more for English lessons? Or maybe I could just ride out the war in this room. Would they let me stay? Would anyone mind if I stayed?

It occurred to me that I was so tired my very bones hurt. The muscles that braided their way up my back had tightened and hardened; my jaw had been clenched for so long I sometimes used my fingers to pry them apart. And all this had happened while I wasn't even paying attention. I had been sleeping on the sofa cushions on the floor near a drafty window for weeks now. I had been eating boiled potatoes during my shift at the Aid Society, brick-like bread from the miserable Nowolipki Street bakery. My Mokotów apartment—the books I had collected for half my life, the desk where I had written or studied or daydreamed, my radio, my bicycle, the cameras I had purchased over the years—I had told myself I could give them all up, that none of it mattered. But how could none of it matter? The photo albums I wasn't able to bring with me: photo after photo of Kasia. I had forgotten our wedding album, of all things, the photos from our wedding lunch at Restaurant Honoratka.

Her dresses still lined up in the closet (I had kept her favorites, lined up like they were waiting for her to come back.) The teddy bears she had collected. Gruby, our cat.

"It has been a long week, but good things seem to be happening in the outside world. Perhaps you have heard that President Roosevelt has officially declared that the United States is no longer isolating itself from world affairs. Moreover, they will begin loaning arms to the British. So I think we can rest assured that our plight will not last too much longer. It's impossible to imagine the Germans being able to stand up to both the British and the Americans together."

"Alevai," murmured the woman sitting next to me.

"Alevai," replied the man sitting next to her.

"Meanwhile, of course, we wait, and attempt to make the best of our dire situation. As I'm sure you heard, several children were recently rounded up and taken to Pawiak Prison for the crime of panhandling. The Judenrat were able to bargain for their release but, unfortunately, not before three of them perished of malnourishment. Yehudit, I believe you have the notes?"

Ringelblum's wife nodded. His child, in the corner, still had his face in a book.

"Further, several communities from the Ukrainian border have been liquidated, and others have been deported to our ghetto. With no new resources coming—"

"What do you mean, 'liquidated'? Explain yourself," said a grumpy-sounding man behind me.

"I mean wiped out. I mean every resident shot and killed, or taken into a building and locked in and gassed." He said this without a trace of anger in his voice, and yet somehow it was clear that he was angry. The room fell still.

"What does the Joint say about all this, Ringelblum?" A call from somewhere in the back.

"They plead for patience."

"Patience!" a bearded man cried. "When they are . . . liquidating?"

"They understand our plight, or they are trying to understand our plight," Ringelblum said. "It is not easy."

"Our plight," muttered the woman sitting next to me. She ran a hand through her thin brown hair.

"I can tell you, there is more food coming into the kitchens, which is good news, despite everything. But the truth is, our circumstances are becoming more challenging, and will continue to become more challenging until the United States officially enters the war."

"Did your contacts in New York tell you when that will happen?" asked the bearded man.

"The people at the Joint know almost as little as we do, unfortunately. But, as I said, they did promise us more food. Cereal and powdered milk. They are using every diplomatic channel they have. Our brothers and sisters in New York . . ."

"My actual brother lives in New York," whispered the woman sitting next to me. "He wanted me to join him."

"My brother's in Palestine."

"We should have gone."

"I refuse to keep thinking of the things I should have done," I said.

Without warning, I thought of my cat. The cat who had been there since the week I'd married Kasia, the cat who warmed the pillow next to mine in the days after she'd died.

Henryk promised me he would take care of Gruby. But if I got home and found Gruby had been lost, I would never, ever forgive myself. Or Henryk.

"How can you help it?" the woman asked.

I could have taken Gruby with me. There were other pets in the ghetto. But I hadn't been able to carry everything. I had tried. I stood there, ridiculous, jamming whatever I could into my pockets, into the wheelbarrow I was forced to take across town with my entire life in it, since trams were banned, cars were banned, there were no taxis. What could I do? It was a five-kilometer walk to my new apartment, balancing this wobbly wheelbarrow on streets that were still half-demolished from the bombing, Kasia's pearl necklace sewn into my coat lining, her earrings rolled into a pair of socks. Meanwhile, around me, people were racing up and down streets with carts, some people on horseback or muleback like it was a hundred years ago. Where had so many people found so many mules? Old ladies weeping, babies shrieking. The Jews of Mokotów, as few as I thought we were, had been shaken loose like nests from a tree on a windy day. And now here we blinked, our lifetimes of accumulation on display, hurrying to our new accommodations in the ghetto under risk of being shot.

So what had I taken? *Huckleberry Finn*, *Moby Dick*. Earrings. A necklace.

A man on horseback rode by me that morning like an apparition from another age, a Polish flag draped around his neck.

And yet somehow it was still a surprise to me, to almost everyone, when they locked us in. When they sealed the ghetto. After all this— after being forced to relinquish my home, my goods, after saying goodbye to my job and my cat and my life—I don't know why anything else should have been a horrid surprise. But it was. I had assumed I could at least walk back to Mokotów sometimes. See my cat.

The walls of the ghetto were three meters tall, and we could see the broken glass that lined the top, and anyone caught trying to scale them was shot on sight, and we had heard the shots ring out from the very first hour after the gates were closed.

In the warm room, the Oneg Shabbat meeting swirled around me. The war talk was over, and now we were reporting on what we had learned during the week that had just passed. Two older members, both women, reported on the various soup kitchens: the rye flour speckled with mouse turds, the unexpected delivery of twenty kilos of half-rotten mushrooms. (In fact, I had been on duty the day the mushrooms came in, and had cheerfully pared away the soft black spots, imagining the impossible: mushroom soup with cream, butter, chives.)

We also had reports on ghetto health statistics—with so many doctors in our midst, a sort of approximation of care was available: all the doctors, none of the medicine, and so an expected uptick in diseases of the skin, lungs, kidneys.

A few reported on the Nazi activities they observed, the random beatings, the harassing of our more attractive women. Meanwhile, others were collecting whatever paraphernalia they could find: posters, pamphlets, German directives printed out and passed around to the denizens of the ghetto like whispered threats. Newspaper photos of children who had been shot sneaking across to the Aryan side. Café menus: wine and goose and chocolate.

The Oneg Shabbateers all had their white notebooks on their laps, were going through their notes, giving updates.

"It would be useful to have a statistical understanding of the calorie rations," Ringelblum said. "Who goes to the soup kitchens and on what days, who has the money for black-market food."

During my shifts at the Aid Society, I sat behind the desk outside the kitchen and collected ration cards. At the end of my shift, I was given a bowl of soup. At home, there was bread and sometimes hidden biscuits. So far, I had not been too hungry, although I had forgotten what it was like to feel full. I reached in my pocket for my other apricot.

"We could also use more information on schooling, couldn't we?" said a man across from me, near the fire.

"We could," Ringelblum said. "That's one of the things we've asked Pan Paskow for." He gestured to me. "Everyone, perhaps you've noticed our newest recruit. This is Adam Paskow. He was the head of the foreign languages division at the Centralny Lyceum for fifteen years. He has a degree in English literature from the University of Warsaw, and a master's degree from the same. Currently, he is teaching English literature classes several times a week for our boys and girls." Ringelblum knew everything about me, even what I hadn't told him.

Everyone turned to me, made appreciative noises, and I felt my cheeks warm. I was generally one to underplay my hand.

"That is wonderful," said Yehudit. "How many students do you have?"

"The most I've had is ten. There are always at least four regulars. The others come and go as they're able."

"How did you advertise the school?"

"One of my students, Szifra Joseph, had attended Centralny before the war. She asked to continue studying with me and told some of the other young people she knew. And I am sharing housing, currently, with several children. Some of them attend my classes."

"Szifra Joseph? The daughter of Avram Joseph, the uniform magnate?"

"Yes," I said. "She speaks quite good English."

"She's the beautiful girl with the blond hair?"

"I saw her cozying up to a guard on the street the other day," said the man across the room. "She should be careful."

"I doubt she was cozying up."

"Ask her," Ringelblum said.

"Ask her?"

"We are creating a three-dimensional portrait of everyone's activities, everyone's survival," Ringelblum said. "We are not painting some fanciful portrait of the last of the Polish Jews. We are telling the truth."

"The last of the Polish Jews?"

"Ask her," Ringelblum said. "We want her story."

"We want everyone's story," said the woman sitting next to me. "Nobody has any privacy here."

"I know that," I said. Of course I knew that.

The apricots were passed around again.

I pocketed a few more this time.

Before we left, we were given our stipend: twenty zloty each. I was surprised at the generosity. "Thank our friends at the Joint," said the woman sitting next to me. "Apricots and zloty when what we really need is a goddamn escape plan." She put the money in her pocket. "I'm spending mine on more wine at the café. You should join me."

She was clean. She smelled nice. I was lonely. Still, the idea of drinking wine with her made my jaw start to hurt again, and made it easier, for some reason, to leave the room where moments before I had been so comfortable.

Name: Szifra Joseph
Date: December 30, 1940
Age: 15 years, 10 months
Height: 175 cm?
Weight: 55 kg?

Szifra Joseph is the oldest of three children born to Irina and Avram Joseph, previously of Konstancin-Jeziorna, Poland. Before his death, Avram was the president and founder of the Joseph Apparel Company, situated in Praga, Warsaw, which for years produced and supplied the bulk of the uniforms for Polish hospitals and sanitary units. The family, therefore, was financially quite successful and lived in a large villa with a swimming pool, a greenhouse, and a gazebo on its grounds. The family employed a chauffeur, a cook, and several maids, all Poles, and found it especially distressing when the Germans decreed that Poles could no longer work in a domestic capacity in Jewish households.

Szifra describes herself as practical, which is why she still tends to her appearance, fends for her brothers, and studies English. She had planned to be an actress before the war and still intends to go to Hollywood after it's over. Evidently, there is a family connection to the Wansol brothers—now Warner—in California, and Szifra's goal is to make use of that connection as soon as we are liberated.

In the meantime, she has consented to be interviewed by me in our classroom on a Monday afternoon, as she has, she laments, "no other plans."

A.P. What has been the hardest part for you about being here?

S.J. I try not to dwell on the difficulties.

A.P. That's a good strategy.

S.J. Well, it's just not going to get me anywhere. If I lie about and moan about how *awful* it all is, if I can't get out of bed and I just *cry* all the time I'm not sure how I'm supposed to get on with my life. And this is my life, correct? This is the only one I'm going to get.

(Here, I should mention that Szifra is conducting our interview in English, even though I had asked my initial question in Polish. I know from our previous interactions that she speaks at least four languages fairly well—Polish, Yiddish, German, and English—and that she has a plan to learn French as soon as such a thing is possible—"even though the pathetic French couldn't hold off the Nazis for 10 minutes.")

A.P. Where did you learn to be so resilient?

S.J. Well, when I was a girl, my father did everything, to the point where my mother can barely make a decision for herself. She's completely helpless. And I knew I never wanted to be like that.

A.P. Isn't your mother working in the brush factory?

S.J. Only because she needs the working papers to secure our apartment. And the stipend, I suppose. But really, what is she making there? 2 zloty a day? And what is she spending it on besides sawdust bread and heating coal?

A.P. You have to admit, it's good to have coal.

S.J. I'm just saying, there are smarter ways to make money.

A.P. Such as?

S.J. You know my younger brother? Eli? He takes 6 of my mother's zloty every week and bribes the guards to look away, and then he sneaks back in with 5 kilos of sugar and sells it for a zloty for 20 grams. And I must say, *that's* how you make things work in this market.

A.P. Your brother is risking his life.

S.J. He is *not*. Don't be an alarmist. As long as he keeps bribing the guard, he'll keep selling sugar, and as long as he keeps selling sugar, he can keep bribing the guard. Or as long as my mother keeps making brushes. I mean it's not very difficult.

A.P. What if there's no more sugar?

S.J. He'll sell potatoes! Or apples! Whatever—it doesn't matter.

A.P. What if he can't get those?

S.J. Then he'll find something else!

A.P.

S.J. Sometimes I think you like to be intentionally dim.

A.P.

S.J.

A.P. Do you mind if I ask another question?

S.J. Go on.

A.P. What's the thing you miss most about your old life? Before you and your family came here?

S.J. Are you serious?

A.P. I am.

S.J. (Throwing her head back as though waiting for a vampire to take a bite from her throat) Everything, obviously. I mean, I miss everything.

A.P. Yes, but what . . . what specifically?

S.J. Are you trying to torture me? I miss all of it. Obviously. I miss my bedroom. I miss my bed. I miss my closet. I miss the household help. I miss school—even your old class, Pan Paskow. I miss our piano. I miss ice cream. I miss my friends. I miss . . .

A.P. Your father?

S.J. My father? Sometimes. I suppose. Well, honestly, not much. I never really saw him at home, you know. He was always working. And it was so pathetic what happened to him. I mean, one setback—one little setback—and he *shoots* himself. In the gazebo, for my brothers to find. Like a coward.

A.P.

S.J.

A.P. Isn't that a little . . . unsympathetic?

S.J. Is it? Clearly, my father loved his business more than he loved me or my brothers. Because if he really loved us, he would have stuck around and tried to protect us. But no. No. Shoots himself with his army rifle. Such cowardice.

A.P. Maybe he couldn't live with the humiliation?

S.J. I don't care what the excuse was.

A.P. Well . . .

S.J. I'll tell you, since you're curious, the thing I miss most is—it might sound silly, but it's the cinema. When they told us that Jews couldn't go to the cinema anymore, that was the very worst of all the rules.

A.P. Yes, it was particularly insulting.

S.J. I did it anyway.

A.P. What do you mean?

S.J. I just . . . I knew I could get away with it. Nobody was going to demand to see my papers. And there were so many films I wanted to see! "Holiday," did you see that? With Cary Grant? Ooh, I loved that. And "Jezebel," with Bette Davis. And "Profesor Wilczur," did you see that one? I don't always love Polish cinema—I prefer American—but that was really good. Very romantic.

A.P. I missed it.

S.J. Well . . . if you get the chance . . .

A.P. And you just . . . snuck in?

S.J. It wasn't hard. For instance, one day last summer, I told my mother I was going to meet a friend, and instead I went to the Odeon near Theatre Square—you know the one?—and I saw there was a gendarme by the ticket booth checking papers, and I thought to myself, "I shouldn't. I mean, I shouldn't. I mean, it's so dangerous I shouldn't." But they were showing "Swing Time," with Fred Astaire and Ginger Rogers, and they're my favorite. The way he dances? Oh, I wanted to go so badly. So I took off my armband, and when the gendarme asked for my kennkarte I gave him a look, you know, a serious *look*, like "How dare you, sir." Because I knew I could. I just had a feeling.

A.P. That's incredibly risky.

S.J. I know. I couldn't even enjoy the movie after that, honestly. I was too nervous. What would happen if he came in looking for me? I mean, even though I wanted to stay—I mean, Fred Astaire is my *favorite*. But I was really nervous. I snuck out during intermission and raced home.

A.P. Did you ever go back? See another film?

S.J. No. But I'm telling you, Pan Paskow, it's the first thing I'll do when I get out of here.

A.P. That sounds like a good plan.

S.J. Well, maybe I'll take a bath first. Have a decent meal. You know what I mean.

A.P. Of course.

S.J. So are we done? Not to be rude, but I do have some appointments to see to later—

A.P. Szifra, have you had any more encounters with the soldier who thought you were an Aryan? (I just blurt this question before I properly plan what to say, Ringelblum's mandate to "ask her" having weighed heavily on my mind in the days before the interview.)

S.J. (Perhaps predictably, turning her most ferocious look on me) Why would you ask me that?

(Here, I stutter something unhelpful to my cause.)

S.J. As I said before, I am making the best of things. I have made decisions during this hideous moment in our history to help myself and my family survive. As you know, Pan Paskow, it is *not easy* to survive.

A.P. I know that—

S.J. As we've already discussed, my father killed himself. My mother is in the midst of a complete mental breakdown. (Szifra switches to Yiddish, her first tongue and the one she speaks most fluently.) I have two young brothers who are pulling much more weight than they should be: Jakub is smuggling, as I mentioned before, and Eli is selling the smuggled goods on the black market and managing our family's finances. My brothers are 9 and 12 years old. This is not a position they or any other children should ever be put in.

(I mumble something apologetic, which does not interrupt her protestations.)

S.J. It seems to me that if I can make an ally of a German soldier—someone that will certainly be *advantageous* to my family as our circumstances continue to deteriorate—it is the very *least* I can do to help out in what has become an unexpectedly prolonged situation. Do you understand?

A.P. Of course.

S.J. Moreover, I refuse to believe that, even in this situation, the German soldier whose acquaintance I have made is necessarily evil. I won't believe that *everyone* is either good or evil all the time.

A.P.

S.J. The German soldier, as far as we know, has been put in an impossible situation himself, as anyone with any understanding of the German political system would understand. German boys are forced to either sign up for a morally bankrupt war or be ostracized, perhaps imprisoned. Did you know that some German conscientious objectors have been *shot*?

A.P.

S.J. And while I'm at it, I might as well tell you that I object to the idea that every Jew is a good person. That's simply untrue. Just because we're the so-called victims here doesn't mean we all have the individual moral high ground. It's true that we are in a lousy position through little to no fault of our own, but that fact doesn't necessarily make us all *good people*. What I mean is that you can also be a *bad* person in a *bad* position. I refuse to see every Jew as some sort of angelic martyr.

A.P. I'm not sure anyone's arguing—

S.J. You are! You're arguing. By suggesting that I've had "encounters," you're implying that I'm doing something that I shouldn't be doing. I reject that. The Germans are on their side and the Jews are on theirs via twists and accidents of history, but that doesn't mean that as individuals we can no longer make our own choices.

A.P. Szifra, nobody thinks that the Jews are all perfect, but certainly we can agree that what the Germans are doing is immoral and should be stopped.

S.J. Of *course* it should be stopped. But until it's stopped, it is my choice to take charge of my life and my goals and protect my family and rely on the good graces of whomever can help me, German or Jew or Pole or Brit or American. I am not allying myself with any particular Jewish cause just because Jews are the good guys here. I don't believe all Jews are the good guys, anyway.

(An old colleague of mine, Wisniewski, taught debate at the Lyceum, and clearly he had done an excellent job. I am so turned around by Szifra's logic and protestations I have nothing else to say, even though I'm certain I didn't collect the information Ringelblum requested of me.)

S.J. And now I wish to conclude this interview.
A.P. Of course. I understand.

EIGHT

═══

Friday morning, I woke to an unexpectedly enticing smell in the apartment: chicken bones boiling in broth. I knew the smell from Kasia's endless attempts to perfect her chicken soup, which she made with little dumplings and lots of dill. My watch said it was six in the morning; on the other side of the curtain I heard Emil Wiskoff snoring, and surely the kids were still asleep. My instinct said that the soup was Sala's doing, not Pani Lescovec's. I pulled on my dressing gown and walked quietly past Emil's cumbersome slumber into the kitchen.

"Where on earth did you find chicken?"

Sala grinned. "Arkady bartered for some." Arkady was her older son, I believe about twelve. He had his father's pale-green eyes and his mother's oval-shaped face. "I'm not sure *what* he used to barter, and I don't really want to know."

"And there are carrots in there?"

"Yes, and onions. And I have matzo meal for knaidlach. I even found olive oil. Or at least the bottle says it's olive oil."

"Are you going to share?"

"Depends," she said, still grinning. "Everything here is on a barter system, mister. What do you have to offer in return?"

"I can teach your children English."

"We can't eat English."

"I can find you more apricots."

She grinned, exposing her gray tooth. "You're on."

I watched her for a little while: the regular movements, the practiced, almost thoughtless way she dipped a ladle in to taste.

"Where did you learn to make soup?"

"Where did any of us learn?" she said. "My mother, I guess. And my grandmother. We all lived together when I was a girl."

"In Warsaw?"

"Near Kraków, actually. In Oświęcim. We were religious, you know."

"I think you mentioned that."

"Very religious. My father wore a shtreimel. My brothers spent all day studying Talmud. It wasn't until I married a Litvak that I was able to get a little breathing room."

"You felt suffocated by the religious life?"

She shrugged, rinsed the ladle off in the leaky tap, and dipped it in again. "I did once I met Emil. Before him, I didn't know enough to know I wanted more."

"Ah, once again my name is on everyone's lips." Pounding feet and labored breath behind us: Sala's well-upholstered husband sitting down at the kitchen table. "Smells like our old kitchen," he said. "Gut morgn, Paskow."

"Gut morgn, Emil." I wasn't sure why he insisted on calling me by my last name or why I insisted on calling him by his first, but that was the system we'd settled on the day we met, and we'd stuck to it.

"Chicken soup for Shabbos?" he asked his wife.

"Chicken soup because we have chicken," Sala said, leaning over to give Emil a kiss. They were a comfortable-seeming couple, married for almost twenty years. (Emil, a Lithuanian—a Litvak—had met Sala while following the trade route from Vilnius to Warsaw, selling sewing machines and sewing-machine parts to the endless supply of tailors in the endless supply of sztetls along the way.) Once they'd married, Emil opened a sewing-machine supply warehouse, importing American brands like Singer and General Electric. When the economy faltered and clothing stores went out of business, more and more Poles started sewing their own clothes, and Emil prospered. The family had lived in the Saska Kępa neighborhood of Warsaw but sent their boys to Jewish schools, had kept kosher and all the rest.

"What are we talking about?"

"Oh, my old life. You know," Sala said. "Before you came and rescued me."

"She was a damsel in distress, certainly," Emil said to me.

"That couldn't be less true. I wasn't in distress. I was just bored."

"Fine, she was a damsel in boredom. Then I came along and spiced things up," he said, and kissed her hand.

In our new environs, Emil kept himself busy as a counselor to the Judenrat and spent most of his days going over lists of petty infractions committed by Jews, which were supposed to be reported to the Germans, alongside petty demands made by Jews that were also supposed to be reported to the Germans. In truth, the lists were busywork; the Judenrat didn't have much power to deliver services and had no interest in securing German justice, but the making and keeping of lists helped the ghetto supplicants feel heard and Emil feel useful.

The head of the Judenrat, Adam Czerniaków, was a bald, red-faced man who had been a senator in the Polish government before the war. Whenever he dared appear in public, he was swarmed by his fellow ghetto dwellers and their pleas for medical care, food, housing, and remediation of neighborly disputes. Therefore, we rarely saw him outside his office. How could he stand it? What an impossible position—especially because, as anyone knew who could look at the situation dispassionately, it was clear the Germans were not going to give Czerniaków resources. It was not as if they had a secret store of medicine or food for the Jews, and if we just begged hard enough it would be forthcoming.

The problem was that it was hard for us to realize that we did not matter to anyone outside our own small company. For so long, we had lived under the illusion that our lives were still worth something to the broader community of mankind, and even though that illusion was shattered brick by brick (a 5:00 p.m. curfew, no going to the movies, no mailing letters abroad, no libraries, no telephones), we still refused to let go of it. Even though the truth was right in front of our faces! How could this ghetto be anything but the logical end of all that we had endured from the moment the Germans invaded. But we refused to believe it, because we had survived so much before, and because we had managed to make our lives rich and fulfilling despite the rules set up against us. We could live—we could *thrive*—under any conditions. We had been doing it throughout our history. And so it was easy for us to decide that what was happening in our city, in our country, was more of the same. Jewish schools shut down? It had happened so many times before—the learning continued, just underground. Synagogues closed? Jews could pray wherever ten men assembled. In our history, it had become a way of life to abide being harassed. We knew ways around it. We advanced only where we could, and were always, if not looking to retreat, clear that we might have to, despite our protests.

And so the restrictions piled on (no walking on sidewalks, no speaking directly to Germans), and we dodged and swerved but did not run away. (Most of us, anyway.)

I thought, for the hundredth time, how relieved I was not to have children.

Emil made tea for Sala and me and sat back down heavily. He had bad knees, I knew, and the trips up and down the five floors to and from our flat had only made them worse. "You're going to the Aid Society today, Paskow?"

"This afternoon, yes."

"I believe the Judenrat has secured new supplies for the kitchens. Flour, some eggs."

"That's good," I said.

"Who does the negotiating for supplies?" Sala asked, but she was interrupted by the sudden appearance of the five kids who lived in our flat—"Not now, boys; this soup is for later"—who rummaged through all our bins and shelves like furious mice, taking everything worth eating and disappearing back into the flat. Filip, I noticed, had his whittling knife in his shirt pocket.

"Where are you off to?" Sala called after them. "Arkady! Raf!"

But they were gone, out into the courtyards or sewers. Many of the kids seemed to have adjusted much better to their circumstances than their parents had. The ones who could count on food a few times a day, who had the bravery to escape to the other side for supplies (and I'm talking kids five, six years old), who could turn ghetto life into a sort of adventure game, who had lived briefer lives before this and therefore had less to miss or to regret—these kids were the princes of the ghetto. Their very fearlessness made us stand in awe.

"I'm back, Eema," said Sala's younger son, Rafel, sliding against her at the kitchen table. "I didn't want you to worry."

"Aw, you," she said, kissing him on top of the head.

"Can I have some money?"

"Are you serious?"

He gave a goofy, monkey-like grin. "Come on, Eema."

"What do you need money for, young man? Money isn't exactly easy to come by here."

Emil spread his large hands out on the kitchen table. It was funny to me that such a large man as he could have such wispy children, but then all the children in the ghetto seemed wispy to me—lean, fast, able to hide in shadows.

"Just fifty groszy. I can't tell you why. I mean, I can, but you won't like it."

"Now you have to tell us," said Sala.

"Dog races," Rafel said, still with that monkey grin, a child who could get away with anything.

"Dog races?"

"I told you you wouldn't like it."

"What do you mean dog races?" said his father. "What on earth are you talking about?"

Rafel sighed deeply. "It's at a secret location. I can't tell you more. I mean, I could if I knew more, but I don't. It's all kept secret till the last minute."

"Secret by who?" Emil asked.

"What do you mean, *dogs*?" said Sala.

"I mean dogs," Rafel said. "There are kids across the courtyard who have these fat, lazy dogs. I think maybe beagles? They lived here before, you know, so it's not like they had to bring them from anywhere."

"Jews don't keep dogs."

"Shh, Emil," Sala said.

Rafel smirked.

"We just see which one of these fat dogs will cross the room fastest. Sometimes they do it. Sometimes they just sit down in the middle of the floor and refuse to move. We take bets. Winning side takes all. There's like ten or twelve of us. We've done it three times already."

"When's the dog race?" Sala asked.

"Eleven."

"I'm coming."

"Eema, you are *not*."

"Adam, when do you have to be at the Aid Society?"

"One."

"Great, you're coming with me."

"Eema . . ."

"Do you want my groszy or not?"

Rafel turned pink. "I never should have told you about this!"

"Someone actually has dogs here?"

"Sala, if I may," said Emil.

"I have a good eye for dogs," Sala said. "At least, I think I do. I'll probably win."

"Eema, none of the kids are ever going to speak to me again if I bring two *grown-ups* to the dog race."

"Tell them you didn't know I was coming. Tell them we followed you there."

"Eema . . ."

"Come on. I haven't had any fun in ages."

"You're making chicken soup!"

"Who told you that was fun?"

Which is how, at eleven in the morning, we found ourselves in the dank broad basement of the old Federation Building on Zelazna Street, where twelve kids had gathered to watch two overfed mutts loll about the room.

"Shh, shh, you mustn't upset them!" yelped one of the boys, presumably the dogs' owner, but unlike most of the dogs I'd met—and most of the people too—these dogs were fat and uninterested in their own predicaments.

"Upset them? Who could upset them? They're barely conscious!" screamed one of the kids, and the rest of them burst out laughing.

The children—ten boys, two girls—all looked to have eaten breakfast, and were wearing generally neat clothing. These were the kids of the ghetto who could spare a few groszy, and they were currently standing in an eager circle around the two walrus-like dogs across the concrete floor. A few of the children flashed concerned eyes at Sala and me, and then at Arkady and Rafel, but the boys gave them a signal to ignore us and go back to their business.

Money was thrown into a bucket in the side of the room: groszy coins, for the most part, and one precious zloty, whose provenance was confusing. What kid still had money to throw around so carelessly? I looked around the room and noted one of them, blondish, with a familiar shape to his eyes, and I realized he was Szifra Joseph's younger brother, the sugar baron. Careless carrier of zloty.

"Come on, let's throw some money in," Sala said, nudging me. She was wrapped up in her muffler and coat, but I could see the glint in her eyes. "What do you have?"

"Not enough to waste on this."

"Oh, come *on*," Sala said. She looked younger here. It was the first time I'd ever seen her outside the apartment. "Here. I'll front you ten groszy."

"It's okay, it's okay," I said, digging out a few coins from my satchel and throwing them into the bucket. The kids looked at us appreciatively, and Rafel sent his mother a secret thumbs-up before returning to the crowd. I could see how much they liked each other, this mother and son—both of Sala's boys, actually. This was a bit of a revelation to me. I had never particularly liked my mother, certainly not when I was nine or ten and eager to escape her grip. Moreover, she hadn't seemed to enjoy us particularly—our constant demands, our endless needs. Did she ever think to have fun with us? Could she have known such pleasure?

"Eema," whispered Arkady, coming up behind us to tug on Sala's coat, "put a little more money on the one with the spotted face. Supposedly, he pooped on the walk over here and that makes him faster."

"Is that science?" Sala asked, and Arkady nodded.

"Let's get started!" the blond boy shrieked, as imperious as Szifra. (He was clearly her brother.) "Rosenzstayn, get your beasts over here."

"They don't want to move," Rosenzstayn whined. "They're tired from the walk."

"How did you find dogs even lazier than you?"

This insult created a new tumult of heckling and laughter, as poor Rosenzstayn (a type I recognized from teaching, bespectacled and eager to please) begged his dogs (not at all beagles, more like overstuffed retrievers) to please get up and go to the corner of the room for the race to begin. "Please, puppies, please, good boys, just get up, won't you, please?"

Sala elbowed me in the side, grinning like a schoolchild, as she joined in the crowd's remonstrations of Rosenzstayn and his lazy dogs. Finally, the pair waddled over to one end of the room, and the children assembled themselves at the other end.

"Eyns, tsvey, drey . . . ," Rosenzstayn started. One of the dogs licked his rear, to the hilarity of the assemblage.

"Come on, Rosenzstayn! Like you mean it!"

"Eyns, tsvey, drey!" shrieked Rosenzstayn, desperate to get out of this with a morsel of his dignity intact. "Churchill! Pilot! Let's go!"

"The dogs' names are Churchill and Pilot?" I said to Sala, who was laughing so hard she had to wipe tears from her eyes.

But now either Churchill or Pilot was giving his nether regions a thorough licking and could not be bothered to move. The other one let out an enormous yawn.

"Churchill! Pilot!"

"Nobody listens to Rosenzstayn!" someone yelled. "Not even his idiot dogs!"

But slowly, mercifully, one of the dogs, the butt-licking one, roused itself and began to swagger its way over to Rosenzstayn in no particular rush, much to the delight of half the crowd and the despair of the other. They screamed and yelled at the dogs and yelled at Rosenzstayn, but mostly they were laughing, and it had been months since I had heard this much unbridled laughter. Everyone seemed to be in on the joke— Sala, the children, even the dogs. (What was the joke? Were *we* the joke?)

And just as either Pilot or Churchill was about to saunter across the finish line, the other dog looked up, seemed to notice the cheering of the crowd, and rose to his feet, which caused such a commotion that the first dog turned around and headed back the way he came, just to see what the bother was about. At this point, dog number two decided to bound over to Rosenzstayn, who covered him with kisses and was rewarded with great big sloppy dog licks. I had never been a dog person and found the whole sticky display rather disgusting, but I was the only one: half the crowd was whooping with joy and divvying up the purse, while the other half was cursing Pilot or Churchill, cursing Rosenzstayn.

"Here, Adam," Rafel said, handing me fifty groszy, or twice my investment.

"Oh, that's okay, Raf. You keep it."

"No, it's for you. We promise a fair return."

"It's not necessary," I said, but I took the money anyway, thinking of this strange economy. At the Lyceum, where I taught, children of privilege spent endless money on sweets and movie tickets and beautiful woolen scarves. Here, it was dogs—no, it wasn't dogs: it was joy.

"Fifty groszy!" Sala said, winking. "Spend it on something nice."

Szifra's brother was still heckling Rosenzstayn, which seemed a bit unfair; after all, he had managed to get the two dogs to follow him the three blocks from Sienna Street, which was not an easy thing, considering the laziness of these dogs and the general imperative not to stand out in the ghetto. As far as I knew, there weren't any directives for Jews to give up their dogs (Jews weren't known, it must be said, for having many dogs), but still it was easy to imagine a Nazi giving Rosenzstayn and his animals a hard time—especially if they heard one of them was called Churchill.

"Enough," Sala said. "Kids, get out of here before someone finds you."

"Who's going to find us?" asked Szifra's brother—was he really Szifra's brother?—but he stopped picking on Rosenzstayn and turned his attention again to horsing around with some of the bigger kids, and we watched as they filed up the stairs out of the basement, looking so much like any group of kids filing out of any big room (laughing, teasing, slapping each other's backs) that it was transporting to watch them, and if it weren't for the fact that they were trailed by two big dogs I could have told myself that they were leaving my old classroom and even fooled myself into believing it.

THAT NIGHT, ALL ten of us gathered in the kitchen—adults at the table, kids leaning against the counters—for a Friday night meal. Sala had contributed the soup, of course, and Pani Lescovec contributed fish cakes, which she had made out of smelt and potatoes. And there were more vanilla biscuits, and even some terrible wine made in the bathroom of one of the doctors who lived upstairs, which Emil had purchased for the exorbitant price of twenty zloty.

There were Shabbos candles lit and prayers said, in tandem, by Sala and Pani Lescovec, and when it was time to say the blessing over the bread (one of those horrible brick-like loaves from Nowolipki Street), the five boys stood and, as one, recited the prayer. And I couldn't help but find the whole thing moving. We had never eaten dinner together all ten of us before.

After the meal, the kids disappeared to wherever the kids disappeared to, but the adults—brought to a truce over the shared meal and the awful wine—stayed at the table and talked for hours about things that people in normal times might have talked about: jokes they half remembered, salacious rumors, stories from their childhoods, complaints about their aging bodies. Sala and Emil held hands on the table for a little while, and Pani Lescovec nudged her husband affectionately.

"You know, it was wonderful to see the kids so happy today," Sala said. "I'd forgotten what it sounds like to hear so much laughter."

"They're strong," agreed Pani Lescovec. "Isn't that what they say about children?"

"I suppose," said Sala. "But still, it's amazing to me they're able to continue on the way they have. Just figuring out new ways to get by, all the time. And your Filip, he's such a good provider! Isn't he the one who found this oat flour?"

"Yes, but your Arkady is the one who traded for the chicken!"

"He came into some money yesterday," Sala said.

"And instead of buying candy for himself, he bought us all a chicken," said Pani Lescovec. "That is a very good boy you're raising there, Sala."

And they continued to murmur in satisfaction at the boys they were raising, a moment of harmony in our fractious household.

As for me, I stayed with them for another thirty minutes or so, but soon enough an ache I hadn't felt in quite some time started to descend on me. I made my apologies, complimented the chefs, and went to bed in my wintry alcove, with the hope that I would dream about my wife.

I DIDN'T. I couldn't. So I looked out the window instead, over the gates of the ghetto, to the Ferris wheel outside our northwest gates. The wheel, brightly lit, circled round and round. I thought I could detect faint laughter crossing the apartment into my alcove. It was Friday night.

NINE

═══

There's a poem by Wordsworth I often teach called "Surprised by Joy." Despite the title, the poem is not about joy specifically, but about the strange combination of feelings that accompany joy in the midst of grief—when a person who has been deep in grief feels unexpected joy. Wordsworth wrote it after he had been grieving for his daughter for several years. During a walk in the woods (Wordsworth found endless time to walk in the woods), he stumbled upon some fleeting but profound happiness. A happiness so profound, in fact, that he forgot, for just a moment, that his daughter was dead. He turned to share his happiness with her, but she wasn't there—and then he remembered. And that feeling, he wrote, "was the worst pang that sorrow ever bore" except, of course, for the sorrow of her death itself.

For a while, I experienced that feeling all the time—a minute, two, when I forgot Kasia was dead and the impulse occurred to me to remember something in detail to tell her later, or to purchase the kind of flowers she liked, or the kind of ice cream, or I would pass a scarf or a dress in a shop window and think how nice it would look on her. The worst, actually, were the small funny things that would have made us laugh together—a good dirty joke, something ridiculous that one of our colleagues did. She did wonderful impressions of all sorts of people: our grumpy neighbors, her father, even Gruby the cat.

Before the accident, I'd often sit with her and listen to the radio while she worked on her translations, a pencil in her mouth, looking up to ask what the English was for *annexation* or *regression*. And if I didn't know the answer, we'd hunt through our dictionaries together. It was in this way that we discovered words we liked, like *mellifluous* or *churlish*. Then, because it amused us, we would find new opportunities to use these English words with each other—"You are sounding very mellifluous today, my dear"—and it made us happy to have these small jokes with each other and nobody else. Now if I hear the word *churlish* in Polish (*chamski, grubianski*), I smile or I sigh and remember my wife.

There should be another word for this feeling—a sort of sorrowful happiness, or a happiness that only deepens someone's sorrow. The closest I can come to it is the Portuguese word *saudade*, which nears this feeling but tempers it with nostalgia, a wish for something that was and can never be again. A grieving person lives in a permanent state of saudade, but saudade does not incorporate joy. And grief might be simpler if joy never tried to intrude.

Kasia had grown up wealthy and had a wealthy girl's attitude to things money can buy: she was often careless with our funds and took great pleasure in unnecessary luxuries. One weekend afternoon she bought six copper pots from the shop on the high street and brought them home with great flourish, as they reminded her of the pots that one of the cooks on her father's estate had used to make bigos and zurek when she was growing up. When I pointed out that we had no cooks, and that it seemed unlikely we were ever going to procure the boar and venison for a proper bigos, she shrugged and said that maybe one day we would—and even if we didn't, the pots would make for nice decoration. And then I found the receipt on the counter, showing that the pots had cost a month of my wages, and I was angry for a few minutes, and then I stopped, because there was no point in being angry. Her father slipped her, slipped us, I suppose, a few hundred zloty a month, for no other reason than she was indulgent with him, she loved him. And because he wasn't allowed to see her all too often—his ill wife having rejected Kasia on my account—the money was the simplest way he knew to show her he loved her too.

She started having migraines in the spring of 1935. This was a particularly tense time for everyone politically, and she wasn't sure if the government would continue to employ her as a translator, which certainly was stressful for her. She loved her job. Moreover, she had been—we had been—trying to conceive a child for so many years at that point and had failed again and again, and this was stressful too. We weren't sure why we couldn't conceive. One doctor said Kasia wasn't drinking enough milk; in response, we ordered the milkman to come every day. Another doctor then suggested it was too much milk, and we switched almost entirely to beer. The final doctor, wall full of diplomas, did a full and rather invasive examination of my wife and then suggested, delicately but not too delicately, that perhaps a woman of such fine Polish stock as herself (tall, gray-eyed, descended from descendants of the Sobieski dynasty) was simply unable to conceive with a Jewish husband. It was perhaps possible that owing to the divine wisdom of God and the female body, Kasia's eggs would not implant, having been inseminated with Jewish sperm.

She told me this laughing, even though by then our four-year struggle to become parents was nothing we ever laughed about. "Can you imagine? The ignorance!"

But the doctor had degrees from the University of Warsaw and Jagiellonian University. He was on the obstetrical board of the Hospital of the Holy Spirit. It had taken her father two petitions to get us an appointment.

"What if it's true?" I asked, which was not like me. I was not in any way a scientist, but I did put my trust in science.

"Adam . . ."

"Not that. Not the Jewish sperm idea—"

"Sperm doesn't have religion."

And we both laughed a little, uncomfortably.

"But what if we're not . . ." I started again. "What if we're not sup-posed to have children together?" This was something I had thought about on those rare nights when Kasia seemed unreachably sad. All her friends had children, all her sisters. "What if there's some incompat-ibility there?"

"Adam . . ."

"I just can't figure out any other reason—"

"Adameczek," she said, as if I were an adorable child. We were sitting on the couch, Gruby between us, Kasia's stockinged feet (striped wool socks) on the table in front of us. A fire in the fireplace. Soup murmuring in a copper pot in the kitchen. Domestic warmth.

The forces arrayed against us had been anti-Semitic, anti-rational. Her mother, her sisters, the first judge who refused to marry us. Our own bodies. Our own bodies?

"What if there is a God after all, and he decided—"

"It doesn't work that way, my love. You know that. Anyone can have a baby with anyone. We learned this all too well in high school. I believe the nuns said that a girl could get pregnant by the devil himself if she wasn't careful."

"And by the devil, they meant a Jew?"

"Probably," she said, putting Gruby on her lap so she could snuggle into me.

"If you want to have children with someone else—"

"Adam—"

"I would understand—"

"Adam!" She put Gruby on the floor; he skittered away, offended. "I will not have this conversation with you again. I don't want just any-one's children. I'm not some sort of brood mare. I'm a wife, and I want to have children with my husband." She was so beautiful when she got upset. Sparkling eyes, pinkish cheeks. "We will have children together somehow. Forget what that idiot doctor said. I could tell he was an idiot by his accent, by the way. He slurred his *r*'s."

I hugged her closer. "Maybe we could steal one of your sister's kids." Her sister Lena, who barely talked to us, had seven; we suspected she did this to spite us.

"Her children look like turtles."

"We'd steal the cutest one. The least turtle-ish one."

"They act like turtles too. They bury their chins in their collars."

"So what shall we do?"

"We should keep trying," Kasia said, raising an eyebrow at me.

So we went to the bedroom and tried. But it was impossible to believe the effort would be successful, as it had never been successful before and now we were older, our bodies were older. I was thirty-four, and Kasia, thirty-three, and she had lately been plagued by those migraines. And in fact, as we dressed again in the fading daylight, she grew tired and squinty.

"Another?" I asked, touching her gently.

"I know," she said. "I have no idea where this one came from. I suppose I'm feeling anxious."

"Yes, but why . . ." And then a horrifying idea came to me. "Did the doctor . . ."

"The doctor?"

"Did he touch you? Hurt you?" I could imagine this as well as I could imagine anything, the famous doctor hurting my wife for the temerity of trying to make a family with a Jew.

"Adam, cut it out." She put on one of her silk robes, another casual luxury, purchased from the shop on Mokatowska Street where she also procured her corsets and stockings. She tied the robe around the waist, bent to straighten our sheets.

"Why are you so anxious, then?"

"A million reasons!" she said. "My job. The government. The fact that no matter what I seem to do—stand on my head, eat nothing but eggs—I can't seem to get pregnant."

"Oh, Kasia . . ."

"Can you turn off the soup?" She stopped straightening the bed, sat down. "I think I want to sleep now."

"But it's only seven."

"I think I want to sleep," she repeated, lying down across the blue linen coverlet. On the bedside stand were stacks of books; she reached out a hand as if she were going to read, but then her hand retreated.

"Are you really going to sleep for the night?"

"Turn off the soup. And the light. I'm getting that strange feeling behind my eyes."

And soon enough, she was taking deep sleepy breaths, the kind I knew so well, the kind I used to match to my own in order to fall asleep myself.

One day, soon after I moved into the ghetto, I asked the doctor upstairs about it—he had been a neurologist at the new Jewish Hospital before the invasion—and he said there were no good treatments for migraine headaches, and that Kasia's accident had been sadly predictable. Statistics showed the rate of fatal accidents was much higher among the migraine-prone. Over a glass of his bathroom rotgut wine, he told me, in his matter-of-fact medical way, that there was nothing anybody could have done.

Name: Charlotte Grosstayn
Date: January 20, 1941
Age: 11 years, 10 months
Height: 144 cm?
Weight: Too thin

Charlotte Grosstayn has shown up to my English classes regularly since I established them in late November 1940. She lives on Śliska Street with her parents and her older brother, Roman, another student of mine, in an apartment they lived in before the relocation. In this way, and in others, Charlotte is luckier than most ghetto children: she never had to abandon her childhood bedroom, and her parents did not have to rid themselves of most of their belongings.

Charlotte herself reminds me of the students I once taught at the Lyceum: smart, polite, neatly dressed, aware of the social relationships that surround her and her own place within them. She is bullied occasionally by her older brother, but I've noticed as the weeks have passed that she is able to withstand and even return some of the teasing and insults he delivers. (I don't believe he means much harm, by the way, nor does she—the situation here is rather stressful, and children lash out at one another as a way to relieve that stress but seem to forgive one another quickly.)

Charlotte has agreed to be interviewed for the Oneg Shabbat project before our English class convenes. I meet her at the café on Nowolipki Street, which still opens occasionally; today it happens to be serving drinks, and I am able to buy her a small glass of raspberry-flavored kompot, which she refuses once, politely, before accepting.

C.G. Thank you, Pan Paskow. This is so nice of you. I haven't had kompot in a while.

A.P. Well, thank you for agreeing to talk to me.

C.G. Yes, of course! I'm flattered that you would ask. (Charlotte takes a very tiny sip of her juice, pats her lips.) I don't know what I can tell you, of course. I'm not so interesting.

A.P. You'd be surprised how many people say that, Charlotte. Or, to be fair, how many women and girls say that. But of course they're the most interesting of all!

C.G. (She smiles, looks down at her juice.)

A.P. Well, anyway, I'm just here to ask you a little bit about your life, about school, that sort of thing. Your family. Whatever you want to tell me about.

C.G. My family? Sure. I mean, you know Roman.

A.P. I do.

C.G. And you haven't met my parents, but I guess you will one day.

A.P. Perhaps. Are they faring well, in the midst of all this?

C.G. My parents? Well, you know what's funny, and I probably shouldn't even say this, but the worst thing that happened to our family happened before the war, when my older sister left. I mean, honestly, I'm not sure this even compares. They never really complain about living here, but they still talk about my sister all the time.

A.P. Is that so? I didn't even know you had an older sister.

C.G. Yes, nine years older. She was the daughter from my father's first marriage, which I didn't know about for quite some time. I didn't know, I mean, until after she left. He was married to my aunt before he married my eema. But then she died in childbirth—my aunt did—so he married her younger sister. Who would be my eema.

A.P. I see.

C.G. You know, it's just the way things were back then. In the 1920s.

A.P. Indeed.

C.G. Anyway, my eema agreed to raise my sister like she was her own. Remember, the baby is not just her new husband's daughter—she's her own niece! She raises my sister from the time she's a little baby, and then she has Roman, and then she has me. I never even knew the story of my dead aunt or the fact that Rachel—that was her name, Rachel—was my cousin *and* my sister.

A.P. My goodness.

C.G. Because, you see, they thought I was too young to understand.

A.P. But you understand.

C.G. Sure! Your wife dies, you marry her younger sister, you pretend the whole thing never happened. That's just how it is!

A.P. I suppose so.

C.G. So we all grow up, and my sister and I go to secular school, and Roman goes to secular school *and* Jewish school, which he hates, but that's what you get for being a boy. And Rachel is really smart. I mean she is *really* smart. She finishes high school early, and she wants to go to college, and my parents say, "Well, what do you need college for?" Because they just think she'll get married and have babies. But she yells at them that they're old-fashioned and she doesn't just have to get married and she wants to be a journalist, which is, of course, crazy, but okay. They let her take university classes—

A.P. A journalist!

C.G. Oh, yes, she really was so smart. She was almost as smart as you, Pan Paskow. Her Polish was perfect, and she spoke German too, and her teachers were always telling my parents . . . Well, anyway, she started going to university—she was 16—and then she started spending more and more time away from home, which my parents didn't like, but what could they do? They already gave her permission, right?

A.P. I suppose. Although—

C.G. And then . . . And *then* . . .

(The waiter comes by and looks at us: Do we want more raspberry drink for the girl? More powdered coffee for the gentleman? Charlotte looks at me with big eyes. Of course we do.)

A.P. You were saying?

C.G. And then one of my father's coworkers happens to be in the university district, and he sees a girl who looks *a lot* like Rachel—I mean, he doesn't want to spread rumors, but *a lot* like Rachel—sitting alone with some boy who is definitely *not* Jewish, some blond boy, and they're speaking Polish. And this coworker tells my parents about it, and they go berserk. I mean *berserk*. They confront Rachel and have this huge fight and tell her: (1) no more university classes, and (2) they're going to find a matchmaker for her, and she is getting married *immediately*.

A.P. I assume she found this distressing?

C.G. Distressing? Pan Paskow, she was absolutely going crazy, screaming and crying. I thought she was going to break glass she was screaming so loudly.

A.P. Oh dear.

C.G. It was terrible. She and I share a bedroom, and she locked me out of it—locked me out of my own bedroom!—so she could scream and cry and protest.

A.P. This sounds very dramatic.

C.G. And it went on for days! She wasn't eating. Not bathing. Only came out of the room to urinate—excuse me for saying. My eema is pleading with my abba—"Maybe you should just talk to her, find a compromise"—and he says no way. And then the day comes where the matchmaker is supposed to visit, and to all of our surprise, Rachel comes out of the room—which is good, because I've been sleeping on Roman's floor, which is *awful*! And she comes out of the room and she takes a bath and brushes her hair, and we're so happy she's come to her senses, and maybe if she just *calms down* she can even start going to university classes again or something before she gets married.

A.P. Your parents would have made a deal with her.

C.G. Yes! They're not unreasonable people! They would have made a deal. So the matchmaker comes over, and we all have to be on our best behavior, which we are—even Roman—and my mother serves her szarlotka, and the matchmaker talks about what a nice family we are and says she knows some boys from very good families, and Rachel plays it cool, utterly cool: "Yes, thank you. That's a nice idea." The matchmaker even asks her what her goals are for her future, and she says she just wants to be married to a nice Jewish boy and have lots of children, and the matchmaker says, "Oh, very nice." But this is when I know that something is brewing, because I know my sister—I mean, we're not very close, but I *know* that she's not telling the truth. And I think my eema knows too, but there's nothing we can say about it right now, because the matchmaker is there and my abba just has this relieved smile on his face the whole time.

A.P. And how old was your sister at this point?

C.G. 17? I think she was 17. Because I was 8, and she was 9 years older than me, and even at 8 years old I knew something was up, you know? Thank you again by the way for the kompot. It's delicious! Isn't it funny now how things are even more delicious than they were before the war? That's a good thing, I guess. I used to hate potatoes, but now they're so tasty to me! And liver! I used to hate it too, but my abba found some beef liver the other day—he wouldn't say where. Anyway, where was I?

A.P. I believe—

C.G. Oh, right, the matchmaker. So the matchmaker leaves, and my abba says, "See, wasn't that nice? Aren't you excited?" And my eema and I exchange looks, because we just *know*, but what can we do? It's like we had a crystal ball, like we could see into the future. But Eema doesn't want to start anything right there, and I guess she's hoping she's wrong. But no. The next morning I wake up, and her side of the room is empty. Somehow, Rachel has managed to slip out without me even noticing, and half her things are gone, and there's a note for me and a note for Roman and a note for Eema and Abba. And the basic story is that she's leaving to run away with her *Polish boyfriend*, and there's nothing we can do about it, and that's it. And she's not even going to be *Jewish* anymore! She doesn't want anything to do with our backward religion! She'll get in touch with us one day, or maybe she won't. The end.

A.P. Goodness.

C.G. I know.

A.P. What did her note to you say? If you don't mind my asking.

C.G. It said that when I'm her age I should do the same thing, that it was 1937 and I didn't have to just follow my parents' ideas about what women were or who they should be.

A.P. Hmm. What did you make of that?

C.G. I don't know. I thought it was sweet. That she would wish that for me, I guess. And also crazy. Like I would ever do what she did. I mean, that I would ever do that to our parents.

A.P. And Roman's letter?

C.G. It was all about respecting women and respecting their autonomy, which was a word we didn't even know, and how women were more than housewives and baby makers—she actually said that! She said "baby makers"! And Roman was blushing so hard when he read that letter.

A.P. And what about your parents?

C.G. Well, after they were done crying and screaming and yelling at each other, and yelling at her—even though she *wasn't even there!*—they sat down me and Roman and told us about my abba's first marriage, and Rachel's real mother. Which was shocking, of course, but also made sense, because there was always something a little different about Rachel. Not just how she looked—although she had lighter hair than we did, and she had gray eyes, and Roman and I have brown eyes—but also just in the way she behaved, in her attitude. She was much more willful than me or my brother were. She liked to fight. She liked confrontations. My brother and I were always pretty cowed by her, if you know what I mean.

A.P. She seems like she had a commanding personality.

C.G. Oh, yes. Yes. And then that night, I can't sleep. It's weird to be alone in the room I've shared with Rachel since I was born. I mean I've never slept alone before in my life! And it still has so many of her things, her dressing table and her mirror, and some of her clothing—like this lacy dress I always wanted to borrow but she wouldn't let me. But she isn't there, so I put on the dress, and it's so big on me, and I go out into the kitchen in it, and I see my eema, and she's just sitting at the table, crying. It's almost midnight. I say, "I'm sorry, I'll take off the dress," and she says, "No, it's not that. Keep it on. It's fine." And she starts crying again.

A.P. Were you able to comfort her?

C.G. Well, what was strange was she wasn't even crying about Rachel. She said she knew in her heart that Rachel would be fine. And I did too. I understood.

A.P. So why was she crying?

C.G. Because she missed her sister! This sister I hadn't even known about until earlier that day. But she said that this was the *exact* sort of thing her older sister would have done, had she been born a generation later. How her older sister never really wanted to get married either, but how her own parents—my grandparents—how they forced her, and how my mother always suspected that she died in childbirth from a lack of will to go on with this lot in life. She never really wanted to be a mother, or at least she didn't want to be one so young, but she didn't have a choice. She was married off at 19, and then she had Rachel when she was only 20, and . . . and she just gave up. She died a few hours after Rachel was born.

A.P. Did Rachel know about her real mother?

C.G. No. They never told her.

A.P. Ah.

C.G. Which I think is wrong, just to be clear. And my eema sometimes wanted to. I think she missed her sister so much. They were only two years apart in age! But my abba thought it would be too disruptive. So my eema could never really talk about her own sister. And when Rachel was growing up, my eema couldn't . . . I mean she couldn't mention the ways that Rachel reminded her of her dead sister. Which she did. All the time. Evidently, they looked alike and did things the same way, brushed their hair, sang while they washed the dishes. My eema and I just stayed up all night talking about the dead sister. Her name was Rachel too.

A.P. Really?

C.G. Yes. They didn't name my sister until her mother had died. And then they named her for her mother. Which just made things harder for my eema, I think—to sorely miss one Rachel while raising this new Rachel as her daughter.

A.P. This is quite a story, Charlotte.

C.G. It is! They sat shiva for her and everything. For my sister,
I mean. Black fabric on the mirrors. The rabbi came.

A.P. Did you ever see her again?

C.G. No. But we got some letters. She told us she was
marrying the Polish boyfriend and they were moving to South
Africa together. Can you imagine? There was an opportunity
in some sort of copper mine there for her husband. They were
taking a boat from Danzig.

A.P. Wow.

C.G. They went to Johannesburg—we got another letter—
and had a baby. Which means my parents are grandparents!
Anyway, my abba refused to read the letters, but my eema read
them and was happy for Rachel, I think, and kept a photograph
of the baby hidden away. They had a boy. They named him
Bernard, which was my grandfather's name. I don't know. I hope
she's happy. It's lucky for her she gets to miss all this mess.

A.P. Would you have taken her advice, do you think? Run
away and gotten married?

C.G. Me? Are you kidding?

A.P. No, not at all. I'm just curious—

C.G. Never! No, never. All I want is to get married one day
and have a nice Jewish home. I'm not like her at all. I'm not brave.

A.P. Of course you are, Charlotte. Every child here is brave.

C.G. Thank you. But, no, not like that! Well, I guess what I
mean is that I'm not rebellious. I want to get married as soon as I
can and have at least 10 babies.

A.P. That sounds like a good plan too.

C.G. Do you think I could name one of them Rachel? For my
sister?

A.P. Of course you could, Charlotte. You could do whatever
you want.

C.G. (Swallowing the very last of her kompot) That's
something Rachel would say.

TEN

===

During my Lyceum days, the coming of spring brought with it a certain frenetic energy—pear trees in bloom, coats coming off. But here, as the late winter days progressed, my students seemed to retreat into themselves. For one thing, a typhus outbreak was racing through the ghetto despite our best efforts to contain it. The Germans, when enclosing us in their walls, told the rest of Warsaw they were doing it for the protection of the Polish citizenry: Jews were covered in lice, a public health menace, et cetera. That hadn't been true then, but now there were a few hundred thousand of us locked into three square kilometers with only the most haphazard sanitation, limited running water, and corpses in the street—of course we had become an epidemiologist's worst nightmare.

We went to lengths to address the outbreak. Many men and boys shaved their hair off to deny lice a place to hide, and even some of the girls did the same, or had shaved heads forced upon them (Charlotte showed up to class wearing a cap of her father's, so mortified was she by her new haircut.) After purchasing a razor from a Polish guard named Nowak (one zloty), Sala shaved my head in the kitchen sink, with the help of the strong-smelling soap she made herself. It was odd, and oddly pleasurable, to have someone touch me this way. I hadn't had hands on my head in years, and had forgotten how much tension the scalp holds, and how easy it is to release it. Water, soap, warm hands on your temples, behind your ears, at the bony places where your head meets your neck. I was sorry when it was over.

"Here, take a look."

She left a few scratch marks on my forehead, but overall I found I didn't look terrible. I had a more nicely shaped skull than I'd dared to imagine.

"Like a football!" Sala said, cheerfully.

"Thank you very much."

She proceeded to shave her boys, but Emil resisted, claiming his position in the Judenrat meant that he had to appear a certain way, that he couldn't present himself looking like an invalid or a convict ("No offense, Paskow.")

"Emil, this isn't for you," Sala said. "This is for all of us, to keep us safe."

"Are you shaving your head, then, Sala? If you're so worried about our safety?" he said. Which I thought was cruel.

"I am, yes," Sala said.

"Eema, no," said Arkady.

"Of course I am," Sala said. "It's for public health. Hair grows back. Pan Paskow said he'd help me if you kids won't."

"Eema," Rafel said, but Sala handed me the razor.

"I'm not watching this," said Emil as the boys scurried out of the room.

"Cowards," Sala said, gathering a towel and a trash bin.

"You really want me to shave your head?" I asked as she released her hair from its knot. It had grown longer, was down past her shoulder blades, and heavily streaked with silver. The soap she used left her hair particularly shiny, almost a bit greasy, and smelling like lye.

"I'll cut most of it off first," she said. "Then you can do the rest."

"I think you made your point to Emil," I said. "You don't really have to do this."

"My mother shaved her head every week," Sala said. She took a hefty pair of scissors out of a drawer—they looked like poultry shears—and, without any more fuss than she'd use to slice an onion, made a neat cut over her left ear, releasing a sheet of silver-brown hair to the floor. "All the religious women did it. Because hair, you know, is erotic. No man should see it besides your husband." She bent down to examine a strand of her hair. "Hmm. There's more gray than I thought."

"I guess you're really doing this."

"I guess I am."

"Well, then," I said. Alarmed at the imprecise way she was holding the scissors, I took a hank of her hair in my hand—"Should we do this over a newspaper or something? Never mind, I can sweep"—and began cutting through it, carefully.

I had never given a woman a haircut before. Kasia used to get her hair cut at a shop downtown every five weeks, like clockwork; she favored the same short style she'd worn since she was five years old, and it suited her. I used to love running my hands through it, playing with the curls at the nape of her neck. But Sala's hair was different—longer, obviously, and smoother, and as I cut it I had the absurd fear that her hair was a living thing and I was hurting it.

"Don't be so delicate. You've got to cut more off," she said. "You're going to shave it next."

I collected myself, kept going, so that all she was left with in the end was a sort of chicken-feather fuzz around her skull.

"Do you want to look?"

"I do not," she said.

But I looked. Without hair on her head, Sala's eyes seemed extraordinarily wide, and her cheekbones sharp and high. I had not realized how her graying hair had made her seem older until it was gone, and she suddenly looked frighteningly young to me, and vulnerable. She was seven years younger than I was, but without hair she looked to me almost like a child.

"What? Is it that bad?"

"No," I said. "It's . . . becoming."

"Stop." She laughed and ran a hand over her chicken feathers. "Ha! I had no idea my head was so . . . so bumpy."

"You have the razor? We need to shave off the rest."

"I have the razor."

We draped a towel around her neck, and she sat in a chair by the table. As I was foaming up her scalp with soap from the tin pot, Pani Lescovec walked in, shrieked, turned around, and left.

"Mariam!" Sala called. "Mariam, it's okay! It's just for typhus!"

"That's her name? Mariam?"

"You didn't know?"

"I never asked, and then it felt like it was too late to ask."

"You've lived with this woman for almost five months—"

"Well, it's not like we actually live together—"

"You do! You live together!"

"That makes it sound intimate, Sala. We didn't actually *choose* to live together. We were just sort of . . . you know, thrust together."

Sala started laughing. "I'm sorry, dear, but 'thrust' sounds even more—"

"Stop. You know what I mean. Stop laughing. I'll scrape your head."

"Thrust," she repeated, still giggling. "With Mariam Lescovec."

Slowly, I ran the razor over her scalp, which was warm and wet and bumpy. After each stroke of the razor, I put my hand on her smooth head to make sure I'd gotten a clean scrape, and I could feel the blood coursing there, just under her skin. There were lots of blood vessels in the head—Kasia's pulsed whenever she fell ill. But I had never felt a warm scalp like this, so clean, with a heartbeat pulsing under it. I wondered if this was what it felt like to put your hand on a newborn baby's head.

"Oh God, Eema, you really went through with it?"

Arkady was back. I removed my hand from his mother's scalp quickly, feeling caught.

"It's for public health," she said. "We can't give the lice a place to hide."

"Yeah, but you look—I mean, I don't want to sound mean, but . . ."

"Oh, who cares," Sala said. "I'll wear a scarf on my head. It doesn't matter."

"Abba's not going to like it."

"Abba would like it less if I caught typhus," she said, and used the towel from her shoulders to dry off her head. "Stop looking at me like that."

"It's just . . . you look so *strange* . . ."

"Get me a scarf, then if you're so scandalized." The boy retreated and returned with a scarf, which Sala tied around her head quickly, then she disappeared to the hallway mirror. "God, I look just like my mother," she said.

"With the scarf on," Arkady said, "you look good, Eema."

"You liar," Sala said, but she hugged the boy to her—he was almost her height—and kissed him on top of his own shaved pate. The two of them did look like a pair of invalids or convicts, but without their hair they also looked more like mother and son than I had ever noticed before.

"I better get to the Aid Society," I said.

"Thanks for the haircut," Sala said.

ELEVEN

O ver the weeks and months, as the days started ever earlier, I found myself rising with the sun and heading for the
kitchen. Sala was always there first. When there was tea, we drank tea
together; when there were powdered coffee granules, we drank coffee.
When there was nothing at all, we pretended not to want anything.
Emil had smuggled in a transistor radio, and we listened, silently, to the
dispatches from the BBC and the free Polish Radio, trying to discern the
trajectory of the war. There were battles in Africa ("Africa?" asked Sala,
like she was imagining the moon) and western Europe. Bulgaria had
joined the war on the German side. There was still no movement from
the Americans, which was both perplexing and infuriating.

According to Ringelblum's welcome, if mysterious, updates to Oneg
Shabbat, the Joint Distribution Committee was lobbying Roosevelt for
action, or at least to make a statement on behalf of Europe's Jews. So
far, however, no word was forthcoming. The Joint did, however, manage to negotiate the delivery of three thousand kilos of flour and oats,
which meant the soup kitchens would have bread for much of the spring.
Upon hearing that, the entire group let out a small happy noise, almost
like a cheer.

I continued teaching. As the days warmed, so did my students' attitudes toward school, and soon enough I had six or seven regulars most

classes. It helped that the Nazis really had no interest in Jewish schooling or lack thereof; what happened in our apartments and municipal buildings seemed to be of little use to them. What they cared about, really, were the kids who tried to escape, the adults who disrespected them, the pretty girls who didn't smile demurely when they were harassed on the street. They were bratty teenagers, the soldiers, or at least that's how they behaved, asking for total deference but too bored or lazy to care about policing our interior actions or lives—which any good soldier would know was where the real danger lay. And so we managed a pathetic equilibrium.

One day, a German photographer came and took pictures of the ghetto, and even though some of us had to step over starved corpses on the sidewalk (not everyone here could afford the bribes, and the soup kitchens didn't always have enough to go around), many of us smiled thinly or even waved at his camera. We did not know what the pictures were for, but we decided that if they were going to kill us all they probably wouldn't bother to take pictures of us first, and that made us feel better.

On the fifth day of March, a few unexpected students showed up in my basement classroom: Arkady and Rafel Wiskoff, who had until then refused their parents' entreaties that they come and learn something useful while they were stuck in the ghetto. And Szifra brought her brothers, Eli and Jakub. That meant I had nine students in all, something like a real classroom; at the Lyceum I used to teach thirty at a time.

"What brings you all here?" I asked in English. They blinked at me. I repeated myself in Yiddish.

"My mother made us come," Arkady said. "She said she couldn't stand us running around like animals. She said this was a better use of our time than risking death in the sewers."

"That's very flattering," I said in English, again to blank faces. "As s'sayer fayn."

The kids blinked again, sarcasm a different foreign language.

They had assembled themselves on the floor in a rough circle, and I joined them, leaning against my overturned barrel. Arkady and Rafel had both been furnished with notebooks and pencils, while the rest of the kids, used to the bare-bones nature of my teaching, had nothing in their hands. They leaned back casually. Some of them, I knew, also went to ghetto cheders, with desks and pens, and rulers that the rabbis could use to slap them across their palms.

With the arrival of the newcomers, it was impossible to teach entirely in English, so I asked the new ones to introduce themselves as best they could in whatever languages they felt comfortable using. Arkady and Rafel spoke in Yiddish; Eli and Jakub spoke in Polish, until Szifra glared at them and they switched to halting English.

Eli, the older one, hard and glinting like his sister, described himself as "tough and smart, I am tough and smart," which, while fluent, didn't sound exactly like how an English speaker might present himself.

"In what ways are you tough and smart, Eli?" I asked. He turned his haughty head toward me.

"In every way," he said.

"Could you be more specific?"

"That's not really what he means," Szifra interrupted. "He's not a bully." But Eli glared at her, and she stopped defending him.

"I make people do the things I need them to do," he said, then folded his arms across his chest and looked down at the floor.

Meanwhile, his brother, Jakub, only nine years old, was able to introduce himself both more fluidly and more sympathetically: "My name is Jakub. I am nice boy."

"You seem like a nice boy, Jakub," I said, and the kid smiled.

"Thank you," he said in English. Then he looked around rapidly, nervously, and sat back down. My guess was that he wasn't used to stealing attention.

"That was very good."

Jakub had clear pale-gray eyes, rosy cheeks. What must it have been like for him, surrounded by so many overbearing personalities? The dominating sister, the snake-eyed brother, the mother weeping in the brush factory? The father who had killed himself in the gazebo for the boys to find while they were playing hide-and-seek? And the fall from comfort: a mansion in the suburbs to a shared squat on Elektoralna Street. Obviously, other children had it worse, but somehow my heart went out to this boy. He was darker-haired than his siblings, and a bit chubbier too, with less of the leanness and foxiness that marked so many ghetto kids. I knew he smuggled—most of the kids here smuggled. But I hoped the other kids watched out for him, kept him safe.

"Who wants to recite a poem for me? Prize is a biscuit."

Hands shot up, which pleased me.

"I can do it!" Young Roman, head shaved to protect against typhus.

"In English!"

"I'll do it!" Charlotte, skinnier than before.

"No, I will!" Leo and Rivka, newer students, said together.

I thought: *These children, raised in fire, will be some of the finest Jews who have ever lived. They will be the strongest and the toughest and the smartest. They will be the most proud and will have the most to be proud of.*

"Pan Paskow? May I recite?" Filip Lescovec said, whittling knife folded in his pocket.

"Yes, Filip, why don't you?"

So Filip cleared his throat and, with a gentle flourish, began to recite Rudyard Kipling's "If—," a poem that was a bit bluff for my taste but did seem to provide a reasonable set of goals for children:

> "'If you can keep your head when all about you
> Are losing theirs and blaming it on you,
> If you can trust yourself when all men doubt you,
> But make allowance for their doubting too;

If you can wait and not be tired by waiting,
Or being lied about, don't deal in lies,
Or being hated, don't give way to hating,
And yet don't look too good, nor talk too wise—'"

"Why shouldn't you give way to hating if you're being hated?" Arkady said, in English that was better than I would have guessed. "Is that the right word?" He looked around the room. In Yiddish: "Farakht?"

"I had that question too," said Roman. "And why wouldn't you want to talk too wise?"

"What does this mean?" asked Eli. "To 'talk too wise'?"

I translated the poem into Yiddish as best I could; the students may have been able to pronounce the words, but most of them had not fully understood what Kipling was saying.

"Is he saying we shouldn't hate the Nazis?" Roman asked.

"He's saying . . . It's not that you shouldn't hate the Nazis. I don't think this poem is a prescription. He's just saying that sometimes it's better not to hate."

"I'm sorry, but I hate the Nazis," Rivka said.

"Of course you do," I said. "But hate isn't a particularly useful emotion. Perhaps it is better to . . ." I searched for the words. "Perhaps it is better to have some sort of reaction that isn't hateful. Perhaps it is better to . . ."

The children waited.

"Forgive?" I said, the word sounding stupid as it escaped my mouth. I felt nine sets of eyes on me, narrowing.

"In Yiddish?" asked Rafel (Rafel, whose grandmother was killed by a blow to the head). But I couldn't ask them to forgive in Yiddish.

"Listen, it's just a poem. Not everything in poems has to be accepted as truth. Some of them are just silly ideas."

"I thought you said poetry was the fruit of the tree of truth," said Szifra, leaning lazily back on her hands.

"Did I say that?" I probably did; it sounded like me.

"You said that poetry might not always tell us what we want to hear, but if we listen closely enough it would tell us what we needed to hear." That sounded like me too.

"Look, this is a simple poem for a simpler time."

"Or it's a poem for a simple man," Szifra said.

And maybe that was true, but it hurt, a little, that the ideas in this poem (self-reliance, forgiveness, kindness) seemed ridiculous—ideas that, when I had taught them to the comfortable children of the Centralny Lyceum, had seemed so noble.

"I have another question—what does this mean?" asked Leo. "'Wait and not be tired by waiting'?"

"It means we should be patient."

"And what is 'patient'?"

"Patient," I said, and, oddly, for a second I couldn't remember the word in my native tongue. "Cierpliwy."

"Well, of course we're patient!" Rivka said.

"What choice do we have?"

"I'm so impatient I'm going to go to the guard and say, 'I'm sorry, I'm impatient to leave. Can you open the gates, please?'"

"I don't think Kipling was thinking about the ghetto," I said.

"Nobody thinks about the ghetto!"

True enough. Every day, we gathered around radios and newspapers, waiting for our deliverers to start delivering. Where were the Americans? The British? How did nobody in the world know what we were going through except for a committee of politely concerned Jews in New York? And why on earth was corralling some kilos of flour the best they could do for us?

Didn't they know how desperate we were to go home?

"Who was this idiot who wrote this poem? Who doesn't understand how the world works."

"He wasn't an idiot—"

"He must have been," said Szifra, "to think that forgiveness solves anything. It solves nothing. It proves that you are willing to roll over when people are walking on your back."

"If I were going to rewrite this poem," said Rafel, in Yiddish (I didn't correct him), "I would say 'Stop waiting! Start hating! Don't keep your head! It's not worth it!'"

The children laughed. "We could call the poem 'How to Survive in the Ghetto,'" said Charlotte.

This struck me as an excellent assignment, and I said as much out loud, wishing I had at least a chalkboard so we could write a poem together, collectively. And then Arkady raised his hand and reminded me that both he and his brother had entire notebooks full of paper, if I wanted to use them, and his father had borrowed enough pencils from the Judenrat offices for an entire class, so we handed out pencils and paper, and my students began writing their own variations of the poem.

Unsurprisingly, they were not nearly as gamely self-reliant as Kipling's original, but they were clever in their own way, and although they were all written in Yiddish (save Szifra's, whose English was spelled phonetically, and therefore almost impossible to read), I felt they were an appropriate use of our time together. After all, how often did these children have an opportunity to write poetry? Or to respond to the stupid ideas of a long-dead grown-up?

> *If you can dream, you are clearly getting a good night's sleep*
> *and not stuck in a room with eight other people, four of whom*
> *snore so loudly they wake each other up.*

> *If you can think, you are not stuck in a cheder with Rabbi*
> *Horovitz, who says that there will be no thinking in his class-*
> *room, only studying,*

> *If you can bear to hear the truth you've spoken, then you're not*
> *talking to a Nazi.*

I read them out loud to laughter and cheers, and asked the students if they minded if I kept them. I thought they would make an excellent addition to Ringelblum's project—after all, I knew we had diaries and newspapers and drawings, but did we have any poetry? And wasn't poetry, after all, the fruit of the tree of truth?

"Pan Paskow! I must go!" Szifra shouted suddenly, breaking free of her languor to pull her hair back in a clip and yank on her coat. "I have an appointment. I'm so sorry—"

"Szifra, it's not even five . . ." (This was a guess; we had no clock in our classroom.)

"I know, but I must." And up she went, up and out the door at the top of the stairs, and the curious children couldn't help but climb on my barrel and hoist one another up to the narrow basement windows to see in which direction she disappeared. I'll admit it: I was curious too. I joined them by the window, peering out.

"Where's she going, Eli?" Filip asked.

"What am I, her babysitter?" Eli was on his tiptoes.

But we didn't have to watch for long to see her meet, in the middle of the street, a striking young man in a Nazi soldier's uniform. Neat and straight-backed, with clean, slicked-back hair, he held on to her arm and leaned in to say something to her. She said something to him, and then they disappeared together down busy Miła Street. A broad channel opened around them. They were parting the sea together.

"Eli?" Filip questioned, but Eli was already halfway across the room, running up the stairs to find his sister. Jakub, the baby, just sat in the corner, eyes wide.

"Jakub," I said, "do you know where they're going?"

He stared at me. I repeated myself in Polish.

"I don't know," he said, and his little face crumpled. "I don't know. How am I going to get home?"

"Do you have any idea where she's going?"

Where could the soldier be taking her? The interaction seemed friendly enough, and Szifra had gone willingly, but still, the thought that any of us might be safe in the company of a Nazi—it was unthinkable.

A ripple of laughter rang out across the classroom, disorienting against the cold shock of my fear. "What's so funny?"

Arkady was smirking.

"What's funny?" I repeated in Yiddish.

Roman gave me a foxy look.

Okay, okay, I knew the joke. Szifra was being sluttish with some Nazi, and slutty women were always good for a laugh. And maybe that was all it was—but still I felt in my bones she was in danger.

"Jakub, where do you live?"

"I can't go home," he said. "I was told I mustn't walk home alone when it's getting dark out."

"Do you know if they're coming back for you?"

Another snicker from the corner of the room.

"Someone will walk you home," I said, but I was met with seven reluctant faces. "Fine, then," I said. "I will walk you home."

THE SUN WAS already setting as we made our way down the street toward the Joseph family's apartment on Elektoralna. They lived in the nastiest little corner of the ghetto, newly crowded with refugees from the rest of Poland and, rumor had it, festering with typhus. I felt myself grow itchier as we walked south, toward their house; there were corpses on the street, covered with newspapers that fluttered in the wind. We pretended not to see them. A withered arm, a leg. On the sidewalk, children begged for scraps of food. I realized I had never given away my biscuit prize and handed it to a boy so ghostly I might have thought I'd imagined his existence but for the clawlike grasp of his hand as he reached up.

Jakub Joseph held tightly to my hand.

"Pan Paskow! Pan Paskow!" Did the children know my name, or was I just imagining I could hear them calling for me? Calling out to me in the encroaching dark, begging. I had a few zloty, but it was my turn to buy candles and tea the next day. Nowak smuggled in food every Thursday to the gate at Twarda Street and sold it to the highest bidder; due to our fortunate circumstances, we were usually able to secure a bit of what he sold. But as we crossed Nowolipki now, I stepped past a mother and a baby sitting against a wall. I would have kept walking, but I heard the whimper of the baby, or maybe it was the mother, and I thought, *I cannot do this*. I reached into my pocket.

The woman stared at me blankly as she received the zloty. Perhaps I hadn't heard her crying after all.

"My mother is sick," Jakub said as we approached his building. "You shouldn't come in."

"What's wrong with her?"

"Typhus," he said. "We think, anyway."

I nodded. If his mother had typhus, it was possible Jakub had it as well, although his head was shaved and he smelled clean enough. "Have you been bathing?"

"My brother takes me to the bathhouse."

"That's good," I said.

"It's crowded there."

I thought about how we still had plumbing on Sienna Street. "I know," I said.

"What do you think my sister is doing with the Nazi?"

"My guess is she's trying to figure out a way to help you and your brother."

"Is she going to get hurt?"

"I don't know," I said, frankly. The boy sat down on the street in front of his house, assuming the position of a thousand other beggars. I sat down next to him. The night was growing very dark very rapidly, and I was glad, because you couldn't see the rest of the street in the dark. But soon it would be curfew, and I'd either have to find a place to stay put through the night or walk home hidden by shadows.

"My mother is very sick," Jakub said again. "When she dies, I'll have no one to take care of me but Szifra."

"Why do you think she's going to die? People recover from typhus."

"Not always," he said. "Szifra said they only recover if they don't want to die, and our mother's just looking for a way out."

"That can't be true."

He shrugged. He took a muffler out of his coat pocket and wrapped it once around his neck; the muffler was hand-stitched.

"Who made that for you?"

"My bubbe," he said. "She died before the war. Which is good for her."

What could we do about typhus? The Judenrat had tried to enforce a quarantine among new arrivals, but there was no way to do that, nowhere to isolate people, and, anyway, life in the ghetto meant a constant search for food and news. You couldn't find either if you locked yourself in a room.

"Who will take care of me?" Jakub asked again, plaintively, and although part of my heart went out to him, I was surprised by a competing urge to slap him. He was nine years old, which was old enough to know that nobody, in the end, would or could.

Rapid footsteps approached: Szifra, flushed, racing through the streets. No sign of the Nazi.

"Jakub! There you are!" As if there were anywhere else for him to be. "Thank you, Pan Paskow. It was very kind of you to walk him—"

"Szifra! Szifra, what on earth do you think you're doing?" I said. In English, so that nobody else could understand.

It was too dark to see her face clearly, but I could imagine the narrowed eyes, the prissy and impervious mouth. "I am protecting my family, Pan Paskow."

"You left your brother to walk home in the dark."

"I didn't realize that Eli was going to chase after me."

"Did he find you? Where is he? And what on earth were you doing with—"

"I do not wish to discuss it any further," she said.

"Szifra, it's dangerous. You cannot trust these people."

"I know what I'm doing."

"Szifra—"

"Enough!" she said. "Pan Paskow, I urge you to hurry home. It's not safe to be out after curfew." And with that she grabbed her brother's arm and whisked him inside their decrepit building. Somewhere in its bowels, their mother lay feverish with typhus. Jakub was right; I felt sure she wouldn't make it.

I walked quickly, head down and hiding in the dark as best I could, careful not to trip on refuse or bodies or starving beggars. I tried to think of Kasia, of her blessed memory. It was cold, but I could feel sweat behind my neck. I had never been out this close to curfew, as the punishments were random: you could be shot on sight, thrown in Pawiak Prison, receive a blow to the nuts or nothing at all.

The exhaustion of it all. I stayed on the darker side of the street, close to the buildings, trying to look down at the sidewalk and out into the night at the same time. There were a few buildings with open doors. I saw Pan Finkelstayn sweeping up in the back of the old sundry store. I thought about going in, asking if I could spend the night on the floor.

"You!" a German soldier, somewhere behind me.

I turned, slowly, saw his outline in the dark. Neat, brushed-back hair. Ramrod posture. *Christ.*

"What are you doing out after curfew?"

Could I tell him that a Nazi had confiscated my watch? I had no idea what time it was. I never really knew.

"I am a teacher," I said. "I was helping a student home."

I felt the soldier take a step closer. It occurred to me that he might kill me, but suddenly I felt all fear leave my body. Everything around me seemed cinematic, as though I were watching from a distance. I could hear the man's footsteps, imagine him reaching for his pistol. I imagined him holding the pistol in the air somewhere beyond where I could see.

"Your name?"

"Adam Paskow."

"Papers?"

I handed him my kennkarte. He took it from me, and I felt his gloved fingers brush against mine. He examined it with a tiny flashlight, a pinpoint of light that contained my whole world.

"Paskow," he said. He took another step toward me. I braced for the blow, but instead he simply handed back my identity card. "Szifra's teacher."

"*Ja.*"

He was quiet. Then: "Hurry home," the soldier said.

I turned and ran.

THAT NIGHT, I found it more difficult than usual to sleep.

IN THE MORNING, I looked at myself in the mirror: Dark circles under my eyes. Stubble on my cheeks. I washed in the trickle of icy water in our bathroom, dressed in dank clothing. I could hear Emil on the other side of the curtain, breathing heavily as he looked over Judenrat papers.

Every day, a game of cat and mouse, interrupted by meaningless busywork.

I TOOK THE long route to the soup kitchen; there was a refreshing breeze, and I needed to escape the crowd in the apartment. Sometimes, I managed to achieve a measure of solitude by hiding in my curtained-off alcove, but this particular morning, when the children were all hanging about and Sala and Pani Lescovec were squeezed into the kitchen together, both trying to make soup—it felt suffocating. Emil was sitting on his bed, red-faced, crying for his mother over his documents.

And so the fetid air of the ghetto felt better than the stultifying air of the apartment, and I felt myself unknot a little just by leaving. I passed a newspaper stand and picked up a week-old copy of *Varsovia*, as I liked answering the trivia questions on the back page. In the old days, I often stopped at the café near my house—back when I was allowed in the café by my house—and spent a leisurely afternoon with the newspaper, the trivia questions, a beer or two, my own thoughts. Pierogis or pretzels. I don't think that I ever took the luxury of that time for granted, as I hadn't always been able to spend time so pointlessly. But for a while, after Kasia's death and even before it, my solo afternoons with a newspaper and a beer were one of my fondest pleasures.

"Paskow!" I was walking by the Twarda Street gate, where Nowak, the Polish guard, stood with his poorly hidden bags of food. (His inflated prices included the price of buying it off the Nazis.) "Paskow, what do you need?"

I reached into my pocket for zloty but then remembered. "I gave away my money yesterday, Nowak," I said. "I'll come next week."

"You gave away your money? Are you a fool?"

I actually liked Nowak, or at least didn't despise him. He usually exchanged a bit of banter with me as he overcharged me for essentials, and in this way made me feel a bit more human. "Nowak, there are children dying on the streets here. I'm not a monster. They need money, I give them money."

"I didn't say you were a monster." He grinned, showing off a mouth full of gold fillings. "I said you were a fool."

"I'll have money next week. I'll need soap. And razors—"

"I actually have a message for you, brother."

"I'm not your brother." I laughed. "What kind of message?"

"Come closer," he said, and I did, as my body was getting used to periodic floods of fear. "So Paskow," Nowak said conspiratorially, "I found out you are an associate of Henryk Duda." His breath smelled like beer and cheese.

"Yes," I said. "Henryk was my father-in-law."

"You were a member of the Duda family?"

"In a way," I said. "Not a very welcome one."

"But Duda was fond of you."

"I suppose," I said. "Really, he loved his daughter. My wife."

"And she's dead now."

"She is. An accident."

"Terrible."

"Nowak, what is this about?" I could feel eyes drawn to us, as it was rare for a Jew and a Polish guard to converse this freely for more than a minute. "What's your message?"

"Duda says you still have her necklace."

I felt myself lurch. "He says what?"

"His daughter's necklace. I think it was an inheritance of hers. Pearls or something?"

"He's taken everything. I have nothing left." This was a lie, but I couldn't believe that Nowak had a total inventory of every valuable I'd ever owned.

"He says he's working on legitimate papers for you."

"Nowak, that's bullshit. He's been working on papers for me for almost a year."

"These things aren't always easy to procure."

"Where is he now?"

"I don't know," Nowak said.

"Is he okay? What's happening to him? Why does he need every last penny?"

"I don't know that either, to tell you the truth. I receive my messages from another messenger. My suspicion, of course, is that he's in some sort of trouble. Otherwise, he would not be pestering a pathetic Jew, no offense—"

"None taken."

"—for his dead daughter's necklace. But he did want me to offer you this." He reached into one of the bags he carried with him, full of oats and sugar and other luxuries, for which he would charge fifty times their worth. He pulled out a brown package tied with twine, stained with grease.

"Meat?"

"Veal sausages from Triatka," he said. "You know Triatka?"

"Of course." It was the most famous butcher shop in Warsaw. Kasia loved it there.

"Duda wanted me to reassure you that these sausages are veal, not pork."

"And they're for me?"

"They're for you. And they are very fresh, very good."

"But why?"

"I assume to convince you of his good intentions. Or else he's worried about you."

"I'm worried about him."

"We worry about each other," Nowak said. "I doubt it does us any good."

I felt the weight of the sausages in my hand. "I'm grateful."

"Next week, you should come with the necklace."

"Bring me razors and soap," I said.

"I will."

"And cheese! And candies. As much candy as you can find. I need it for the children."

"I will speak to Duda. Or I will speak to the people who speak to Duda."

Veal sausages! How long had it been since I'd tasted such a thing?

"When can you come back?" I said.

"As soon as you have the necklace."

"Come back soon."

"I will."

I nodded at him, hurried back to the apartment, grabbed Sala, pulled her into my alcove, showed her the package hidden inside my coat.

"What are you doing, Adam?"

"Kielbasa cielecina," I said, opening the package to reveal the white sausages flecked with herbs, at least one kilo of them. Her eyes grew wide.

"Who'd you have to kill?"

"Nobody," I said. "At least not yet."

"Are we going to share these?"

"I don't know," I said. "Are we?"

Outside the alcove, I could hear the children running around like lunatics. Pani Lescovec was in the kitchen, muttering over the stunted pilot light.

"I don't think so," Sala said.

The urge to kiss her then came over me as suddenly as any urge I'd ever felt, so suddenly I had to put a hand over my mouth to stop myself. "Don't tell anyone we have this," I whispered, removing my hand, pretending to stifle a cough.

"I won't," she whispered back, standing all but fifteen centimeters away from me, curtained off against the world.

Her warmth. Her smooth skin. Her oval face. We stood there in the alcove for as long as I could manage it, until finally it became too much to bear, and I bent down to her and I kissed her.

"What on earth are you doing? I'm a married woman!"

"I know," I said, and then leaned forward and kissed her again, put my hands behind her back, and for just the slightest moment I felt her entire body relax.

And then we both remembered ourselves. She hurried out of the alcove, past the curtains, the secret delicacy of the kielbasa cielecina concealed under her apron.

Name: Sala Wiskoff
Date: March 7, 1941
Age: 35
Height: 160 cm
Weight: Not telling

Sala Wiskoff, who describes herself as a "formerly active housewife," agreed to be interviewed at the table in the kitchen she shares with nine other people, including me, in a converted one-bedroom flat on Sienna Street. Formerly of Saska Kępa, Sala was born and raised in Oświęcim, in the southern part of the country. She was the fourth child of Shlomo, a scholar, and Malka, a scholar's wife. Her parents both died before the invasion; she believes her remaining brothers and sisters either perished in September 1939 or are surviving somewhere in hiding.

For our interview, Sala wore a blue housedress that smelled like the soap she makes herself in a tin pot in the kitchen. She is scrupulous about cleanliness, especially in our cramped quarters, since she is, like so many of us, both terrified of typhus and desperate to maintain the dignity of a tidy home. In addition to the housedress, she wore her glasses on a chain around her neck. (She needs them only to read but wears them most days so that they don't get lost, new glasses being almost impossible to secure in the ghetto.) She wore a scarf around her shorn head.

It was a bit of work to persuade Sala to sit and be interviewed; after some initial reluctance, she met me at the kitchen table, as she so often did for no particular reason, at 5:45 a.m.

S.W. You just want me to tell my life story?

A.P. You can tell me whatever you want.

S.W. And what is this for again?

A.P. It's just to have a record of our time in the ghetto. So that we can remember what happened to us.

S.W. You think we could forget?

A.P. Well, the best way to remember anything is to write it down while it's happening, so memory doesn't shift around and become unreliable.

S.W. Shift around?

A.P. I mean, you know what memory does. How much we forget—

S.W. Actually, my memory refuses to leave me alone.

A.P.

S.W.

A.P. Well, then, why don't you just start at the beginning?

S.W. The beginning of what?

A.P. Whenever you . . . whenever you think your story begins.

S.W. My story? Hmm . . . I've never thought I had a story. Although it's certainly a nice idea. Well, I guess the most important thing to say is that for a long time in my life I just didn't know any better. I mean, for years and years I didn't know anything at all. I was a child for longer than most children are.

A.P. Meaning?

S.W. Oh, Adam. You wouldn't believe how small my life was until I left Oświęcim. How each day was like the next. I woke up in the morning and helped my mother make breakfast for my younger brothers and sisters. Then my sisters and I did laundry with her—which was an endless task, since we had nothing but a tub and one of those awful scraping boards, and we just scraped all morning until our fingers were sore. Or, if I wasn't doing laundry, I would have to clean up from breakfast and then take care of my little brothers. In the afternoon, I got started on dinner preparations. We had chickens in the yard, and it was often my job to kill and pluck them.

A.P. Which was worse, the laundry or the chickens?

S.W. Probably the laundry. Because the chickens, you know, it was amusing to chase them through the yard. And they were so dumb it didn't feel cruel to kill them. Now, my oldest brother worked at a ritual slaughterhouse, and he killed lambs and cows, and I don't know how he did that—he'd come by the house with blood on his apron, and I just cringed—but the chickens, that was nothing. Or you'd get to the henhouse in the morning and find that a fox had killed half of them in the night, anyway, so you were having cabbage for dinner.

A.P. What was your town like?

S.W. Oświęcim? It was . . . just a town. Not much. Brick houses, a town square, a synagogue, a mikvah. A haberdasher, a distillery. Not too many Poles—maybe half the town? But they had their church. It was a very fancy church, and everyone lined up on Sundays in their fine clothes. Sometimes, I wondered what it was like in there, but I never dared peek in.

A.P. Did the Poles harass you?

S.W. It was said in the olden days they would sometimes chase after the Jews, but by the time I was born, occasionally someone would spit at us, kick over a few gravestones in the cemetery, but for the most part they tolerated us. We were their trading partners, you know. Some Jews even employed Poles. The Great Synagogue had a Polish janitor who could work on Shabbos.

A.P. Did you have friends?

S.W. Oh, there wasn't much time for those sorts of things, really. It's not like with my kids, who had so many friends, who played football, who went to school all day. We didn't live like that at all. Sometimes, I wonder how the world changed so much in just 20 years. Cars, films, outings—the things that my children took for granted before we came here are things I could never have imagined in my life. We didn't have electricity, even! Or plumbing! And now we just expect those things. So . . . I wouldn't have believed it when I was a girl. What it would be like for me in so short a time.

A.P. Were you happy? When you were a girl?

S.W. (Sipping tea) I would like to say that I was happy, because nobody wants to admit to an unhappy childhood. And it wasn't torture, I suppose. But there wasn't much joy.

A.P. Why not?

S.W. Because my parents had 12 children and no money, until my brothers were old enough to earn some of their own. And my father wanted his sons to be scholars, like he was, but there is no money in being a scholar. My mother wanted them to go into business, to provide for their families and help us out too. But when she said that, of course, my father felt she was betraying him. So there was no winning. They fought a lot. They'd had an arranged marriage. I never thought they were particularly well-suited to each other, to be honest. My father was so devout, and my mother never even went to the synagogue.

A.P. Did she believe in God?

S.W. I never asked her.

(Because Sala is easy to talk to, and because she is also good at being quiet, it is a simple thing to sit in the kitchen and just be with her without talking. She has a very lovely, expressive face, and if you watch her closely, you can see her thoughts flit across her eyes.)

A.P. What do you remember the most?

S.W. I suppose just the severity of everyone's life. The

constant struggle to feed the kids, which I felt was very much on my shoulders, since I was the second-oldest girl.

A.P. Did you go to school?

S.W. I did, until I was 13. It was a Beis Ya'akov for girls. I learned how to write and read, which gave me a leg up. My older sister and my mother never went to school. They were illiterate. I had to read for them, and so did my brothers. But in a way, knowing how to read and write just made everything worse. Because the world wasn't hidden anymore. We had newspapers in Oświęcim. There was theater. I wanted to do things, go out, be part of the world, but I knew it was impossible.

A.P. It wasn't impossible—I mean, eventually you did get out.

S.W. Yes, but that was really mostly luck.

A.P. How'd you do it?

S.W. (Smiling) I never told you this story?

A.P. Tell me again.

S.W. Well . . . my brother needed someone to help him on market day. And that was something I could do when I was done with my chores. And my brother gave me 2 zloty, which I then turned over to my mother, so she let me go. My brother sold pins and thread and bobbins, things he traded for in other towns. Small stuff. He brought me along to help make change or to converse with the Poles who came by, since I had picked up a little Polish by then. And I used to be pretty, so people would stop and talk to me—

A.P. You're still pretty, Sala.

S.W. (Blushing) And then one day, this young man came by. He was selling sewing machines. Sewing machines! Nobody I knew had a sewing machine. He was a Litvak, straight from Vilnius, and he had two huge horses and an enormous cart with these machines on them. Brand-new, from America! Like nothing we had ever seen in Oświęcim. He put one out in the middle of the square and started demonstrating how to use it, and it was like he was giving away zloty, the crowd that surrounded him.

A.P. It was Emil.

S.W. Of course. Emil. I watched him from our stall, and he caught my eye and called to me to come help him demonstrate his newest model. A Singer 200, off the boat from New York. He took a piece of fabric and wrapped it around me—I had never stood so close before to a man I wasn't related to—and then he took a few measurements and made me a shawl in about 30 seconds. It was a silky fabric, the likes of which I had never felt. And considering I had worn the same black dresses from the time I'd hit puberty—

A.P. It must have been something.

S.W. It was something.

(Sala is prone to embarrassment, and sometimes, when she begins to feel shy, she stands and fusses, rearranging an already-neat countertop or putting water on to boil. Here she stood, looked in the icebox for something to eat, and returned with a sliced piece of carrot.)

A.P. Did you get married straightaway?

S.W. Have some carrot.

A.P. I'm still interviewing you. When did you get married?

S.W. (Sighing) Three weeks after we met. It sounds like something from a fairy tale, a story for children. But I was so young, and so desperate to escape from our crowded house. 14 people in three rooms! And Emil was kind.

A.P. It makes sense.

S.W. You wouldn't have recognized Emil if you had seen him. He's put on quite a bit of weight, you know. But back then he was slender and fit. So tall. And he had so many promises for us. A house of our own in the city, a car—a car! Nobody had cars back then. A fur coat. Vacations by the sea. A radio.

A.P. Did you believe him?

S.W. I wanted to.

A.P. Were you afraid to leave Oświęcim?

S.W. I wasn't.

A.P. Were your parents reluctant to let you go?

S.W. (Laughing) Emil promised he'd send them a stipend every month for as long as we were married—meaning, I suppose, for the rest of their lives he would support them. I guess they sold me, in a way.

A.P. Did you feel like you'd been sold?

S.W. I didn't care! Who would have cared? I was bound to be betrothed eventually to someone—at least this someone had money. Or was going to make money. And he had dreams! He was going to get me out of Oświęcim. And he seemed to really like me, for whatever reason. I mean, at that point, who knew, he could have had a harem in the back of that cart, girls from every city between Vilnius and Oświęcim, but it wouldn't have mattered to me. I would have joined the harem and gone.

A.P. And he didn't.

S.W. Have a harem? No.

A.P. So what happened next?

S.W. Well, I don't want to give the impression that everything was perfect from that day on, but to tell you the truth, it was fairly perfect from that day on. I helped him with his sewing-machine demonstrations. We picked up more merchandise at the port in Danzig—it was more of the world than I had ever seen! And Emil was kind to me, he was charming. He was so ambitious! I had never seen ambition like that. He wanted to make thousands, millions! He wanted to build a stucco house with gardens in the back. He wanted a maid for me, and jewels. And I was dazzled by all of it. What I had expected of married life: drudgery, children—

A.P. You didn't have children right away.

S.W. I was not going to live like my mother, who'd become a mother herself when she was 16. There was no way! And I knew from the other girls—I think they learned from the Catholics— that there were certain ways around getting pregnant if you wanted to avoid it. So we decided to live like it was 1925, not 1825. We weren't just going to start spitting out babies.

A.P. Wow.

S.W. Listen, I had spent my life taking care of babies and—

A.P. I wasn't trying to—

S.W. So we spent those first several years making our dreams come true. Emil opened the import office in the business district. We found the house in Saska Kępa. It was so beautiful— seven rooms, and a water closet with running water! No more carrying water in from the well! No more outhouse. And then Emil found a maid for us, which seemed outrageous—I mean, there I was, already living a life of luxury I could never have imagined, and suddenly there's a maid? But the business had taken off, and he wanted to spoil me, you know. He really loved me. I couldn't figure out why, but I decided not to ask questions I didn't want the answers to.

A.P. Sala...

S.W. Well...

A.P. And then?

S.W. Well, I mean, good things don't last forever, of course.

A.P. Meaning...

S.W. No, no, nothing scandalous. It's just that in our seventh year of marriage we got word that Emil's father had died.

A.P. What happened?

S.W. I don't know. People just died in those days. Don't you remember how people used to just . . . die?

A.P. Of course.

S.W. So Emil went up for the funeral, and when he came back, he had his mother with him. I had never met her before. She was this tiny lady, seemed half of Emil's size, but I could see the strength in her just by looking at her. One of those miniature women with a will of iron. She moved in with us, and Emil, being Emil, had to give her the nicest downstairs bedroom, the one with the east-facing windows and the stained-glass lamp. The one I read in when I couldn't sleep. I loved that bedroom. It was the only place in the house that was entirely mine.

A.P. You didn't argue with him?

S.W. How could I argue? He had given me everything. My entire life! I wasn't going to tell him he couldn't have his mother live in the nicest downstairs bedroom in our house.

So Reva moved in, and pretty soon she took over the household. She had decided I didn't know what I was doing—which was true, but of course how could I ever learn if she was there doing everything? Cooking, bossing around the maid. Testing the mantelpiece with a white glove to make sure it had been dusted. Sometimes, I went to the import office with Emil, and she would throw a fit—"Business is no place for a woman," that sort of thing. So for the first time in my married life, I started to despair.

I tried to talk to Emil about it, but he was Reva's only son and very close to his mother. He couldn't tell her to let me live as I wanted. In fact, he told me that initially the reason he wanted to make so much money, you know, was to take care of her. They hadn't been poor, like I was, but in Vilnius they were the sort of just barely middle class that makes you feel poor.

A.P. I grew up the same way.

S.W. So then you understand. For me, everyone around us in Oświęcim was just the same as we were, so we never felt particularly down-and-out, even though we were nearly destitute. Meanwhile, in Vilnius, Emil's mother was surrounded by rich Jews and knew she was looked down on. All her life, she'd wanted a maid to boss around. Now she had one, and she was a pig in shit—excuse the expression.

A.P. So what did you do?

S.W. I decided to have a baby.

A.P. Ah.

S.W. I knew I was going to have children eventually, and even though I'd wanted to wait a few more years, once Reva arrived there was really nothing else for me to do. I couldn't just read all day. And with the maid around, it wasn't like there was any housework.

A.P. So you had a baby because you were bored?

S.W. (Smiling) There are probably worse reasons.

It took a few months for me to become pregnant, and I was surprised by that. That this thing I had been avoiding so carefully turned out to be harder to achieve than I thought. But then, in October, I started to feel so exhausted, and I knew. My body was different. I told Emil, and he was overjoyed. He went to the synagogue to give thanks. I didn't mind.

Anyway . . .

Arkady was born at midnight, July 31. There was a full moon, and I stared at it through the window as I labored. The moon was so big and bright it was almost like it had a personality. Like it was a living thing. I felt like the moon was ushering me onward, like it was whispering to me that I could do it, that I could see the process through. Isn't that crazy? It was a hard delivery. When the midwife wasn't attending to me, she was keeping Emil and Reva out of the room. They both wanted to burst in—neither one has any self-control.

A.P. Well...

S.W. Emil heard me screaming, and he was frightened. And his stupid mother—may she rest in peace—she didn't have the decency to tell him that it was normal, that it's always like this, that a woman's curse is pain during childbirth. Humans aren't very efficient about delivering babies, you know. At home, I'd watched the ewes deliver their lambs, and it was like one, two, three, and it was done. But for women, it can take hours—days, even. And the pain is unreal.

A.P. I've heard.

S.W. So I stared at the moon out my window, and I prayed. Which was surprising to me. Because I had never in my life resorted to prayer. Not when I was being forced to kill chickens or clean the outhouse, not when I had to sit in those horrible stuffy Beis Ya'akov classrooms. Never. I don't even believe in God, honestly. Emil does. My kids might. I never did. Maybe I shouldn't say that out loud.

A.P. So why did you pray?

S.W. (Standing again to fetch more food, looking into the icebox as if for a miracle) It couldn't hurt, could it? And I guess it felt like the only thing I had left that might save me from the pain.

A.P. Do you remember the prayer?

S.W. I do.

A.P. Would you say it?

S.W. Why?

A.P. I'd just like to hear it.

S.W.

A.P.

S.W. Baruch atah Adonai elohanu melech haolam, ha tov v'ha meiteev. (She is quiet for a moment.) Do you know it?

A.P. I don't know Hebrew, unfortunately.

S.W. Ah. And you the language teacher! Well, it means something along the lines of "Blessed is the Lord, king of the universe, who is good and who brings us good."

A.P. That's it?

S.W. I know. It sounds more imposing in Hebrew. I said it again and again. Even when the pain was so intense I could barely breathe. Baruch atah Adonai elohanu melech haolam, ha tov v'ha Meiteev.

A.P.

S.W. When Arkady was born, I'm telling you, the moon was so bright it was like a beam direct from the heavens through the window. You know what I mean? Have you ever seen a moon like that?

A.P. I have.

S.W. The midwife took the baby to wash him, and I was alone in the room for a minute, and that was the only minute of my life I felt the presence of God. Does that sound silly? I don't know. It might have been the hormones. Or the rush of energy leaving my body. Or blood loss. I lost so much blood the midwife was afraid I wouldn't survive.

A.P. Or maybe it *was* God?

S.W. Adam, come on. (Sala smiles. She does have a very sweet smile.) When the midwife came back and placed the baby in my arms, I felt . . . for the first time in my life, I felt like I knew what love was. Actual love.

A.P. Ah.

S.W. I mean, I was fond of my husband. I felt affection for him, certainly. And I cared for my parents and siblings. But Arkady, he was this tiny, shriveled thing—really not very beautiful, if I'm telling the truth—but to me, I had never seen anything so beautiful. I couldn't believe he was mine. He was all mine! Not Emil's, not Reva's. Not my mother's. He was mine. I had done this. I had made this person in my own body.

And as he's grown up, he's brought me the sort of joy I could only imagine feeling when I was a child myself. I have never known any happiness like the one I've known watching this child grow. He's so smart, and he's kind. And he's funny. He's funny! Neither Emil nor I are particularly funny, so we're not sure where he gets it.

A.P. Sala, why are you always putting yourself down?

S.W. Adam, stop. It's true. I know what's true. Anyway, Rafel was born three years later, and I felt the same thing, the same amazing rush of love. And the two of them have given me more happiness than I could have ever imagined. They really are the reason I feel I was born, to bring them into the world. Does that sound crazy?

A.P. It doesn't.

S.W. Maybe it does.

A.P.

S.W. As soon as we get out of here, we're going to do so much, we're going to live so much life. I feel like I owe them a year back of their childhood.

A.P. They're still having a childhood, even if it's in the ghetto.

S.W. No, no, this isn't right. This isn't . . . This isn't a childhood. This is some sort of strange hell that we try to make as normal as possible so as not to face the truth of it. But it's not childhood. Often when I'm feeling helpless, I think, "I have to survive it so I can make it up to them."

A.P. I don't think kids see this the way we do. To them, it will be a year or two where they lived a different way.

S.W. We're going to go to Palestine after this. Emil and I decided.

A.P.

S.W. We're going to turn brown as almonds.

A.P. I'll miss you.

S.W. You can come.

A.P. Maybe I will.

S.W. I hope . . . You should. You should come.

A.P. We just have to survive until then.

S.W. I promise, we'll survive. Of course we will. I always survive. So do you.

A.P.

S.W. Why stop now?

TWELVE

The next morning, I put the necklace in my satchel, still unsure whether or not I could actually give it away. I walked to the Twarda Street gate to see if Nowak was there, selling supplies, but instead it was the fat old guard who threatened to shoot you if you made eye contact. Relieved not to have to make a decision, I looked down, away, met the eyes instead of a small boy who had spread all his belongings on the sidewalk. What did he have? A few trinkets, some bobby pins, keys to a house he no longer lived in. "Pan?" he called, gently. I was such a sucker. I bought a bobby pin for ten groszy and gave it to the next beggar I passed.

"You have to be careful, Pan Paskow," said an older man watching the scene from an outdoor table by the Café Muzyka, closed for many months now. "You won't survive if you keep giving these filthy children all your money."

"I'm sorry?"

"You can't have a big open heart in this place. Come sit."

He was an older man with a throaty voice and a face half obscured by a scarf. He seemed familiar, but so did everyone. "Do I know you?" I said.

"You don't recognize me?" he asked.

I was reflexively embarrassed, but also annoyed—how was I supposed to recognize anyone when it was ghetto policy to keep your head down and your eyes averted? "I'm one of your colleagues at Oneg Shabbat. Ignatz Forman. I used to be head librarian at the University of Warsaw."

I took the other seat at the table, holding tight to my satchel as I sat. "I'm sorry, Pan Forman. It's hard to remember . . ."

"Ah, that's all right. Let me buy you a coffee. Oh, that's right—there isn't any coffee." He let out a dry chuckle at a joke I was sure he'd told many times. "So how are you holding up these days? I see you can't keep these little fuckers from guilting you out of your money."

I was surprised at his casual obscenity but tried not to show it, instead nodding vaguely. "They have so little," I said.

"Let them go, Paskow. You think your groszy will save them?"

I shrugged. There were other ghetto nihilists, but I tried to avoid them—the ones who thought we all were doomed, or that there was no point in charity or kindness, since in the end it would keep the suffering alive only to continue suffering. These people were exhausting to be around, and confused their own darkness for wisdom.

"Let me ask you a question, Paskow. What do you think of our little Oneg Shabbat project?"

"What do I think of it?" I didn't, really—I had a job to do, and I did it, and was rewarded with apricots and a warm fire and the opportunity to ask nosy questions of my students and friends. "Well, Pan Ringelblum is certainly an impressive figure."

"Ha!" said Forman. "He's a self-regarding fool."

I tried not to look surprised.

"Listen," Forman said, "Ringelblum thinks this is a noble cause, trying to write down the history of this place. And, sure, I'm willing to help if it gives me something useful to do. But the truth of the matter is, nobody gives a shit about what the Jews have to say. Nobody ever has, and nobody ever will."

"I'm not sure that's—"

"You're not sure? Has anybody in the entire two-thousand-year history of the Jewish people been half as impressed with them as they are with themselves? The chosen people. Chosen for what, exactly?"

"Pan Forman, I don't know—"

"I don't mean to offend, of course," he said in a way that suggested he didn't care one way or the other if he offended.

"I'm just not particularly religious," I said. "If you're looking for a theological argument."

"Theology!" He shook his head. "No, not particularly. I'm more interested in men than gods. Self-pitying Jewish men in particular." He looked at me through narrowed eyes to see if he was shocking me; he wasn't. "Our rot has been thoroughly exposed, Pan Paskow."

"I'm not sure what you mean."

"Our rot! Our failures. The lies we tell ourselves to keep going. Our self-pity. All of it. The Nazis have exposed us for what we really are."

"Pan Forman . . ."

"You're a language teacher—isn't that right, Pan Paskow? So you tell me, what's the language you hear most of the time in the ghetto?"

"Polish, I suppose."

"Polish. Yes, Polish," Forman said, leaning toward me, his hot breath puffing against my face. "All this time and effort we put into teaching our children Yiddish, put into Hebrew, and yet here we are, Jews, all of us, speaking the oppressive stupid language of the goyim. Polish."

"Well, but there is a lot of Yiddish too."

He waved a hand in the air, as if to cut off my naivete. He had a face marked with the brown spots of age, longish gray hair, moist red lips. He was wearing a plaid cap and a thick woolen scarf, even though it was warm out. He reminded me of a million old teachers I'd seen come and go at the Lyceum, made contemptuous and cynical by time.

"And you tell me, Paskow, what kind of Jew would let another Jew starve in the street?"

"Nobody is *letting* anybody—"

"Please," Forman said. "Don't give me that nonsense. Of course we are. Of course we're letting it happen! What kind of Jew would hoard food when he sees a child starve? And yet do children starve every day here? And do you doubt that there are many people with enough food to last the week?"

"Didn't you just say, when I gave the child the groszy—"

"Oh, I'm rotten too. Believe me, I'm rotten too." He coughed softly into his hands. "I can sit here all day, not a care in the world, because I know my wife will have soup on the stove when I get home. We had money before this. And so did you, I assume. Otherwise, you wouldn't walk around here clutching that bag so tightly."

My stomach roiled, but I did not loosen my grip on my satchel. "I'm sorry, but I don't really see your point."

"My point is that Oneg Shabbat is trying to create a memorial to a hollow people," he said. I didn't respond. "That's right," he said. "A hollow people. A hollow people who prefer to think of themselves as mere victims instead of moral actors like everyone else."

I did not have anything to say to this. In front of us, on the street, two nicely dressed girls walked by, chatting. They had clean-looking hair, done up in braids, and were wearing soft wool coats.

"Ach," he said, eyeing the girls up and down. "What I would give for a slice of Sacher torte right now. Can you imagine? Sacher torte, with a little whipped cream on the side."

"I'm sorry," I said, "but I must be off."

"You wouldn't like a little slice of cake yourself?" he said, his eyes still trailing the girls.

"I really must go."

"I understand," Forman said, turning back to me. He tightened his scarf a bit. "Have a wonderful day, Pan Paskow."

I hurried down the street away from the Muzyka, stepping over the string-thin legs of starving children, never not dwelling on the diamond-and-pearl necklace in an inside pocket in my satchel. The necklace was worth . . . how much? The life of a starving child? My own life? Would it buy me a new kennkarte? Kennkartes were the small books identifying us by name and religion, our photographs stapled in: flimsy, stupid, crucial. Fake ones went for five hundred zloty, and everyone knew the fake ones were no good.

I had no idea how much it would cost to make a real one. I had no idea how much it would cost me to hope.

Forman was right; perhaps he was right. We Jews might not be better than anyone else. But on the other hand, given these circumstances, we certainly weren't any worse.

(Even as a mother and her baby, puffy from starvation, sat on the sidewalk weeping quietly, expecting nothing.)

I paced the ghetto like a fool, the necklace in my satchel, looking for Nowak (what if I were robbed? thrown in jail? shaken down by the police?), trying to imagine what I would do with a kennkarte, trying to imagine how I would get out of here (a sewer? a bribe?), trying to imagine what my life would look like on the outside when I had nobody to help me. Unless Henryk would still help me. But why would he help me when I had nothing left to offer him?

Unless he still wanted to be kind to me, in honor of his favorite daughter, who had loved me.

And when I thought that, I wanted to slap myself for the sin of sentimentality. We had all become so sentimental here.

Our big open hearts were going to get us all killed.

Or we were going to be left to rot.

THIRTEEN

===

"**W**hat's with your face?"

"My face?"

"You look pale. You're not eating."

I smiled, despite my glum mood, and felt my glum mood lift. I rarely saw Sala outside the confines of our flat, but she and I were walking toward the building at the same time and, for once, I didn't have my head down.

"Sala, nobody's eating."

"There's not eating, and there's *not eating*. Come on. I have bread."

"From where?"

"I made it! Mariam Lescovec decided to let me use the stove for four whole hours, and the gas was on."

"You baked bread."

"I can't promise it's good."

"It's home-baked bread."

"It might be a little raw in the middle. But it won't kill you."

"And if it does . . ."

"At least you'll have eaten first."

We marched up the five broad flights of our seven-story building together, both slowly losing our breath but doing our best not to show it. Our building had been handsome once, a graceful limestone with mullioned windows and decorative archways. It had withstood the 1939 bombings relatively well, as had many buildings of its age and pedigree, but now there were chinks in the walls and the general stench of despair lingering in the hallways. Still, the women of our building, anxious to fend off decrepitude, kept the public areas dusted. Occasionally, Pani Lescovec ran a mop up and down the foyer floors.

We made it to our apartment, graciously pretended not to notice the other's wheezes, then followed the smell of bread to the kitchen. The flat was gloriously empty—this never ceased to feel like a miracle— and I watched in amazement as Sala removed a towel from on top of a browned loaf and set it on the kitchen table.

"Where did you get the flour?"

"I had a silk scarf I decided I was done with."

Silk for flour. She had gotten the better of the deal. I watched as she sank a knife into the bread. It gave off wisps of steam. The richness of the smell made me feel the tiniest bit dizzy, but I did my best not to show it.

"Tea?" I asked.

"Tea, yes."

She passed me a mug and the warm piece of bread, and I sank my teeth into it like it was made of butter, made of air. I would allow myself only one slice, and I knew I shouldn't eat it fast. On the other hand, the luxury of eating something fresh-baked while it was still warm . . .

"I could tell you were hungry."

"Sala, do you think the Jews are rotten?"

"Excuse me?"

"Nothing. I—"

"Is this because you kissed me?"

I coughed; I thought we had made a silent pact to never mention it, but she was smiling.

"I'm sorry about that. I was just so—"

"Oh, don't be," she said. "Nothing that exciting has happened to me in a long time! Here, have another slice of bread." And I was surprised that I felt stung by her dismissal of a moment I suppose I had been savoring, quietly, in my memory—one of those small golden moments sprinkled throughout your life that may never be repeated but will live forever in your mind's replay and be enlarged there.

I looked at Sala: pale skin, huge eyes, high cheekbones. A cheap burgundy rag around her head. Blue housedress. Thin, chapped lips, gray tooth. I looked down at the table and tried to remember Kasia's robust, beautiful face, and was frightened to find I could not immediately bring it to mind.

"Here," she said, putting another slice of bread on my plate.

"Sala, this is for your boys. I shouldn't—"

"But I made it for you," she said, and she touched my arm. And I looked at her again, at those pale chapped lips—

She blushed and looked away. "I just thought you weren't eating enough," she said. I found my arm tingling where she had touched it.

"That's very kind of you," I said. "But, really, I couldn't."

There was a new kind of heaviness in the air around us, heavy with the sweetness of the bread, and her breath, and the fizzing centimeters of space between us. I would not kiss her—I would not do that again—but I would enjoy the desperation of wanting to.

And then the door opened, and the raucous crowd of boys, followed by a hearty, "Sala! Sala! Is that bread I smell? Ah, hello, Paskow."

The fizzing air fizzled away, and Sala was at the counter, slicing thin pieces of bread for all the hungry boys and for her husband.

Name: Emil Wiskoff
Date: March 8, 1941
Age: 48
Place: Kitchen of our shared
apartment building, 53 Sienna
Steet, Warsaw, Poland

Emil Wiskoff is an imposing figure. He stands at least 2 meters tall and weighs perhaps 115 kilos, and boasts consistently excellent posture. He has a ruddy complexion, thinning brown hair, a trim, well-greased mustache, and green eyes that project authority. He is often clothed in a well-fitting suit, which he wears to his position at the Judenrat. His laugh is as sharp as a dog's bark. His voice is loud.

    E.W. So you want to know my history for your files. Is that right?

    A.P. Well, I'm trying to put together the story of our time here, and I thought . . .

    E.W. You want to know about my family, then, Paskow? My lineage?

    A.P. Not really. Just your own—

    E.W. You see, from 1648—and probably from long before, I'll tell you—the Wiskoff family was based in Vilna, in what was alternately the Grand Duchy of Lithuania, the Polish-Lithuanian Commonwealth, and so on. Constantly being invaded and then reinvaded. But the Jews just minded their own business, built a very close-knit community. Sometimes times were good for us, and sometimes not so good, but we persevered. We had synagogues, yeshivas, the rest of it.

A.P. I have always wanted to see Vilna.

E.W. You should visit after the war. It's a beautiful city. Beautiful! I'll take you there.

A.P.

E.W. So, as I said, from 1648, and quite likely before then, there were Wiskoffs in Vilna. My family kept a record, you see— a generational record, on parchment, like a Torah—so we could know our own story. Like the kings of Europe! Every birth and death, every marriage, we had it written down. The patriarch of the family would bring it to the scribe on Yiddishe Gan—that was the Jewish street there, near the Great Synagogue—and have the parchment inscribed with the relevant names and dates. So we knew everything: who was born to whom and when, and who died and when, and how they were related to whom.

A.P. Impressive.

E.W. Yes. A very rare thing for a Jew to have this kind of information, passed on from father to oldest son. That was the rule, you see. Father to son.

A.P. But what would happen if there were no sons in a generation?

E.W. That's a good question, Paskow. And I'll tell you the answer. It never happened. Not once in 300 years. Wiskoff women knew they were responsible for birthing at least one son, and for almost 300 years, God provided.

A.P. Wow.

E.W. A miracle, how God provides. I am the oldest son in my family. The only son, in fact. Four sisters after me.

A.P. Do you still have the parchment?

E.W. Ah, well, that's the tragedy, what happened to our family record. Not the first tragedy and not the last, but a tragedy nevertheless. Perhaps you're familiar with the pogroms that used to come through Vilna, especially after Russia took over the territory.

A.P. Yes, I—

E.W. The moronic Russians blamed the Jews for the death of Tsar Alexander. Which is quite something, considering most of us wouldn't have known Tsar Alexander from Alexander the Great! But, really, it was just an excuse to cause destruction, wouldn't you say? The Russians. There has never in the history of the entire planet been a stupider people than the Russians. There's a museum in Leningrad where they have babies in jars of formaldehyde, babies born without their brains—did you ever hear of such a thing? And even these babies are smarter than your average Russian. Or maybe they are your average Russian. Who can say. Their heads crunched in like crumpled paper.

A.P.

E.W. Where was I? Oh, yes, our family record. So you see, the parchment was in the keeping of my grandfather, who lived just down the lane from our own family, and whenever he heard whispers that the Russians were coming to pillage the neighborhood, my zayde would bury it under the ground with whatever valuables he had. Not that he had much! But then one night in 1908, I believe, the Russians came too fast, those idiots, and, like idiots, they burned everything they couldn't steal. Our parchment went up in flames. My grandparents were lucky to survive with their lives.

A.P. My goodness.

E.W. My own family hid in the wheat fields behind the lane. For some reason, our own house was untouched.

A.P. That's fortunate.

E.W. I've been through a lot, I don't mind telling you. Quite a lot. My father was quite distraught over the loss of the parchment, as you can imagine, but my mother had been very resourceful. She wasn't a fool. In fact, she was one of the first literate women in the family. And it turned out she had copied down my father's family's record. Really at first, just to practice her writing, but then as it became clear that nothing the Jews owned—absolutely nothing, was safe from these idiot Russians—she did it in order to keep the record safe. As a gift, I suppose, to my father's family. She was a wonderful Jewish wife, you see. So even though we lost the parchment, we still had the information in a tiny notebook. Eyn togbuch. Smaller than the one you're using now.

A.P. What luck!

E.W. My mother kept the notebook in the family vault at the bank, would go visit it to record births and deaths, brought it with her when she left Vilna. It was one of the few things of value she brought.

A.P. Well, that was—

E.W. The truth is, my mother was far more literate than my father was, had more schooling. My father was a good man, a humble man, a tailor, but not particularly entrepreneurial, not able to sell his services among all the hundreds of tailors in Vilna. And he was a large man, like I am. His fingers were nimble, but you would never look at him and think, "Ah! That's a tailor." He looked like a boxer, to tell you the truth.

A.P. So do you, Emil.

E.W. I suppose I do. Yes, I suppose so. (Emil begins to grow misty, which happens frequently but remains surprising, to see a man so large tear up.) But really, my story starts with my mother. Don't all of our stories start with our mothers? Our lives? Our souls? Is there anything more worthy in the world, Paskow, than a Jewish mother?

A.P. I don't—

E.W. My mother was a remarkable woman. Remarkable. She raised five children on my father's meager salary, encouraged me to set up a business for myself when I was only 17, helped me find the investors to buy my first oxcart, my first sewing machine. And it wasn't easy for her. She had to approach some of the big machers at the synagogue—the few among us Litvaks who had any money—and try to sell them on my entrepreneurial skills. She had me do a little performance, try out my sales pitch on them.

A.P. And she was successful.

E.W. Baruch hashem. Yes, she was successful. I was successful. I started the business. Of course, my mother wasn't thrilled when I left Vilna, but she understood: I had to follow the money. There was too much competition at home. So I packed my cart and took off, and it was many years until I saw her again, many years . . .

A.P. Until your father's death.

E.W. Yes, you heard the story from Sala. Yes. My father died, and I went back to Vilna for the first time in a decade to find my mother and bring her to live with me. What else could I do for my sweet eema after all she had done for me? And, oh, Vilna had changed since my departure. So much more modern! But the Jews seemed to be poorer, had fewer businesses, or even basic ways of making money. It was far worse for them up there than in Warsaw, and many of the people I'd known had left for Palestine. All my old neighbors. Three of my sisters. Anyway, I packed my mother up and brought her home, and it was then that I felt right in the world—with my mother in my home, the way it should have been.

A.P. And Sala . . . didn't mind?

E.W. Sala? She loved it! It was so good for her to have someone to teach her the ways of a Jewish housewife.

A.P.

E.W. And when Arkady was born, and Rafel, my mother took that little notebook and inscribed their births. One day—long after this moment in time is a memory—one day, I will give the book to Arkady, and he will keep the record of our family for another generation. And his son, and his son after him.

A.P. You are lucky to have such a strong family tradition, Emil, wouldn't you say?

E.W. Well, Paskow, anyone who knows me would tell you I'm a very lucky man.

FOURTEEN

===

Amid all the comings and goings of the ghetto, the new refugees and the suddenly deceased, the Oneg Shabbat group
remained remarkably stable. At each meeting, we looked a little worse
for wear, of course—a little more tired and a little more sallow—but
none of us had starved to death or been shot, none of us had succumbed
to typhus or the flu. It was impossible to know whether this was because
we had been recruited from the ranks of the lucky or because our record-
keeping provided us a purpose that made us want to stay alive.

In the library on Tłomackie Street one bright afternoon in late June,
we gathered, as usual, to give our reports and share news. I had grown
to look forward to these Saturdays, even though there were fewer treats
to pass around and we no longer received our stipends. The library still
felt like a world apart from our world, and my Oneg Shabbat colleagues
felt not exactly like friends, but like compatriots. Ringelblum maintained
his sources in the outside, and usually knew information about the war
that had yet to trickle down to the rest of us; he had recently told us, for
instance, about the fall of Yugoslavia, and that the London Blitz seemed
to have ended for good.

Now, as we assembled ourselves on our customary chairs and
couches, exchanged good wishes and dark jokes, Ringelblum called us
to order. His hooded eyes seemed even bleaker than usual. I noticed

that his wife and child hadn't joined us, and my decent mood started to wane.

"It seems . . . ," he began without preamble, as was his way. "It seems the Germans have decided to invade Russia."

Startled silence in the room; rapid blinking.

"Last Sunday, the Nazis invaded Russia across three thousand kilometers of their border, bringing troops in from points in Belarus, Latvia, and Poland. The Allies seemed not to have had any advance warning. Remember, Stalin and Hitler signed a pact two years ago. So this was, of course, unexpected."

I looked around the room for some clue as to how to interpret the news: Would the Russians repel Hitler, thereby ending the war? Was it foolish to imagine the Nazis could somehow claim Russia? Was this good news? Bad?

"It's impossible to successfully invade Russia," someone said, breaking the silence. "Remember Napoleon."

"Napoleon didn't have Panzer tanks," someone else said.

"We cannot know what this means for us," Ringelblum said. "Allies continue to lobby the Americans to join the war. Churchill, especially, has increased his lobbying, and we know that Roosevelt has, at the very least, committed to sending more munitions to the Allies."

"But not soldiers."

"No," Ringelblum said. "Not soldiers. At least not yet."

We absorbed Ringelblum's words, trying to determine, still, how to feel. I was certain I wasn't the only one who thought some nice dried apricots might make the moment less fraught.

"There is more," Ringelblum said, for there was always more. "Our sources tell us that the Germans have begun building poison chambers in some of the prison camps. These poison chambers are rooms that can hold several hundred people at once. Prisoners are told that they are taking showers, stripped naked, and then suffocated by the release of a noxious gas. This is happening now in Auschwitz, the prison camp that the Germans have set up in Poland, just outside the Jewish area in Oświęcim."

"Oświęcim?" I said, startled.

"Yes. The Germans call this place Auschwitz."

I felt a lurch in my throat.

"The Germans have begun bringing trainloads of people in from around Europe. Some people they use as slave labor, but the people they decide are not useful are marched to the gas chamber. This would be older people, children, the disabled—"

"Children!"

"Yes, of course, children," Ringelblum said, sounding disgusted both at the news he was relaying and our disbelief. "Children are generally not useful workers."

"This cannot be," someone protested from the back. "They are trucked in and simply . . . murdered? Immediately?"

"Do the Allies know about this?" demanded someone else.

"If I know about it, the Allies know about it."

"And they're not stopping it?" asked a man from across the room.

"It seems to me, Pan Klosterman, that the best way for the Allies to stop it is to defeat the Germans in the war."

"Yes, but in the meantime—"

"Yes," said Ringelblum. "This is what's happening in the meantime."

"But children?" wailed Klosterman.

"Pan Klosterman, last month in Nowy Wostok all children under five were locked into a synagogue, which was then set on fire."

Tears rolled down the face of the woman sitting next to me. (I knew her name now; she was Marysia Hoff, a former reporter for the *Folkstaytung* newspaper.)

The day, which had been sunny and cloudless—how grateful we always were for sunny, cloudless days—seemed suddenly bleak. I could no longer make out the sun outside the windows.

"Where is this information from, Pan Ringelblum?"

"Some is from escapees—"

"Ah! So people are able to escape!"

"Barely," Ringelblum said. "It is a case of extreme chance and extreme luck. But, yes, we have spoken to escapees. To spies from the Polish resistance. Reports from German POWs captured by the British. The intelligence is filtered down and—"

"And who are these prisoners? Tell me who they are taking to these places."

"As I told you," Ringelblum said, puffing his cheeks and letting out a breath, "it seems to be a combination of resisters and their families, political opposition, Roma, and Jews. Some of the communities that might have been sent to the ghetto are now being sent to these places instead."

"But why? Under what pretext? This violates the rules of engagement!"

"It's unclear," Ringelblum said. "I can't pretend to understand the logic of mass killing—neither Jews nor Roma are military threats, and surely we would be more use to the Nazis as captive labor. Even those of us who can't work very efficiently can still work. But of course to understand the rationale behind Nazi decisions is to understand insanity. We can't do it."

"Yes, but surely—"

"Pan Klosterman, if you are asking me to argue for the Nazi position, I apologize, but I cannot."

I looked around the room, couldn't stand it, looked instead at my own hands.

"So it becomes ever more urgent to continue to push the Americans into the war with whatever means the Allies have. The Allies are, of course, a shifting force, as we can assume now that the Russians will join their side, having been invaded. But as the Germans have continued their pursuit of European domination, they have also moved into North Africa, the Maghreb. It has even been said that they've sent U-boats to the coast of North America, perhaps trying to engage the Americans in war. So the German forces are certainly widespread."

"As you say, Ringelblum," said Klosterman, as if to make peace, "no sane person can understand the Nazis."

"Unless the Nazis subjugate Russia," Ringelblum said. "In which case their insane decisions will be looked back on in history as not only decisive, but brilliant."

"Impossible," someone protested. "We're talking about a territory of seventeen million kilometers."

Next to me, Marysia Hoff was still leaking slow tears. I touched her hand to try to offer comfort, and she turned to me. "I thought . . . ," she whispered. "Somehow I had just always thought . . ." She didn't finish her sentence.

"These are, of course, neither actors nor actions we can affect," Ringelblum said. "Which means we must continue to concentrate on the things we can do, the stories we can record, the history we can record. I know that this is a difficult time for all of us, but we need to continue to do the work that will outlast this moment in history."

"Pan Ringelblum, do you know if Stalin has officially denounced Hitler?"

"I do not."

"Do you know how many people are being transported to these death camps?"

"I do not."

"Do you—"

"Unfortunately, I have told you all that I know. If I had any better information I would share it."

"But do you . . ."

Ringelblum looked at Marysia Hoff, who was wiping a tear from her face with her wrist.

"I'm sorry, Marysia," he said gently. "I do not."

It seemed natural, of course, that we would want a leader at a moment when we were rudderless and despairing, but the leaders we had were fragile and impotent on all sides. Ringelblum knew what he knew, but not more. The Judenrat seemed less and less able to perform even their basic functions. The soup kitchens were running low on supplies, and the food that we once ladled generously was now cut back to a cup or two of broth each day. We had gone through the American supplies too quickly. We had once fed people eggs, potatoes, bread: now, we had water, cabbage, the rotted tops of beets and onions. From the outside, our smuggling children reported that there was less and less to trade for, and prices had gone up precipitously. Once-proud housewives stood on the street to sell their silk dresses and lace curtains. Nowak, at the Twarda Street gate, had almost nothing useful in his bags. I'd grown used to the taste of rotten apples.

On the streets, German soldiers grabbed us and forced us into conscripted labor: building roads, building dams. We heard of a teenage boy taken away for the crime of tripping in front of a Nazi and, in the process of falling, touching the Nazi's shoes. In the Pawiak Prison, he was made to walk in circles for three straight days until he died from exhaustion. His story was not the only such story we'd heard. Black cars moved slowly down our streets, taking those who looked healthy enough to work (but if you didn't look healthy, you might be shot for sport) and those who looked peaceable (but if you didn't look peaceable, you might be shot as an agitator).

Adam Czerniaków, the head of the Judenrat, a man who had once been known for his preference for fine wine and cigars, never appeared on the streets anymore. Emil told us that he was hiding not out of shame but out of sorrow, although the difference didn't seem apparent to us.

"So what do you have for our archive?" Ringelblum said. "Pan Forman? Pani Hoff?"

We reported on the notes we had taken during the previous week:

The Yiddish Shakespeare Society had put on a performance of *Macbeth* in a courtyard on Zamenhof.

Five hundred new refugees from Lvov were being housed in a half-destroyed warehouse near the cemetery.

Typhus was raging—there had been a block of cases on Chłodna Street—and we'd learned that many dozens, perhaps even hundreds of people per day, were dying of the illness. There was a renewed push to quarantine incoming refugees, but where? There was still no space for that, and people were resisting even shaving their heads.

Lieberman, our resident ornithologist, said that there had been sightings of night herons in the skies above the ghetto this past week, which was unusual; usually, these herons were in Scandinavia by this point in the year. Lieberman suggested that the herons' migratory patterns had been disrupted by the air campaigns and bombings across Europe.

Three children had been born in the apartments around Grzybowski Square between Tuesday and Friday. All mothers were reported to be in good health, although one of the babies had jaundice, which doctors were trying to cure with taking him into sunlight as much as possible. Rabbi Aron Brauer, a trained mohel, was due to perform the Brit Milah for the two newborn boys in the coming days.

The great pianist Wladyszlaw Szpilman held an impromptu concert at the café on the corner of Nowolipki Street Wednesday evening before curfew. As word had gotten around that Szpilman was playing, crowds had gathered and gathered—even the Nazi and Polish patrolmen, it was said, stopped to watch. Szpilman played Brahms and Bach, and when the crowd shouted, "Bravo!" and "More!" he closed with Chopin's Revolutionary Étude, even though the Nazis had banned public playing of Chopin. Perhaps Szpilman assumed that they were too poorly educated to recognize the music, or perhaps he did not care. Regardless, the Nazis did not stop him.

Two dogs were shot in the head in the middle of the street by a Nazi who seemed to be drunk. The Nazi also fired at the dogs' presumed owner, a child, but he was firing from a distance and the child's parents managed to pull the screaming boy away in time.

I reported on my students: Most of them were still attending my class, still learning their poems. Their English was variable, but some was quite strong.

I was thinking about Churchill and Pilot.

Ringelblum asked me what poetry I was teaching. I told him that I was teaching only happy poems these days, as the children needed whatever happiness they could find, and so did I. We should prepare our children for joy, I said. Children need happiness, and poetry can provide that. I readied myself to recite an example, but Ringelblum didn't ask me to.

Instead, he said, "You might want to expand your repertoire."

As we left the room, I looked for Pan Forman, just to see what he'd made of the latest reports of our war and our despair, but I did not see him then, nor, in fact, did I ever see him again.

FIFTEEN

====

As there was less food for distribution at the Aid Society, there was, accordingly, less demand for my services, and while I didn't mind skipping my depressing shifts, I also didn't like having time on my hands. So I tried to make any spare hours pass as quickly as possible by hiding in my basement classroom, reading. While this was not a particularly productive use of my time, it did have the advantage of being peaceful and transporting: it was occasionally possible to shut out the shots and screams and wails of the ghetto above me and try to lose myself in the cold basement air and the words on the page. I had an endless supply of mediocre books from the traveling librarians who visited the apartment every few weeks with their stuffed briefcases. While the selections were slim, occasionally there was something decent among the offerings. That week, for instance, I was halfway through a Polish translation of *Gone with the Wind*. Such an idiotically romantic war story! I found myself quite enjoying it.

Yet it occurred to me, as I was reading, that I had never met an actual American. Which was strange! I had seen them in the cinema, of course, and in the newspapers, I had heard them speak on the radio and on countless newsreels. I could even differentiate the way they spoke: the short, clipped consonants of President Roosevelt sounded very different from the languid vowels of Scarlett O'Hara, at least as I imagined her.

When I pictured Americans, I pictured tall people with smooth skin and blindingly white teeth. Full heads of hair, sweet breath. Could it be, an entire race of people like that? I was certain there was. Goodness shining around them like halos.

Americans, in short, were wonderful company. Therefore, it was my plan that Sunday afternoon to escape the ghetto and the increasing horror of the world both inside and outside with an afternoon in antebellum Georgia. After the horror of the Oneg Shabbat meeting, I had almost convinced myself I deserved it.

I followed the maze of streets to my classroom, and pushed open the heavy basement door, covered over in advertising posters, newspaper posters, propaganda posters. The dank basement air flew up at me, as it always did, and the cold, but something else too. Human voices. Husky whispers.

I took one step down the stairs, then stopped, frozen. The voices were speaking German. One voice was a woman's.

And then there was quiet, except for a sort of moist panting sound (a sound I dreaded hearing from the other side of the curtain, a sound I had only rarely heard in the eight months that I had shared a living space with Sala and Emil). The ambient glow told me that the lightbulb was on. Carefully, slowly, I crouched, lowering my head over the banister to see if the people I'd imagined were the people who were there.

Once I had confirmed that it was who I'd thought it was, I backed up and out into the ghetto afternoon.

I had always assumed that Nazis would know better places for their assignations than the cold floors of basement classrooms, but then again Szifra had spread out her lovely camel coat.

Poor, dear Szifra.

The Nazi was on top of her, his white buttocks pumping up and down. I saw her splayed legs, stockings rolled down around her ankles, shoes still on, face turned sideways; perhaps she even saw me, but her expression was so blank and so dead. Her blond curls spread out on the floor. Her dress crumpled up beside her. She was not protesting. I doubted that she had ever protested. The Nazi's gun lay on top of her dress.

Whatever she was going to get out of this connection—whatever she thought she was going to secure—she was only sixteen years old. She was still a child.

I wondered if her mother was still alive. I wondered if her mother would have the energy to care if someone told her what was happening.

I wanted to run, but I found, to my surprise, that my usually sturdy legs were weak. So I leaned against the basement door, tacky with the glue from the advertisements and propaganda, and stayed that way for several minutes, until my heart slowed down and I was able to walk without fear of falling. Then I made my way to Chłodna Street to see if I could find Szifra's mother. I had never met the woman before, but surely she would want to know what her daughter was up to. This wasn't a game. People were being trucked away and gassed to death.

I prepared a speech in my head: "Mrs. Joseph, you don't know me, but I am your children's English teacher, and I am here with alarming news."

But when I got to the Joseph family apartment, I saw Eli and Jakub sitting on the sidewalk. Jakub was crying. Eli, face steely, told me only that they were waiting for the coroner; their mother had died of typhus early that morning, and in the heat, her body was starting to smell.

SIXTEEN

════════

"**M**y God, those poor children," Sala said.

I had persuaded her to come up to the rooftop with me, as I was afraid of talking about Szifra in the house (her classmates were my housemates), but I had to tell someone what I had seen.

"How did the boys know what to do?" she asked.

"Everyone here knows what to do when someone dies."

"Yes, but . . . they're so young. How old are they?"

"Twelve and nine."

"My boys' ages."

"Almost exactly."

"And both their parents gone."

"And the boys left to clean up their deaths," I said. "Twice."

When my wife had died, after days of unconsciousness, I'd sat with her body for hours before calling anyone, paralyzed even though the doctors had prepared me for how to handle the inevitable: Call the coroner. Call the church. Her father wanted her buried in the family plot by the chapel at Saint Krzysztofa's, and that was fine—I had no problem with it. It meant that we would not be buried together, but I had no illusion that our souls' locations depended on our bodies. Further, I had no illusion that our souls would outlive our bodies.

"I stayed with the boys until the coroner came," I said.

"That was good of you," Sala said.

Well, it hadn't been much—I'd simply sat down with the boys where they were on the sidewalk, in the heat, my arm around Jakub, who wept into my sleeve while Eli looked at us piteously.

"When he finally showed up, two hours later, he and his team just threw her on a cart. They have these sort of cardboard coffins they drive around on the back of the cart. Double-decker. Twelve bodies at a time. Have you seen them?"

"I have."

"I've heard they burn the bodies," I said.

"No, they bury them at night, in mass graves," she said.

"The ones with typhus, though. I've heard they cremate them in secret."

"They really shouldn't," she said. "It's against the rules."

"Whose rules?"

"God's," she said. "Or the people who invented God."

"Even in times like this?"

"Well, there are different Talmudic interpretations of it," she said. "In times of plague, some of the sages say you're allowed to burn bodies to keep the living people safe. Because the preservation of life takes precedence over any other rule. That's why you can eat trayf if you're starving. Or so it's said. I've never tried it."

"So then there are exceptions."

"But it feels wrong," Sala said. "The soul needs time to depart the body, and cremation disrupts that process. And with cremation, you might have to leave the body alone for a few minutes, and that's not right. A dead soul needs company at all times. Because, you know, the soul is lonely and confused from having died."

"You really believe all that?"

She shrugged. "It's a nice idea. Doesn't strain the imagination too much."

On the roof, a few crows had gathered, their black outlines stark against the dimming sky.

"When we couldn't retrieve my father's body after he was killed in the war," I said, "my mother went crazy trying to locate it so it wouldn't be alone. She wanted to give him a proper Jewish burial." I remembered it so clearly—I'd been sixteen years old. "But his body was never found."

In a gust, the crows took off into the sky.

"I think that's why my mother stopped believing—it was easier for her to give up her faith in God altogether than to imagine my father's soul wandering the earth, homeless."

"I think the same happened to Emil," she said. "Once he couldn't go back for his mother. It was easier for him to stop believing the same way he had before."

We were sitting beside Filip Lescovec's strange little rooftop shelter, which had grown more elaborate as the months had gone by. He had fortified it with bricks and scraps of tin, and had hidden, in its recesses, small jars of sucking candies wrapped in cellophane. Filip was known among the boys to be the scrappiest trader, and I was impressed by his resourcefulness: it wasn't easy to collect dozens of candies here and keep them to oneself. Still, ghetto rule: finders keepers. I unwrapped a cherry candy for Sala and took a licorice one for myself.

"How old was Szifra's mother, anyway?"

"Thirty-three," I said.

"God," she said, "that's my age."

The dusk, the endless dusk, was still lingering; it was summer, and the sun wouldn't set until nine o'clock. Mothers hung whatever they could find over windows so their babies would sleep. In the distance, I could see other people on rooftops, hiding from the fetid air below. The double-decker hearses now moved through city streets the way the trams used to, making regular stops, collecting the bodies. Although we were still finding ways to outrun it, I couldn't help but worry we were losing our advantage. Health, wealth, companionship: How long could we hold on to these gifts in the face of typhus and starvation? When would we turn against each other?

And now the cemetery had resorted to burning bodies. There was no choice.

After the coroner took Pani Joseph away, a rabbi had come by—how did he know? had he followed the coroner as he made his rounds?—to offer prayers for the dead. Quickly, a minyan assembled on the sidewalk.

"Her name?" the rabbi asked the boys gently.

Her name had been Irina.

"Daughter of?"

But the boys had never met their grandmother and didn't know her name. "Szifra would know," Jakub said, but there was no time to wait for Szifra. The rabbi had his rounds to make.

The rabbi commenced the prayer, ten of us standing in a circle on the sidewalk, the boys in the middle. Surrounding them, holding them up. I had heard the words of the psalm every so often since my childhood, and they returned to me like a reflex: "The Lord is my shepherd. I lack nothing. He makes me lie down in green pastures. He leads me beside still waters. He restores my soul. He leads me in the path of righteousness for his name's sake. Yea, though I walk through the valley of the shadow of death, I will fear no evil."

The words were a comfort, which surprised me.

And when the prayer was over and the minyan had dispersed, the rabbi took the boys to him, and placed his hands on their bald heads, and murmured a small, private prayer, and in the distance I saw Szifra running, racing toward us, and I quickly turned and walked the other way down the street, because I was afraid of what I would say or do if I spoke to her, and in front of a rabbi, no less.

I wondered if she arrived while the rabbi was still there. If the rabbi would manage to spare a prayer for her as well. I hoped he would, and that someone was listening.

MY WIFE'S FUNERAL had been at Saint Krzysztofa's chapel; it was the first Catholic funeral I had ever attended, and Saint Krzysztofa's was the first church I had ever stepped foot in. Kasia and I had lived our lives away from any particular religious calendar; when she visited her family for Easter, I made my excuses. Still, we had decided that when we had children, we would raise them Catholic, as it was simply easier to be a Catholic than it was to be a Jew, and we wanted to give our children every advantage. It was possible, I'd thought, that I would even convert, although neither one of us felt strongly about that point.

Anyway, her funeral: hot, slow, turgid, mostly in Latin, a language I had studied years before but could not follow when spoken out loud. Very few words were spared on Kasia; instead, the crowd appealed, again and again, to God's grace and mercy. I sat in front, Henryk on one side of me and Kasia's sister Lena on the other, both sniffling into their handkerchiefs while I sat there, stony, unwilling to cry. Lena had not visited at any point during Kasia's decline, claiming that she was too busy with her seven children at home. And perhaps she was, but that did not spare her my antipathy.

When the crowd knelt, I knelt; when they sat, I sat; when they crossed themselves, I did the same. When the priest finally delivered a few generalized remarks about Kasia's life, they were so vague that for a moment I didn't realize what he was talking about. She had been a "kind person." (Sure, but kindness was not the most memorable thing about her.) She "loved to read." (Yes, but it was *what* she read that was so distinctive: English biographies, histories of various languages.) She "yearned to travel." (Yes, to London. She wanted to see the British Museum and the Globe Theatre and take a train to Stratford-upon-Avon. There was never any itch to travel like some idiot with a rifle and a bush hat. She wanted to go to London because often she dreamed in English.)

At the other end of the pew, Kasia's mother sat, weeping genteelly into a bit of lace while one of her grandchildren comforted her. Ever since our courthouse wedding—no priest for us, just a judge in his shirtsleeves—Kasia's mother had never missed an opportunity to voice her displeasure about our union and, in fact, often suggested that there might be a warm place in hell for both of us. I thought dully about asking her now: *Do you think, Pani Duda, that your daughter is roasting in the underworld? That her soul is being tortured by a million Satanic henchmen? Is that why you're crying, Pani Duda? Tell me, truly, what do you think?*

Kasia's body was displayed in the front of the church, the mahogany casket wide open. I had selected the clothes she would wear, her favorite gray dress, expensive, from Simeone's on Nowy Świat, black leather shoes, her plain gold wedding band. Her eyes had been open when she died, but I had closed them once she stopped breathing and the coroner had stitched them shut. When I leaned in to kiss her goodbye, I saw the threads, tiny black *x*'s underneath her eyelashes, and I felt a hot punch in my gut. The delicate skin under her eyes.

After the service, we walked her casket to the churchyard next to her grandmother's plot. "My Kasia, my Kasia!" Henryk shrieked while his living daughters rolled their eyes and his wife fanned herself with her bit of lace.

"Henryk, no, you mustn't," I said, and he turned and held me, weeping hysterically. At a Jewish funeral, we would help bury the body together, each tipping a shovelful of earth into the grave, but here we would leave and let the groundskeepers do it. Her casket, closed now, rested at the side of its plot. I felt the wetness of Henryk's tears and snot on the shoulder of my suit jacket.

And then it was over: we were walking back to the cars. There was to be a funeral luncheon at the Duda home, and I didn't think that I could stand it. Henryk had found the courtesy to discuss the menu with me: There would be sausage. There would be cheeses, and pastries, the kind Kasia had loved as a girl.

"Adam, Adam, you made her so happy. Whatever else they say about you isn't true. It isn't. She loved you, and that is all. My daughter loved you."

At the luncheon, I stood on the receiving line while the mourners, mostly Henryk's sycophants, came and kissed his ring while he cried. Sometimes he introduced me as Kasia's widower, but usually he did not. My own mother and brother were in Palestine, and they had wired their condolences.

I stood in the line and saw the days stretch out before me, as alone as this, always.

The Duda home was enormous, and resplendent in its grief; black bows were tied on the mantelpieces and the staircases, and various maids and servants wore black from head to toe as they passed out small bites of food. The crowd included the mayor and the governor-general and a few cowed functionaries who had worked alongside Kasia in the translation department of the Ministry of Foreign Affairs. They knew who I was—we had met, socially—and gave their regrets in whispers, feeling entirely out of place in all this grandeur. Was this who I was: the son-in-law of a great man? Was this who Kasia had been: a great man's daughter? There was no real way to relay that this funeral had nothing to do with her, with us, especially since every so often, Henryk would let loose with an enormous wail and the entire house would fall hushed. "My Kasia! My Kasia!" And then he would stop, monitor the effect his grief had had on the crowd, and go back to shaking hands or accepting the sympathies of another government functionary or sycophant.

I stayed for as long as I could manage and then took the tram home to Gruby. Once back in the flat, I turned the mirrors in our house around. I put away the cushions on the sofa. In the absence of any real rituals for grief, I relied on what I remembered from my own father's death: *We must not be comfortable. We must not think of ourselves.* I took a chair outside to the tiny balcony and looked out at our street.

Without Kasia, and without a funeral to dread, there was nothing in my life but a long stretch of days.

I'd sat on the hard chair on our balcony for many hours, wondering what to do. I would go back to work on Monday. I would donate Kasia's dresses to charity. If there was another way for me to fill the endless days until my own death, surely I would find it.

"Adam! Adam, you're in here?" Only Henryk would burst into my house as if he owned the place. I put Gruby down, stood, and almost stumbled from the stiffness in my legs. I had been sitting for too long.

"Don't you have people to entertain at home?" I said.

"I wanted to see you, to check on you."

"I'm fine, Henryk."

"Don't lie to me," he said. He was still wearing his suit, but his shirt had come untucked over his broad belly. "You covered the hallway mirror."

"Tradition."

"Shiva," he said. "I know the word for it."

"You don't sit shiva for someone who wasn't Jewish."

Henryk shrugged, sat down on the cushionless sofa. He put his hands on his knees. Slowly, his face crumpled. "What are we going to do without her, Adam?"

I could not believe he was here for more of this. "We're going to keep living the way Kasia wanted us to."

"But how, Adam? How?"

I buried my forehead in my hands.

"We'll put one foot in front of the other," I said. What were the clichés? "We'll remember every day is a gift from God."

"Bullshit," Henryk said. "You don't believe in God."

I sat down next to him. "Henryk, I don't know what you want me to—"

"No, no. I want nothing from you," he said. "That's not why I'm here. I'm sorry. I should shut up every once in a while."

"Henryk—"

"She was my favorite, Adam."

"I know."

We were quiet. Gruby wound himself around Henryk's feet. I stood, fed the cat some stewed meat, sat back down next to Henryk, regretted sitting.

"She was funny, my Kasia. She had such a sense of humor! And she loved to learn. My other daughters are wonderful, of course—but she was the one I had dreams for. She was the one who was going to change the world one day."

"She didn't want to change the world," I said.

"She would have anyway," Henryk said. "Just by being herself. In all the small ways a good person can change the world."

I was quiet. I knew I should stand back up, offer to make tea or pour some vodka—we had some somewhere—but was overcome by the sheer exhaustion of all of it: of taking care of Kasia, of watching her descend into delirium and then her coma. And, to be fair, Henryk had come by sometimes and helped, which was astounding to see. This powerful man sitting by his daughter and putting cloths on her feverish head, or calling in the best doctors in Warsaw. They came from the Catholic hospitals and the Jewish hospitals, and all pronounced the same thing: traumatic brain injury due to a fall. When they asked her questions, she blinked and spoke nonsense.

"Do you have anything to drink?"

I stood, returned with two small glasses of vodka.

We clinked, drank, no toast.

"Look," Henryk said. "I want you to know that I'm here for you. That's what I want to say. I'm not here to . . . I don't want to make this any worse for you than I already have."

"You haven't—"

"Shush, Adam. I know this hasn't been easy. I know I've . . . I know I've intruded occasionally. But it's only because I wanted the best for my daughter. I wanted to . . . I kept thinking that if we just found the right doctor. The right treatment."

"I know," I said. He never stopped. Read medical journals on his own as if through the power of his own desperation he could become a doctor.

"You know what I was really thinking: we should have taken her to the States."

"Henryk, come on."

"No, really. The doctors said that's where the innovation is. New York City. Jewish doctors there. Of course. But they would have seen Kasia because of you, right? A Jew treating another Jew?"

"Henryk, we were not going to take her to New York."

His body sagged against the couch.

"The problem with you, Adam, if I may . . ."

I blinked.

"Is that you have no will. You just accept things as they are. You don't stand up and fight. You don't believe in the power to change. You're a realist, which isn't a bad thing, but if the world were only made of realists the world would never change."

"I suppose."

"We should have taken her to New York," he said again.

"I suppose," I repeated.

Gruby, full of dinner, had fallen asleep at my feet. For a while, Henryk and I just watched the cat. Kasia had found him on the street when he was a kitten, part of a feral litter living in the park, and brought him home wrapped in her shawl. It was nearing autumn, already cold. He was skinny then, so we named him Gruby to be funny, and also as encouragement. And now he was enormous, ten kilos.

"My tribute to Kasia will be my fidelity to you," he said. "Whatever you need, whenever you need it, you can rely on me."

"I should be okay here, I think."

"Money, if you ever need money. A passport. If you need permits. Want to move to the country. Whatever it is."

Henryk offered services, patronage, kept people in his debt. "That is good of you, Henryk."

"And it won't change should you remarry. I want you to remarry! A man shouldn't be alone at so young an age."

"I cannot think about something like that."

"Of course, of course," he said. "You think I'm lying, but I'm not. Whatever I can do for you, I will do it." He slurred a little. He was drunker than I'd thought.

"I'll call you a taxi," I said. "You need to rest."

"My driver's outside." As he gathered his coat, he said, "May you never know what it is like to lose a child, Adam."

"I don't have any children, Henryk."

"Of course not," he said again, pulling me in for a sweaty embrace that smelled of vodka. "Of course."

One year later, Kasia's sister Lena drowned in the Vistula River, leaving behind her seven children. I returned to Saint Krzysztofa's for the funeral, watched the children, dressed like dolls, as they stood at the entrance to the church.

When Henryk saw me, he came to me, clutched my hand. "This is my lot in life," he said. "God is punishing me, and I don't even know why. You're the only one who understands this, Adam. Not even my wife," he said. "You're the only one who understands."

I did not ask him why this was or how this could possibly be true, but I held him as he cried, and when he came to my house for vodka that evening, I drank with him until he passed out on the couch where I used to sleep during the months after I lost my wife.

SEVENTEEN

The next evening, Filip strutted into the apartment with two large bags of chicken feet that he had traded for somewhere on the outside. He had recently turned twelve and was starting to grow; perhaps his prosperity as a trader had provided him with the requisite calories for a proper growth spurt, or perhaps the human body would do what it was designed to do even in the most absurd of circumstances. Either way, he was a good ten centimeters taller than he'd been when we'd met, and his shoulders had started to broaden. His voice was changing too, becoming deeper. I noticed it especially when he practiced his English with me. In English, he sounded almost like a man.

"I'll trade you four feet for next week's lesson," I said. (The going price for English lessons was three zloty or, lately, whatever the children's families could spare; I had no idea what the going rate was for chicken feet, since chicken was not legal for purchase in the ghetto.)

"I risked my life for these," he said; he said it casually. "But I'll give you a discount. Four for five zloty."

"That's highway robbery," I said. "Those are just feet!"

Filip shrugged. "You hungry?" He'd grown nervy.

I sighed. My satchel was on the counter; I reached in and handed him his zloty. He plucked four feet out of one of his bags and handed me the skinny, clawlike things. They were fresh, with feathers on their anklebones and needlelike nails on the ends of the toes. They looked, frankly, disgusting. But you could boil them for a while and then fry them, and they would make an edible snack. When I was a child, we ate them frequently when my father was deployed and his government subsidy disappeared in the mail.

"So what's it like right now on the outside, anyway?" I said, using an old kitchen knife to pare the claws off the feet.

"Better than here," he said, watching me work with an expression of mild amusement. "But still not great." His hair was growing in thicker than it had been before he'd shaved it for typhus, and darker too. This had happened to my own hair when I was his age; fine blondish wisps had become the coarse brownish-blondish curls that Kasia used to trim by the sink.

"How so?"

"People seem hungrier," he said, "and there's less in the shops. There are more beggars in the streets, and the Germans beat them up or take them away in police vans. There are still rich people, though. You can see it in the way they dress. They still have cars, jewelry. They're still shopping."

"Any news of the war?"

Filip shrugged. It was one of the luckiest aspects of youth, this ability to be nonchalant. "I don't know, really. I saw some headlines in the newsstand that the Germans are proceeding to Moscow, but it might be propaganda. They have a lot of the same news outside that they do in here."

I sighed and scraped at my chicken. Our contraband transistor had updated us with the same news, German troops mowing down Russians like they were so many toy soldiers, but it was hard to know if this was the truth. Occasionally, we would get a blessed crackle of British news, but this, too, felt like propaganda: The Germans were on the retreat; they had underestimated the number and relentlessness of the Russians. And now that Stalin was awakened to the danger of Hitler, the Russian bear would roar. But how could all this be true at the same time, that the Russians were winning *and* losing, that the Germans were decimating the Soviets *and* losing three hundred Panzer tanks a day? It was all paradox, nonsense. And so we waited in our hot and crowded apartment, stinking, sweating, hungry, waiting for deliverance and unable to know the direction from which it was coming.

"I did hear that the Germans captured Minsk," Filip said, after a minute.

"Yes," I said. "I heard that too."

Filip removed his whittling knife from his shirt pocket and a stick from his bag and began whittling, idly, his motions matching mine. We worked with our knives in several minutes' silence.

"You still carve dinosaurs?" I asked.

He shrugged. "They weren't dinosaurs." He peeled the bark off the stick with long strokes; the bark curled in light-brown rings on the table. I finished up with my chicken feet and put them in a pot, turned on the tap: mercifully, water.

"How did you get this stuff, anyway?"

"I traded for them. A pair of candlesticks. I think they were bronze. Or gold. A golden color, anyway."

"Where did you find bronze candlesticks?"

"People die here all the time," he said. "They leave a lot of stuff behind."

"And you just take it?"

"I don't just *take* it," he said. "I turn it into food."

The water filled the pot—drip, drip, drip—and I wondered if I had scaled the feet correctly, and if I would be able to find the oil to fry them later, or if I would just eat them as they were, pale and bony. I had eaten all sorts of sludge these past months, grateful for every bite: potato-peel soup, beet-top soup, jarred, salted cabbage. And then, occasionally, I celebrated—with illegal chicken or eggs from the proceeds of a pair of Kasia's shoes, illegal white flour from the sale of our old vinyl records.

"You scavenge," I said.

"I guess that's the word."

"Yes," I said. And then, for some reason, I repeated it in English: "Scavenge. You are a scavenger."

"Scavenger," Filip repeated in English, his voice resonant and deep. "It's a nice-sounding word."

We were quiet again. I watched Filip whittle his stick into something fine and sharp-looking.

"What's happening in here?" Pani Lescovec, Filip's mother, bustling in in her housecoat. "Filip, you found chicken? How on earth?" She was damp from sweat, had been cleaning the hallway we shared with three other apartments, where the children played and sometimes slept. Her graying hair stood up in loose curls around her broad face.

"Just chicken feet, Eema."

"Chicken feet—that's not nothing. Where did you get them? How did you get outside?"

"I was careful."

"Were you?"

"I always am."

"Oh, how I worry about you," she said, hugging him close. Pressed against his mother's side, Filip looked like a young child again. "My smart boy."

"I just sold four feet to Pan Paskow. Five zloty," he said, proud of his dealmaking.

"And what are you doing with them, Pan Paskow? Boiling?" She peered into my pot. "They're not properly peeled."

"I was going to fry them next," I said apologetically; in our household, it was known that Pani Lescovec was the most assiduous and talented cook.

"My son risked his life for these!" she said from her position at the stove. "You should treat them with respect."

"Eema, come on. I didn't risk my life."

"You did!"

"I'm sorry, Pani Lescovec," I said, with as much deference as I could muster. "You know I'm not much of a cook."

Assuaged, she used a slotted spoon to pull the feet out of the water and onto a plate. She blew on them to cool them, and then started pulling off the skin and reserving it on a towel (How long would it be until we had to start selling our kitchen supplies? How long until we no longer had towels, plates, slotted spoons, chicken feet?)

"I'll fry this skin for you," she said. "It will taste something like gribenes. Do you know gribenes? I need an onion. Is it possible we have an onion?"

"I'll go find you one, Eema," said Filip.

"No, it's not worth it. I don't want you to go outside."

"It'll take five minutes."

"Make it three minutes. It's getting dark," she said as Filip hurried out of the kitchen. "I have enough stress as it is."

But she was smiling. The thought of an onion, fried chicken skin, a somewhat proper meal.

She returned the chicken feet to the pot and set it back to boil on the rickety stove. Watching her put me in mind of my own mother a million years before: the ease at the stove, the ritual, unthinking nature of her movements. "You know what would really be wonderful? A carrot," she said dreamily. "Two carrots. And maybe some celery. And some noodles. And, of course, a real chicken."

"How did you learn to cook, Pani Lescovec?" It was a question I liked to ask the women—it got them talking.

"What do you mean?"

"I mean, how did you learn to cook?"

She turned, gave me a look like I was crazy. She had a worn, bleached-out face—thin eyebrows, soft, splotchy cheeks. Pale-green eyes, like cloudy water. "I didn't learn to cook. I just started cooking."

"How old were you?"

"Old enough to reach the stove."

"Which means?"

She sighed heavily. "I don't know, maybe five? Six? I made challah. I made soup. What everyone did."

"Would you mind telling me more?" I asked. "While the feet boil?"

"I'm going to fry gribenes out of these," she said. "And make chicken soup from the bones. As soon as my boy comes back with the onion."

"That's okay," I said. "We can talk while you cook."

She turned and looked at me curiously with her pale, worn-out face. "I don't know why you'd want to talk to me," she said. "I don't have much to say that's worth talking about. I'm not educated like you."

"You don't have to be educated to talk to me," I said. "You just have to talk."

"About what?" she said.

"Just . . . anything. Your life before this. Your life here."

Pani Lescovec blushed, her splotchy cheeks growing rosy. "Nobody ever asks me about my life," she said.

I took out my white notebook. "Let me be the first."

Name: Mariam Lescovec
Date: June 30, 1941
Age: 41
Height: Who knows
Weight: None of your business

M.L. I must warn you again, as I see you writing, that there's nothing very interesting about me. How do you write so fast?

A.P. It's like shorthand. I have a system. Everything you say—I don't stop to think. I just write it all down. I'm writing too fast to judge, by the way. So you never have to be embarrassed by what you say.

M.L. And why are you writing down what I say?

A.P. To have a record. I'm trying to collect a record of all the different people who lived here. All the different kinds of lives.

M.L. Because?

A.P. Because we don't want to forget.

M.L. Ha! As if we could forget.

(Pani Lescovec sits down at the kitchen table while we wait for her son to bring her an onion that she can fry with the chicken feet to make something like gribenes, the cracklings that are particularly tasty in soup or with bread. She is a heavyset woman with wide shoulders and a broad bosom; she usually wears a scarf over her hair and one of a series of grayish, worn-out dresses. In many ways, she is a contrast to her husband, who is about the same height as she is but much narrower; he keeps his mustache trimmed and puts on a neat suit to go to his job with the Jewish police. They are not such an odd couple, though, if you think about the types that populate old cartoons or stories of sztetl life: the large, bossy wife and the wispy, browbeaten husband. You see them like salt and pepper shakers, a familiar set. The woman mans the stove with an iron spatula; the man cowers and says, "Yes, dear" and turns over his money at the end of the week.

But this is probably not a fair observation. Once, when the door between the kitchen and the maid's room was left open, I peeked in and saw them asleep there on their tiny bed, folded around each other, her cheek resting on his shoulder. In the spare half second before I turned my head, I thought that this, too, is what love looks like.)

A.P. So maybe start at the beginning? If you'd like?
M.L. The beginning? The very beginning?
A.P. As far back as you can go.
M.L. Well . . .

(She leans forward; the flimsy chair creaks under her. She seems embarrassed about talking but also eager.)

M.L. I was born in Warsaw. Not far from here, actually. Just outside the ghetto walls. My father was a fishmonger, maybe you knew his shop? Grabeski Fish, it used to be called. No? He sold to gentiles and Jews alike. The Jews bought salmon and herring and whitefish. The Poles bought eel and catfish. Everyone bought fish on Fridays—it was the busiest day—and my father had to work fast in the evenings to make it home for Sabbath. Fortunately, our apartment was right above the store.

A.P. Did he touch the nonkosher fish?

M.L. Listen, a zloty is a zloty, gentile or Jew.

A.P. No, I wasn't—

M.L. But he employed a Polish kid to work with the nonkosher fish. They were very close, in fact. The kid was like the son my father never had. My father taught him how to scale and filet the fish, how to pick out the best fish at the wholesalers. And I remember, I was jealous, because I wanted that attention too. I wanted to go to the wholesale market. The things they described! Salmon the size of children, sturgeon the size of grown women. Salmon roe like rubies. Caviar in buckets. I used to dream about it. And the traders were people from everywhere—not just Jews but Poles, Hungarians, Ukrainians, Germans. All speaking their languages. It sounded very exciting to me.

A.P. But your father never took you.

M.L. No, never. I was the only child, you see. He was very protective of me. And very old-fashioned about a woman's work. Which I came to see, as I got older, was appropriate, but back then I felt very depressed, because—

A.P. Why appropriate?

M.L. Because in our culture, Pan Paskow, a woman is the center of the home. Without a woman to take care of the children, to feed her family, to make sure everyone's needs are met, a household cannot function. There can be no family life. And a family life is the most important thing to us. To Jews.

A.P. And so when you realized this, you stopped wanting to go to work with your father?

M.L. When I realized that the most fulfilling role in my life was to be a mother and a wife.

A.P. I see.

(Pani Lescovec returns to the stove, and I watch her for a while. It occurs to me that she might have made an excellent fishmonger. She has an ease with the food that seems inborn, hard to learn.)

A.P. You're good at that.

M.L. You asked me before how I learned to cook. I didn't learn in the way that you mean, someone giving me lessons, step by step. I learned by watching. I learned my whole life by watching. My mother did everything in our house, and when I wasn't in school I just watched her: cook, clean the house, prepare for Sabbath. She ran a Jewish women's group, and I would sit sometimes and watch that.

A.P. What did the women's group do?

M.L. They talked about issues in their homes, in their families, about Jewish ways to handle problems. A husband is a drinker, for instance. A daughter is dressing inappropriately. A son is dating a Pole. No offense.

A.P. Why would I be offended?

M.L. Well, I know about you—I mean, about your wife.

A.P. It's not a secret.

M.L. But it's not something you would have wanted the world to know about.

A.P. On the contrary, Pani Lescovec. I am very proud of my wife. We had a good marriage.

M.L. But you understand that this is something that would not have been accepted in the community, correct? And if you'd had a supportive community, you would have found a proper spouse. A Jewish spouse. I don't mean to talk out of turn, but in my world it is seen as a very big failing when someone marries outside the faith.

A.P. You're not the first to express this to me.

M.L. You know, when the war is over, if you ever want to meet someone—

A.P. That is kind, Pani Lescovec, but the purpose of this interview really is to talk about you.

M.L. I'm just saying . . .

A.P. We shall see what happens when the war is over. Again, I'd rather talk about you. Tell me, how did you meet your husband?

M.L. (She blushes again. She blushes rather easily.) It was an arranged marriage. This might seem old-fashioned to you, but it was the traditional way, and, as I told you, my parents were quite traditional. There was a matchmaker on Chłodna Street, right down the street, in fact, just past the gate—she was the same matchmaker who introduced my parents. She knew of a young man studying to be an accountant, religious, very smart. We met at my uncle's house for 20 minutes, and that was enough. I knew we could have a successful marriage.

A.P. How did you know?

M.L. He was quiet. He seemed pleasant. He clearly had a good future. And that was it. All I needed to know. Sometimes it's best not to think too hard about things, or you can make yourself crazy.

A.P. I've never thought about it that way.

M.L. It's true. It's true. You don't want to poke holes in every argument. I liked him, he seemed to like me. So we were married in February, and had our first baby the following March.

A.P. And two more boys after that.

M.L. Four, in fact. We lost the second one to croup, and the third . . . The third just died. We never did find out why. I went to the crib one morning and . . . and there he was. Not breathing. A week after his bris.

A.P. Oh. Oh no.

M.L. Well, a long time ago, but . . . it was a difficult time. For a long time, I was very sad. But then I had Andrej, and then Filip. So. I still think of myself as a mother of five boys, even though only three are with us. The other two are in heaven. Looking down at their brothers. Watching over us. Speaking of which . . .

(Filip returns with three onions, hands them to his mother. She draws him in for a kiss, which he shrugs off, clearly mortified in the way of 12-year-old boys. Filip disappears, and soon I hear him tramping up the stairs to the roof.)

A.P. Can you show me how you fry chicken skin, Pani Lescovec?

M.L. Oh, it's so easy. You don't need me to—

A.P. I'd like to see, if you don't mind. I never really learned how to cook.

(I stand next to Pani Lescovec then as she removes a small flask of oil from the drawer. She slices the onion into the oil and lets the onions turn pale over the heat. In a few minutes, it smells wonderful, and I tell her so.)

M.L. Now, ordinarily you'd want to make gribenes with chicken fat, the kind from its thighs. The skin of chicken feet is not what you'd use. But in desperate times, we can use what we have. These won't be as tender as real gribenes, but they'll still fry up nicely. Here. You just drop them into the pot, like this.

(As she speaks, Pani Lescovec places the chicken skins in the bubbling oil, where they puff up and turn golden. As soon as they do, she removes them from the pot and places them on a towel to drain. She has salt in a small jar, which she sprinkles over the cooling golden skins.)

M.L. Try one.

(I do, and it is delicious—crisp and salty and fatty on my tongue. I haven't had anything as wonderful in quite some time, and I tell this to Pani Lescovec.)

M.L. Oh, if you think this is something, you should have been there on Friday nights in our old house, before all this. You would have enjoyed it so much. Always guests, always good wine, not like that plonk from upstairs. We started every Shabbos meal with soup, and then there was gefilte fish. You know gefilte fish? From my father's old recipe. Whitefish and pike fish ground together with spices and onions, then wrapped in the skin of the fish and poached until there is a nice sauce. My husband could have made a meal of just that. He would say, "Oh, Mariam, don't make me anything else. I just need my gefilte fish." But of course there was more—I would make salmon with horseradish, or roast chicken, or sometimes we would have flanken in the pot with prunes. And dessert—I made such a good walnut cake. And sometimes lekach. Do you know these foods?

A.P. Hearing the names is like a doorway to my past, Pani Lescovec. When I was a young child, when my grandmother was alive, she would make her own mandelbrot. The chocolate kind.

M.L. Ah, yes. The chocolate.

(And for a while we just sit there, eating the chicken skins, pretending not to notice that we are eating them all by ourselves. We are lost in the memory of the food we ate before.)

M.L. I'll tell you what, Pan Paskow. When this is over, when we get out of here, you'll come to my house and I'll make you a Shabbos dinner. Would you like that?

A.P. I would, of course.

M.L. And maybe I'll invite a nice lady I know.

A.P. Pani—

M.L. ~~Then you won't have to moon over Pani Wiskoff.~~

A.P. Excuse me?

M.L. Nothing, nothing. I didn't say anything. It's not your fault. You never had a Jewish wife before. You didn't know what you were missing until now.

(To be clear, I never missed anything when I was with my wife.)

A.P. So what happened to your father's shop?

M.L. When he retired, he sold it to his assistant, the Polish kid who had helped him all those years. This was, let's see . . . This was in 1933, I think. Or '32? I would still go there, but now I would pay for what I bought. For a while, the kid used to try to give it to me for free, but I wouldn't accept it. I never asked for a handout just because I was the previous proprietor's daughter. And sometimes my father and I would go in together, and then my father couldn't help it: he'd tie on an apron, would go back to saying hello to the customers. And they would be surprised: "Pan Grabeski? We thought you had retired." He loved it. "No, no, I'm back. You need salmon? You need river trout?" And his assistant—his name was Piotr—they would fall right back into their rhythms. Sometimes my father would bring Jerzy to the shop, my oldest boy, and teach him about the business. The way he kept his accounts in a ledger, how he tracked shipments. He and Piotr would take Jerzy to the wholesalers, the way I wanted to when I was a girl.

A.P. And Piotr didn't mind?

M.L. No. It was like a family.

A.P. A Catholic-Jewish family.

M.L. *Like* family. Not a real family.

A.P. No, of course.

M.L. Well, I suppose we were something like a family. For a little while. But then the government changed, and things became a little tense. It was strange. Piotr asked my father to stop coming to the shop. He said it made it more difficult for him to run the store his own way. His own way! It was just a fish store! And of course the items changed. Shellfish, which we had never had before. My father would pass by and look in, still feel like he had some connection to the shop, or maybe he just couldn't let it go, but each time he went past he just felt sadder and sadder. Because he knew he wasn't welcome. And then he saw that Piotr changed the name. It wasn't Grabeski Fish anymore.

A.P. Well, it was his own shop.

M.L. Yes, but for 30 years . . . I don't know. It was sad to see. Piotr changed the name to Riba Piotra.

A.P. That's a New Testament story about Peter and the fish. Calling the store Peter's Fish—it's like a pun.

M.L. Yes, yes. I know it's a pun. But. My father had built that shop, had customers from all over Warsaw who came to Grabeski Fish. And to see Piotr just paint over the sign. Not allow us in anymore. And he was apologetic for a while about it when we saw him—we still lived above the shop, of course. I'm so sorry, Pan Grabeski, but you know how these new rules are. It put a nail in my father's heart. It really did.

A.P. How long had they worked together before this happened?

M.L. 25 years. Since Piotr was 14 years old. The kid—he didn't have any parents, lived with a drunken uncle. Just showed up at the store one day begging for work. My father had been thinking about finding a gentile assistant for a while, and Piotr had strong hands, a good sense of humor. So my father said, "Let's give this a shot," and that was how it started. Sometimes Piotr would sleep in the back room. Sometimes he'd come up and have dinner with our family. He learned to say the blessings, all of it. He was like a little orphan my father had taken in.

A.P. And they were together for a long time.

M.L. Half a lifetime.

A.P. Half a lifetime.

M.L. And then the government changed. And then the German invasion. And after that, after '39, when they would pass each other, Piotr would pretend not to see him. Wouldn't acknowledge him. Saw him coming and crossed the street. And it was then that I knew that this was going to be bad— very bad—if the Nazis could turn Piotr so thoroughly against my father. And my husband always says that it was in the Polish heart from the beginning, that they were always looking for a reason to shun us, to banish the Jews, but I don't think so. I think Piotr loved my father once. But he grew scared.

A.P. Scared of what?

M.L. Of associating with Jews anymore. I don't know. It's easier to think that someone is a coward than a bigot.

A.P. Is it?

M.L. It is for me.

(We have now polished off the chicken skin, but the chicken bones are in the pot with the onions, and we will have a nice broth with onion in it later, or at least Pani Lescovec will, and perhaps so will I if she decides to share some with me. If not, I suppose I'll just go hungry—I don't have any more zloty on me and will have to sell another one of Kasia's pillowcases tomorrow to have money for the week.)

A.P. Where are your parents now?

M.L. My mother died last year, soon after the invasion. My father followed a few months after.

A.P. I'm sorry.

M.L. I think all of it—the humiliation—it was too much to bear.

(Her eyes seem to grow wet, but she does not cry.)

M.L. You know what's funny? Even after all that had happened, I left a note at the fish store for Piotr when my father died. This was about a year ago now, a little longer. February of last year. Isn't that funny? It seems so much longer. Anyway, I wanted to give him a chance to send his condolences. Like I said, they'd been so close. Like father and son almost. For so many years.

A.P. And did he?

M.L. No. Of course he didn't. But what was strange—a few weeks after the funeral, we received a delivery of whitefish at the door. Just a few fish. But I couldn't eat it. I'd lost the taste for it, you know?

A.P. That sometimes happens.

M.L. It used to be one of my favorite things, but for some reason I'd just lost the taste.

EIGHTEEN

<hr>

September: the days cooling and shortening, the hearse vans circling, circling, the children smuggling, the Aid Society kitchens overwhelmed. During the last week of the month, we'd received a new shipment of cabbage and potatoes (oh, for the day I would never again think of cabbage and potatoes), and the good ladies of the Aid Society had brewed vats of a sort of soupy stew. They had a little sugar to add, a little salt. Maybe a little oil. They served the stew out of the bowls they kept under lock and key; there was a shortage of household goods outside the ghetto, and the smuggling kids knew they could steal plates and bowls and trade them for a few zloty at the gates. Same with the Aid Society spoons. Same with our meager potatoes.

My job at the Aid Society was not particularly crucial, but I was glad to have it, as the working papers gave proof of my utility (and helped ease your way out of jail, it was said), and the zloty I earned meant I didn't have to sell so many of Kasia's dresses and sheets and underthings at once. Sometimes, I earned 10 zloty a week; sometimes, 2. Sometimes, when the pipeline between New York and Warsaw shut off, there were no zloty at all, nor even an extra bowl of soup, and these were the times when it was hardest to believe that the war would ever end.

During the last week of the summer, I had been taken off the ration desk from downstairs and moved upstairs to the ladle position behind one of the massive cauldrons; I spooned the watery stew into bowls and handed over the two small crusts of black bread that would make up the day's allotment of 171 kilocalories for each member of the Jewish population of the ghetto. When I was faced with a pregnant mother, a small child, an old man, a woman with kind eyes, I would try to ladle up the bulkiest portion of stew, toss in an extra scrap of bread, but if I did that too often there was not enough bread for the next pregnant mother, the next small child. They looked at me with their huge eyes and usually said nothing, instead of "Thank you."

I kept Kasia's pearl necklace in my satchel, wrapped in her linen pillowcase, and I wore the satchel over my shoulder throughout my shift at the Aid Society, even though my shoulders started to hurt.

You had never seen such cheekbones. You had never seen so many bulging eyes.

At two in the afternoon most days, I took a break for my own bowl of stew, sitting at the end of one of the long tables by the window. Sometimes I heard rapid gunshots, a wail, and then the resigned silence of a ghetto afternoon: the Aid Society building was near the gates, and undoubtedly someone had been caught trying to sneak in or out. Or perhaps someone, despairing, had deliberately provoked a guard. This happened too. If you were lucky, the guard shot you quickly and you were out of your misery, but if you were unlucky, you ended up in Pawiak Prison and returned (if you returned) far more skeletal and miserable than you'd even been before.

There was no winning.

At recent meetings of Oneg Shabbat, we heard that the Germans had closed in on Leningrad, had surrounded Kiev, had murdered all of the Jews in Vilnius. And the good news? The United States had agreed to help convoy ships across the Atlantic. What else? Nothing else. So this was not much good news, really. The British bombed Berlin. The children of Leningrad were said to be starving. We all were starving. Ringelblum made his announcements looking ever wearier; more Jewish towns had been emptied across Poland, Ukraine, Lithuania, and every day more Jews arrived in our ghetto to find rooms in our basements and attics, and when those were full, to take shelter in our streets. Yet we weren't overcrowded, because so many of us were dying and clearing out to make room for the new.

Still, there were the healthy ones. The ones who still managed to smuggle and trade. The ones who still had family wealth hidden below the floorboards. And the few who managed to find papers somewhere, falsified or fabricated. The ones with the good looks and the good luck to convince a new guard of their Aryan-ness and walk out into the world to try to survive on the outside with no friends, no home.

At night, for some reason, it had grown more and more difficult to dream of Kasia, but I would often close my eyes during the day and imagine her with me. We heard that, on the outside, Jews were no longer permitted to live with non-Jews, even if they had been married for many years. Even if the Jew had converted. Even if the non-Jew had converted. But I could imagine Kasia next to me, and nobody would know she was there.

"Pan Paskow?"

I opened my eyes to find the diamond-shaped face of Eli Joseph, across the table from me at the soup kitchen. His head had been shaved, but his eyes were still glittering blue.

"I thought that was you," he said.

"Eli," I said. "How are you? You haven't been to class."

"Yeah, I'm sorry about that. I've been working a lot, you know? Trying to find some money. It hasn't been easy since my eema died. And trying to take care of Jakub."

"Of course. I know. Your mother."

"Yeah."

"It's been terrible for your whole family."

Eli shrugged.

"How's your brother doing?"

"Bad," Eli said. "What would you expect?"

"Bad how?"

"Nightmares, mostly. I told him he has to grow up, he can't still be such a baby, but I don't know. He won't listen."

"You can't just force someone to grow up, Eli."

He shrugged, took a healthy slurp of his stew. "This is pretty disgusting," he said before he took another.

"I know."

To my right, the line by my ladling station kept growing, and I felt bad that I was taking my time over lunch. On the other hand, we all were entitled to a twenty-minute break twice a shift and, oh, how I needed a break from the wall of humanity in front of me. Here, at the table, I was surrounded by the slurps of soup and the occasional furtive kerplunk of someone trying to steal a spoon.

"You know, we're going to get out of here soon," Eli said.

"Is that so?"

"Szifra's going to get us papers," he said. "She told us. Polish kennkartes. We just have to grow our hair back, and then we're out. You know, so we don't look like starving Jews."

"How's she going to find you kennkartes?" I said. (Although of course I knew: the Nazi's buttocks pumping up and down.)

Eli shrugged. "You know Szifra. She can do anything she puts her mind to."

I shrugged back at him, looked into my bowl.

"Hey, Pan Paskow, do you speak any German?"

"A little."

"Could you teach me? I think I might need to know. In case we end up with German kennkartes instead of Polish ones."

"Could that happen?"

"Szifra says anything could happen."

"I'm not sure how quickly you could learn it," I said. "And if the papers say you're German, it might be a challenge if you don't speak the language."

"Well, but Yiddish," Eli said. "It's pretty close. And we're going to pretend Jakub is mute from a bombing injury. I mean, let's be honest, if that kid talks we're gonna get shot, no question."

"I'm not so sure about that."

"But Szifra's going to try to get us Polish papers, she said. So maybe we won't have to learn German after all. I don't know. I've never done anything like this before. I wish I'd studied harder in school," he said. "Although Szifra knows German. She's smart. So maybe . . . maybe Jakub and I will both pretend to be deaf from bombing injuries. Or something."

"Where are you going to go?"

"What do you mean?"

"I mean, after you get out of here. Where are you going? It's not like . . ." I was about to say *It's not like you can go home,* but that was both too obvious and cruel.

"Szifra's figuring it out for us," he said. Unlike Filip, Eli's voice hadn't started to change. It still sounded very much like a child's voice. "All I'm supposed to do is keep my head down until she gets the documents. Not say anything to anyone."

"Including me?"

"Including you," he said. "But you've been nice to us." He took another bite of his soup. "And it's hard not to say anything to anyone. So . . ."

"So . . ."

"But don't tell Szifra you know. I'll get in trouble."

"I won't," I said.

"I'll tell you one thing," he said. "It'll be great to say goodbye and good luck to this stupid place."

"I can imagine."

Together we slurped. Outside the window: gunshots, a scream. We both pretended not to notice.

"Where would *you* go?" Eli asked me, after the screaming died down. "If you could get out of here. Palestine, I guess? Or Switzerland?"

"England," I said.

"England?" he scrunched up his face. "Is that even possible?"

"I don't know," I said. "I've heard if you make it to Sweden by boat—you have to bribe a lot of money, but if you can get into Sweden you can go to the British Embassy in Stockholm and plead your case for refugee status. But the British will only accept you if you have something to offer. Money or skills."

"Do you have money?"

"Probably not enough."

"Skills?"

"Who knows." I spoke five languages, and Kasia had worked closely with the British Embassy in Warsaw for years, translating their materials as she worked to forge connections between the British and Polish governments. Some functionaries even attended her funeral. Not that I could prove it. But still, maybe. Maybe. A boat to Sweden, a plea to the British: this was the desperate plan I had imagined for myself late at night when I thought about sneaking out. I just needed money for papers and money for a bribe. In all likelihood, the necklace pulsing in my bag was enough for only one or the other, if even that.

"I think we're just going to try to go to Palestine," Eli said. "I heard you can get down through southern Europe if you have the right papers."

"That might be so."

"But they have to be German papers."

"That also might be so."

Eli sighed heavily.

"Repeat after me," I said. *"Ich höre nicht gut."*

"Ich höre nicht gut."

"Ich wurde bei dem Bombenangriff verletzt."

"*Ich wurde bei dem Bombenangriff verletzt.*"

Because he spoke Yiddish, his accent was all right: *I do not hear well. I was injured in the bombing.*

"*Es tut mir leid,*" I said. "*Dass ich nicht sprechen kann.*"

"What does that mean?"

"'I'm sorry,'" I said. "'I cannot speak.'"

"Do you think that will work?" Eli said, looking at me hopefully.

I could not lie to the kid; I only shrugged in his manner and turned back to my bowl of stew.

"Will it work, Pan Paskow?"

"Trust in your sister," I said to him. "She's doing everything she can."

AFTER MY SHIFT ended at five o'clock, I made my way to the Twarda Street gate to see what Nowak would offer me for my linen pillowcase, and if it would be enough to keep me fed this week. (Prices were going up and quantities were going down, and although I had indeed earned five zloty for this week's work, I wasn't sure that it would be enough for potatoes, oil, bread.)

We'd had a run of beautiful weather, and this September afternoon was no different: sunny, breezy, maybe twenty degrees. (There had once been a large thermometer attached to a wall by the courthouse, but that had long ago been broken off, stolen, traded, and now we had no real way to know the temperature except by sticking our arms out a window.) I decided to close my eyes and enjoy the air and imagine I was anywhere else. Then a German guard screamed, "*Idiot, öffne deine Augen!*" And I blinked and started to run.

Nowak was at his post. "You still haven't brought Duda the necklace," he said when he saw me.

"Nowak, what is Henryk paying you, anyway?"

Nowak shrugged.

"Is he doing all right?"

"Listen," Nowak said, "it's not an easy situation for anyone right now. The wife isn't well. The grandchildren are terrified. The older ones have been conscripted, and the younger ones are in a bad mood. They can't get the ice creams they like anymore."

"You've got to be kidding me."

"Listen, there's rationing on the outside too."

"Ice creams?"

He made a sort of *What can you do?* face, gestured with his hands. "It's more than that, to tell you the truth. You play as many sides as Duda has over the years, you're bound to make some enemies. Anyway, he wants the necklace. He knows you have it. He's made a careful list of all the items of value you might still have."

"I have a pillowcase."

"What the hell do you want me to do with a pillowcase?"

"It's linen and silk."

"So?"

"So take it, sell it. I don't care. It's worth at least forty zloty."

"Are you crazy?"

"My wife bought it at Vitkac. That's where she bought everything. She probably spent a hundred zloty back then."

"What was the currency even worth back then?"

"Come on. At least a trade."

"What do you want for it?"

"What do you have to sell?"

He looked conspiratorially, side to side. "Give me the necklace," he said.

"Nowak, even if I did have this necklace—and believe me, I'm not saying I do—but even if I did, what on earth would compel me to give it to you?"

"You want a Polish kennkarte?"

"He's been promising me papers for a year now."

Nowak took the linen pillowcase from me, rubbed it between his own meaty hands. "Maybe you'd give it to me because I could kill you any time I wanted to, Paskow," he said. "Let's not forget."

I supposed he could have killed me, but then again anybody here could, at any time, so his threat didn't have quite the sting he wanted it to. "What are you giving me in exchange for that pillowcase?"

"Screw the pillowcase," he said, the menace gone from his eyes. He had never really been that type. "I need the necklace."

"This is a farce," I said. "I don't have a necklace. Henryk doesn't have papers. And if you kill me, you have to tell him that not only did you not get the jewelry, but you also killed his favorite daughter's husband."

Nowak was still for a moment; I wondered if I'd pushed it too far. But then I remembered that I didn't care. Suddenly, he started to laugh. His gold-filled mouth. He bundled up the pillowcase in his hands, crushing it.

"What's so funny?"

"Oh, this whole thing," he said. "Irony. Is this irony? Or is this just insanity?"

"What? Is what irony?"

"Look at us," he said. "Look around!" The ghetto street was filled with starving children and litter. Above us, squirrels leapt from building facades and treetops. In the middle, purgatory, me and Nowak. I understood what he meant. Irony and insanity, both or neither. "All this over a pillowcase!"

I looked at him, unwilling to agree. He stopped laughing, kept the pillowcase crumpled between his hands.

"Look, our friend Duda is in a bit of a spot," Nowak said. "If you have anything of value that you could use to help him out, I'm sure that he would be able to compensate you handsomely in this lifetime or the next."

"The next won't do me any good," I said. "What are you going to pay me for that pillowcase?"

"What pillowcase?" he asked, depositing it into his bag.

"Nowak, come on."

"Bring me money next time," he said. "Something I can use. A pillowcase? What do you think I am, royalty? I'm resting my head on linen? Give me a fucking break."

"My wife used that pillowcase."

"I don't really give a shit about your wife."

"You have a wife, Nowak?"

"Don't ask personal questions," he said. "We're not friends."

I had the necklace in my bag. It was right there. And . . . and perhaps I haven't been as honest as I should have been. Perhaps I've hidden it from this accounting. But it was not really just a pearl necklace. It was a ten-millimeter South Sea pearl surrounded by two carats' worth of diamonds, purchased in Kraków and gifted by Henryk Duda to his daughter on her wedding day. It was worth perhaps twelve thousand zloty. There was nobody to trust with it. Not Nowak, not Henryk. Not even my pen and notebook.

It seems laughable, but sometimes I thought about Filip. Would Filip know where to sell it? Was he my best chance? What if I took him with me?

I could teach him how to say "I'm sorry. I can't hear well. I was injured in the bombings."

How to say "I am German," "I am Catholic," "I am whoever you want me to be."

But even if I taught him all that, the necklace wouldn't be enough to buy us both safety. I had heard boatsmen's bribes were up to one thousand zloty, and bribes in Stockholm twice as much. And I'd still have to buy kennkartes, train tickets, a clean shirt.

"Come back the Friday after next. Bring me the necklace. I'll have papers for you."

"And if I don't?"

"You rot in here," Nowak said. "Your choice entirely."

I was furious with myself for giving away the pillowcase, for being in this position, for having so few friends in the world that the best smuggler I knew was a twelve-year-old boy. But I nodded at Nowak and went on my way—still hungry, with no money to buy food and with nothing to eat. The necklace was burning in my satchel. Couldn't Nowak see it? Feel its heat?

I almost tripped over my own feet and spilled my satchel on the sidewalk as I raced home, a German guard shouting after me, "*Idiot, idiot, steh gerade!*"

NINETEEN

According to the scratchy, half-audible sounds emerging from our radio, the Germans had surrounded Moscow.

"We should get rid of this thing if all it's going to do is tell us bad news," said Sala. Her boys were in the kitchen with us, getting their hair washed in the sink. Mysteriously and miraculously, the typhus infestation seemed to be receding, but still, we were careful, washing as often as we could, keeping our hair cut close to the scalp. Both Sala and Pani Lescovec were doing laundry every other day, even the bedsheets, which might be stolen when you hung them from the windows, which meant they were hung inside, which meant the boys complained of sleeping on damp beds.

"I could sell the radio," Arkady said. "I could probably get a hundred zloty."

"If you sold the radio, how would we hear the news?" Sala had Rafel leaning back over the sink, his head deep in suds. Arkady was next, his shirt already off despite the encroaching cold.

"I thought you didn't want to hear the news."

"Wrong," said Sala. "I don't want to hear *bad* news. Good news is more than welcome. Come here. Let me wet your head."

October now, and we were approaching a year in that stuffy dim flat on Sienna Street. On that first fall evening eleven months ago, if you had told any of us that we would be here for an entire *year*, living side by side in this small apartment overcrowded with heavy furniture, without enough food, without knowing any more about when we would go home, any more about the fate of our families and friends outside the walls, even our own fates—surely at least one of us would have run to a guard and begged him to shoot. But we hadn't known, so we had survived.

A year of sleeping on sofa cushions, my belongings piled around me as though I lived on a sidewalk.

A year of teaching English poetry in a basement, slopping stew to desperate refugees in the Aid Society offices. Selling Kasia's precious things to the parasites by the gates. Forgetting the taste of good bread, strong beer, beef.

I had reread the same books again and again—*Gone with the Wind* twice. I could recite out loud long portions of *Huckleberry Finn*.

A year of talking to Sala in the middle of the night or early in the morning, or sometimes in the middle of the afternoon, when nobody else was around. We smiled, laughed, patted each other's hands, but a friendship that would have once seemed scandalous was now just another eccentricity of life in the ghetto.

A year of listening to Sala and Emil sleep and whisper on the other side of the curtain.

On those nights, I pressed my head against the window seat and closed my eyes.

It had become more and more difficult to find heating fuel, so we had slowly started to burn sticks of furniture: a small table had been the first to go, chopped up and fed into the boiler. It had released nasty, smoky fumes but had warmed the apartment thoroughly for a good several hours; still, Filip was sensitive about the smell and promised to redouble his smuggling efforts in order to find us some coal. We were worried that it would be a cold winter. We were hopeful that it would be a cold winter. A cold winter would mean snow, and snow would mean that, possibly, the Germans would find themselves bogged down in Russian blizzards, just as Napoleon's troops had been almost 130 years before.

(On these matters, Emil, who had once been a promising history student, liked to expound: "Russia is incalculably vast. Incalculably. The largest landmass in the world. Incalculable." There was an outdated atlas in the apartment, and sometimes we would huddle over it as Emil tried to imagine the German maneuvers across the wide barren fields of Mother Russia.)

We had all marked birthdays. We had grown thinner. The boys had grown taller. We had stopped talking very much about the future.

The radio was, as Sala said, full of bad news: in Stanislav, in Ukraine, twelve thousand Jews had been rounded up and shot.

In Kamianets-Poldiskyi, eleven thousand Jews had been rounded up and shot.

In Odessa, forty thousand Jews had been killed; they were either rounded up and shot or burned alive in four separate locked buildings.

Amid this news ("Arkady, turn off the radio!"), we had celebrated Rosh Hashanah and then Yom Kippur; for the first time since my childhood, I fasted for the holiday (a fast made infinitely easier by the fact that I was already used to hunger). Emil recited prayers in the living room. Pani Lescovec baked us bread to break the fast, and together we joined in the small kitchen and welcomed the evening. I was beginning to forget that I had ever lived anywhere but this apartment, ever known any companionship but the companionship of these nine people. It was remarkable to me but also somehow completely natural that we should all still be here; in the same way a child cannot truly imagine that he might one day live somewhere besides his childhood home, I could not truly imagine that we would not always live like this, forever.

But it was impossible that we would live like this forever.

There was a rumor that Jerzy, the Lescovecs' oldest boy, sixteen years old, had started spending time with a young woman who lived on Leszno Street. Flirting, courting, whatever you called it: it was the very thing that was supposed to happen among sixteen-year-olds, but still it reminded us that the rhythms of natural life were impossible. What were these two going to do? Get married? Start a family? (Although people on our block had gotten married and started families, in what seemed to some of us, a glorious rejection of the Nazis' rule over our lives and, to others, pure idiocy.) We whispered about Jerzy and the girl—Rafel had seen the two of them holding hands at a theatrical production of *Yankele* in the old Palace Theater—and we were glad to have something to whisper about.

She was short and slightly hunchbacked, Rafel said. But she had big tits, Arkady said, not knowing that his mother could overhear their conversation. Sala covered her mouth with both hands to keep from laughing out loud.

Some of my students kept coming to class: Roman, Charlotte. Other students vanished, and I didn't have the heart to ask what had happened to them. I rarely saw Szifra anymore, but her brothers still sometimes came to my class. After everyone else left, I would teach them a bit more German.

My parents were killed in Berlin.

I was staying with my grandparents in Warsaw.

I am on my way home.

Hello.

Please.

Thank you.

Later that October, the Germans reached Sevastopol.

The Germans sank an American destroyer.

The Americans still did not declare war on Germany.

Luxembourg was declared "*judenrein.*"

("And what does this mean?" "What it sounds like, Sala. Free of Jews.")

That November, Jerzy told his mother he wanted to propose marriage to the slightly hunchbacked girl from Leszno Street, and his mother started laughing hysterically and then slapped him across the face.

That night, Jerzy didn't come home before curfew. Filip was sent out to find him at ten. The whole house heaved with worry while Emil and

I shared a bottle of upstairs rotgut. Sala joined us at the kitchen table. The other boys headed up to the frigid rooftops to keep a lookout. It was generally understood that Jews caught outside after curfew were rounded up and sent to prison or to labor camps, but it was also understood that everyone broke curfew eventually. The rotgut tasted like dirty prunes, but it fired my belly and kept my face warm even as my fingers and toes grew cold.

Filip dragged his brother into the apartment at midnight.

Jerzy said he would stay out past curfew the night after that and the night after that until his parents understood that he intended to marry this girl, but, in fact, he did not stay out past curfew again. And his father said, on yet another night nobody could sleep, "So what if he does try to marry this girl? What else does he have to look forward to?"

And his mother, Pani Lescovec, started to cry.

That November, I began to truly believe I would spend the rest of my life in this apartment, that deliverance would never come. I would sit in my alcove and look at the pearl necklace and sometimes wonder at its grandeur and sometimes at its impotence. To trade it meant to trust that someone would actually get me a kennkarte, would actually ferry me to Stockholm, would actually keep his word to me, a Jew. Nowak, Henryk, the greed of a stranger, the goodwill of a stranger: none of them seemed particularly reliable to me. Any one of them could take the pearl, surrounded by diamonds, and give me nothing in return. And if I lost this necklace, I was almost certainly lost myself.

So I did nothing.

In December, the Japanese bombed Pearl Harbor. The following day, the Americans declared war on Japan and, a few days later, on Germany.

I put the necklace back in the space under the floorboards in my alcove.

For the first time in a year, I thought that perhaps salvation was on the way.

TWENTY

═══════

Two days later, just as the sun was starting to emerge, an explosion shook the window above my alcove, thrumming the glass and shocking me out of a dream about soup. I stumbled past my curtains and out toward the corridor, finding my tattered loafers along the way.

They had started to shell the ghetto. Served me right for having been optimistic.

"Adam, where are you?" Sala, already in the kitchen, in the half dark. The gas was out.

"You didn't hear that?"

"Hear what?" she said. She was sitting in front of an empty plate.

"The explosion?"

"I heard nothing," she said, smiling gently.

Had I dreamed it? Was I finally losing my mind? It seemed to me to be a reasonable thing to lose my mind, and not entirely awful. The ghetto was filled with crazy people, oblivious to what was happening to them, and pleased enough, it seemed, to drool on themselves in the shadows. Perhaps it was my time to join them. But my heart was still pounding.

"Are you all right?"

"I really don't know," I said. I looked down at myself, quietly mortified. I was dressed in nothing but my third pair of pants, the ones most worn down by overuse, threadbare at the knees, soft enough now to sleep in. My ribs protruded. The hair on my chest had turned gray. My skin prickled from shock and from the cold.

"There was an explosion," I whispered pathetically. "Outside my window."

"Did it break the glass?"

I blinked and tried to remember. "I don't think so?"

"Why don't we look."

"At the window?"

"Come," she said. She was in her dressing gown, but she was not wearing the scarf on her head, and even in the faint light I could see that her hair was starting to grow back in short wisps. She stood, took my hand in a sort of motherly way, and led me back to the alcove, past her snoring husband. We ducked in through the curtains. The glass was intact.

"I must have been dreaming," I said.

"I don't think so," Sala said, kneeling up on the window seat. "Come, look."

I perched on the window seat beside her. Our apartment faced east, and the sun had now risen over the ghetto walls.

"Do you see?"

A tiny spiderweb crack; a tiny smear of something red.

"A bird must have flown into the window as the dawn was breaking," she said. "It rattled the window and woke you up."

"You think that's what it was?"

"Certainly," she said. "Starlings used to fly into our kitchen window all the time. I finally drew a picture of an owl and posted it on the window so they'd stop."

"Did it work?"

"It did," she said. "I don't think starlings are very smart."

"Ah," I said, abashed as a child.

"Poor thing," she said, and I didn't know if she was talking about me or the bird. Her shoulder was next to mine, separated by a millimeter of fizzing space.

"Your hair is growing back," I said.

She turned to me and gave me the saddest smile I had ever seen. I leaned down and kissed her soft chapped lips. Her husband snored behind us, a dead bird lay at the foot of our building, and my heart still pounded, pounded—now for a million reasons. I kept kissing her, and she didn't resist, and I held her close in both my arms. And my heart continued to pound.

TWENTY-ONE

Still, it grew colder.

The boys turned up the hunt for fuel, coal, zloty—anything that could keep us warm. I did my part, finagling a few bags of coal from Nowak in exchange for the last pair of Kasia's boots. We burned only as little as we needed, which meant that we were always at least a little bit cold, and we stopped laundering our clothes and bedclothes, because we had no way to dry them. We worried less about typhus, but only because other worries had taken up room in our minds. Put out one fire, and another one starts to burn.

At the library on Tłomackie Street, our Saturday meetings focused on the aid societies, the distribution of food, the best way to keep the most people from starving.

"Trying to give food to everyone, even the starving," cried a man in the back, his own voice weak from what I assumed was hunger, "is a waste of the few resources we have. We must continue to feed the people who will live! We cannot waste food on people who will die anyway!"

"How could you say that?" screeched a woman sitting closer to me. "To not feed the starving! Have you forgotten you are a Jew?"

"Jewish law says we must preserve the living at the expense of everything else!"

"So you're a rabbi now, Pan Blumstein?"

"No more than you, Pani Auerbach!"

We allowed these fights to simmer even in the relative calm of the Oneg Shabbat group; we had to be angry at *someone*, after all, and it was easier to be angry at one another instead of the Germans. (The only attitudes we could muster toward the Germans were fear and resignation and mystified despair. Why were they doing this? What had happened to them in their lives that they couldn't let us live ours?)

Ringelblum still stood straight, still darkly handsome, still well-dressed, the sadness just barely visible in his eyes. Yehudit still attended our meetings too, with her air of inviolable calm. They were both intimately involved with the soup kitchens and the Judenrat board; they knew the players at the post office and the members of the religious council. Ringelblum still had occasional phone access to New York, and so he knew the most current news of the war. He was a barometer, and we looked to him to know how to feel: When he was hopeful, we were hopeful. When he stood straight, so did we. In the cold of January, there was still a fire in the woodburning stove in the library, still small plain biscuits passed around, which we felt guilty taking but took nevertheless by the handful.

"Shabbat shalom, friends," Ringelblum said. "What news do you have to report?"

"A wedding," I said, startling myself, as I was rarely the first to speak.

Ringelblum nodded, made a note. "A religious wedding?" he asked. "Or courthouse?"

It had been a religious wedding, overseen by a rabbi who lived on the top floor of our building, in the courtyard of the bride's family's apartment building on Leszno Street.

"Wonderful," Ringelblum said. "You attended?"

"The groom has been my housemate for over a year," I said. "I stood in attendance by the chuppah."

"Wonderful," Ringelblum said again. "Wonderful news."

The bride was resplendent in her mother's wedding dress, which had been seamlessly tailored to disguise her mild hunchback. The groom, nervous, wore a borrowed suit covered in a white cloth, to symbolize his innocence. The couple met under a chuppah that had been constructed by the groom's younger brother out of carved wood, and which was covered by a canopy woven out of one of the groom's housemate's dead wife's linen sheets.

The bride circled the groom seven times. Both the bride and groom sipped wine out of a silver kiddush cup. When the rabbi pronounced them wed, the groom smashed a piece of glass under his foot.

To celebrate, all who gathered danced to music played by a four-piece string band that had once been famous outside the gates, and drank wine provided by the doctor who lived upstairs from the groom. We ate vanilla biscuits Sala had scrounged up and oat-flour cakes baked by the groom's mother. The women danced in circles with the women, and the men danced in circles with the men, and then the bride and groom, breaking custom, danced in circles with each other. And when a truck full of Germans approached the courtyard, we packed up quickly and disappeared into the nearest apartments so that the only trace of us left was the abandoned chuppah.

"I live in that building," said one of the Oneg Shabbat archivists, a dark-haired middle-aged woman. "I watched the wedding from my window. I painted . . . I painted a few watercolors of it," she said, almost embarrassed. And then I remembered who she was, the artist who had painted lovely pictures of her toddler daughter. She removed a few images from a folder and passed them around; they were pale and spare, a small crowd in a courtyard, a distant bride, the sun shining in the cold. A group dancing in a circle, furiously, to keep warm and spread joy.

"These are beautiful, Gela," Ringelblum said.

"This is exactly what it was like," I said. "You really captured it."

Gela smiled. "It was so good to paint something happy," she said. "Would you give this one to the bride and groom? Maybe they'd like a keepsake." She passed me a watercolor of a bird's-eye view of them as they walked together out of the chuppah, man and wife. "Tell them to keep it out of the sunlight. I make my own paints—they're not very stable."

"I'll do that," I said, and Gela smiled briefly.

None of us were in a particular hurry to leave the library, so we lobbed easy questions at Ringelblum—and though he was usually impatient with our stalling (did anyone else in the ghetto have so many places to be? so many problems to solve?), he let us stay for an extra hour, debriefing us on our various reports, providing us general information about the war.

Soon enough, though, conversation turned to our fellow Jews in Lithuania, Latvia, Estonia, and this is when we started to look away from one another, when we stopped being able to choke down our biscuits. According to the refugees who had made their way to Warsaw, entire villages had been wiped out: Jews were marched from their homes, made to dig pits, and then shot in the back while they were digging. Then the next line of Jews. Then the next. It was impossible to fully imagine this except in the broadest outlines—when we envisioned the Jews digging the pits, we did not see their faces, only their bodies, and the repetitive motions of the shovels, and the collapse. (At a Jewish funeral, we buried one another; in Lithuania, the Jews buried themselves.)

Some in the room said these stories were predictions about what was soon to happen to us: if the Nazis were to dissolve the Jewish communities of Landwarow, Troki, Niemenczyn, Vilnius, why wouldn't they dissolve Warsaw too?

"Because," said Marysia Hoff, "there's nowhere around here to dig."

"And besides," said Pan Klosterman, an optimist. "I have news from cousins in Białystok that there have been no mass shootings. No liquidations. My guess is that the Lithuanians are behind this, not the Germans. They have always hated Jews in Lithuania."

"The Germans don't hate us?" someone in the back said, a sneer in his voice.

"Not like the Lithuanians."

"Not like the Poles," someone else said, to bitter laughter, and I found myself laughing too.

"As unfortunate as it is," Ringelblum said, "I imagine these liquidations are casualties of what has become an increasingly vicious war between the Germans and the Soviets. The farther east one goes, the more likely it is that one will find Jewish towns at the mercy of either German or Russian vigilantes."

"So you would describe these Jews as 'casualties of war'?" asked Klosterman.

"Well, all Jews are casualties of war, Pan Klosterman—"

"Yes, but these Jews, specifically? The ones being shot in these mass events? They are not the intended victims but, rather, you would say, accidents of war?"

"Sadly," Ringelblum said. "Tragically, yes. Our brother and sister Jews caught in the middle of warring factions, as is so often the case. But as for us, our job is to stay watchful. Take care of one another. And, most importantly, keep writing everything down."

I was writing everything down, obviously—but it did strike me that perhaps writing it all down was not the most important thing we could do for ourselves. The most important thing we could do for ourselves was survive. Not just in words, but in actual bodies. And to that end, the archive was of no use at all. In fact, the archive suddenly seemed to me a sort of capitulation, an acceptance of the truth that we would not be here and so our written words would have to say what we ourselves could not.

And I wasn't interested in my writing, or anyone's writing. I was interested in staying alive! I wanted to stay alive.

I knew better than to say such a thing out loud.

"And now that the Americans have joined the war, Reb Ringelblum, have there been any significant advances?"

"None that I know of," Ringelblum said. "Which doesn't mean that there haven't been any. But whatever moves they are making remain secret."

"But we can assume they are making moves?"

Ringelblum was usually quick to deflate our optimism, but for some reason he chose not to. "Yes," he said. "I think that's a safe assumption." He gave us a tentative smile.

I didn't believe him.

AFTER THE MEETING, I wrapped myself in a double layer of moth-eaten scarves before stepping outside: it had started to snow, and the streets were already coated with a layer of grimy white. I often took the path straight through the ghetto to get home to Sienna Street from Tlomackie; the route was crowded, which made it easier to hide, should the Germans come trolling through, looking for bodies to haul to a labor camp. But today, I welcomed the cold, thinking that perhaps it would clear my piercing headache. I noticed, for the first time, that I had worn a hole in one of my shoes, and thought perhaps I would take the route past the shoemaker on Nowolipki to see if it could be repaired, or if he had a pair of new shoes I could barter for. Or perhaps I could walk toward the Twarda Street gate to see if Nowak had anything new in his bags.

Unsure of which direction to take, I stopped and scanned an intersection, and at a distance of about thirty meters saw a tall blond girl walking languidly across the street. How long since I had seen Szifra? I wanted to see how she was doing, but I also didn't want to run and attract any attention, so I wove in and out of the crowds, following the sheen of her smooth blond hair. I tried calling her name; she didn't hear me. Then, at the next intersection, I lost her.

Which way? Left toward Okopowa? Right on Gęsia? I chose the former, but it was a mistake; Szifra had vanished like a mirage. And then, as soon as I rounded Okopowa, I heard the heart-stopping blast of machine-gun fire. A pause, a silence, another blast. Children were running toward me, followed by a pair of soldiers. I recognized some of their faces, or maybe I just thought I did: all children looked like one another now, half-starved.

"Go," screamed one of the children. "Go!"

Instead, I stepped back as far as I could into the shadow of a doorway, and when the children stopped running and the soldiers seemed to have disappeared I resumed my walk, carefully, down the path left by the shoes racing through the newly fallen snow. The crowd would surely be thinner this way. I kept my eyes toward the sidewalk, saw the snow was turning pink, then darker pink, and then completely a pool of crimson. How many shots had been fired?

There were several small openings at the base of the wall on this part of Okopowa Street, holes big enough for seven- or eight-year-old children to get through. These were the egress points for our youngest and sneakiest smugglers.

These smugglers, these boys, had become the lifeblood of the ghetto economy. We knew that our very lives depended on them: the price they could get for turnips or potatoes, the markets they could find for our used picture frames and books. We didn't like to talk about it or acknowledge our indebtedness to them, or to the fragility of our system, but we also couldn't avoid it. Given the meager kilocalories they allowed each of us, if the children hadn't smuggled in food, we all would have perished.

But then there was the cost.

Prostrate on the street were two boys, boys who looked too old, too big, to fit safely through the holes at the bottom of the wall. How desperate they must have been to try! They'd been caught while wiggling through, stuck under the wall, half on the ghetto side and half on the

Aryan. They'd been shot as many times as children could be shot and still be recognizable, the shots emptying their blood into a pool on the street. A guard leaned casually against the wall beside them, smoking a cigarette. *"Gibt es ein Problem?"*

"Nein," I said. *"Kein Problem."*

The guard returned to his cigarette, a foot balanced behind him on the wall, as casual as I'd ever seen a German guard, as if there were not two dead children two meters from where he smoked. But soon enough, a curious crowd began to draw closer, as it always did when children were killed, and a rabbi came to negotiate with the guard, as rabbis always did when children were killed: not to remonstrate, of course, but simply to beg access so that the bodies could be taken to their families.

The guard crushed out his cigarette and began screaming, *"Geh zurück, geh zurück! Ich werde schießen!"* And I used that moment to take a closer look, because something in me knew already.

Filip, our Filip, his unseeing eyes turned toward the sky. A black-and-red hole where his forehead had been. His whittling knife still in his shirt pocket.

Behind me, the rabbi was muttering, the crowd was pressing. In the distance, cars were coming: Germans to scare away the crowd.

"Geh zurück!" the guard screamed again, but the crowd did not get back. The snow was falling more heavily. The guard would start shooting any second, I knew it. But still I knelt next to Filip. I touched his white cheek. I felt something in me close up and turn to coal. Behind me, the rabbi was still muttering. "Yitgadal, v'yitkadash, sh'mei rabah . . ."

I had never had children of my own, but I had lived with this child for more than a year. Filip on the rooftop, whittling his toys. Filip mastering the art of the smuggle. Filip in my English class, bumbling his way through Rudyard Kipling. Filip dead on the street, half his body obscured behind a wall. I took his knife and put it in my satchel. Its handle was warm.

"Come," the rabbi said, but I did not move.

A familiar shriek behind me. The crowd separated. I stumbled back, away from Filip, flat on my hands on the frozen street.

"Meyn engel, meyn engel! Nein!"

I had heard that voice a thousand times; I knew who it was.

Mariam Lescovec, hurling herself at her dead son, at the wall that contained him. Pulling him out, screaming unintelligibly. Covering herself in the snow and her own snot and tears, covering herself in his blood. Red and black with it. Even the German seemed stunned by the largeness of her display, by her intensity—he simply watched her. We all watched her, encircling her and her dead boy to protect them.

But then she turned, screamed, *"Nein!"* And she ran to the German guard as if to throttle him to death with her hands, and I have no doubt that she could have and would have, but her advance snapped the guard out of his torpor and he shot her in the chest, snuffing her out as casually as one would exterminate a mouse.

She fell centimeters from where her son lay.

The crowd, again, went running down Okopowa Street. The guard, looking at his handiwork, lit another cigarette.

My feet, beneath me, felt unstable; I wasn't sure they would carry me. The rabbi took me by the arm—he was old, he was frail, but still he took me by the arm—and stood me up (I was still kneeling; I hadn't realized) and held my arm as we turned away from Okopowa Street. He didn't say anything, but he kept holding my arm as we made our way through the snow and the grime on the street. The beggars were still there, the starving people still lying there as the snow fell slowly over them. The shops were still open, the ones that stayed open on Saturdays. The ones that had closed for the Sabbath were still closed.

At the corner of Okopowa and Chłodna, the rabbi asked me if I would be okay, if I could make it home from there. I said I could.

I don't remember the rest of the walk, but when I entered the apartment, Sala opened her mouth in a silent scream. I went into the bathroom to wash my face and saw that I was covered with Filip's blood.

We had no hot water for bathing, so I took off my clothes and washed as best I could from the tap. Then I put my bloody clothes in the boiler to burn. They gave off a rancid stink and a heat that lasted the rest of the night.

THE SURVIVING LESCOVECS never returned to the apartment, and we never discovered where they went. After seven respectful days, I moved from my alcove into the maid's room. I covered the bed with my remaining sheets, put my increasingly tattered clothing on the shelves. I hid the pearl necklace in the space between the bed and the floor. Finally, I hung Gela's watercolor on a wall away from the sun. Despite my caution, however, the paint started to fade, and within days the painting was little more than a series of smudges on white paper, a faded wheel of color where a wedding had been.

TWENTY-TWO

S ala started coming to my room soon after.

We were all living underwater at that point, hungry and exhausted even after we ate and slept.

When she lay on top of me, I could feel the bony ripple of her ribs. Under me, I felt the sharp ridges of her hips.

We were so underwater we only rarely thought about her husband or her children, asleep (or were they?) a shut door away.

We were so underwater that we did not acknowledge to one another what we were doing when we saw each other in the kitchen, where we continued to drink tea sometimes and chat about the day ahead or listen to the contraband radio.

It had been many years since I had slept with someone, and I was surprised at how quickly the rhythms came back to me, a melody I had known since forever. She was warm and soft. She tasted like sweat, her short silvery hair bunched under my fingers. She was quiet through-out—of course, we both were quiet—but she closed her eyes tight at the moment of climax and then had to stifle a laugh. I, on the other hand, felt enormous sorrow and enormous love.

When I thought to worry about pregnancy, she said that it had been many months since she'd eaten enough calories to menstruate. She said she wasn't going to worry about it, and neither should I. I decided not to worry.

If Emil knew what was happening, he, too, was underwater, living in this strange underwater world where there were no more rules about right and wrong, where sex with a married woman in the same apartment where her husband slept was simply a matter of not waking anyone up. He treated me no differently than he ever had. He addressed me, jovially, as Paskow in the morning. When he got out of bed, he used both hands to push himself up.

Of course, it was possible he didn't know.

Usually, she crept out of the room a few minutes after we finished, washed herself quickly in the spindly tap, and then sat up in the kitchen, reading or drumming her fingers on the table as she waited for the sun to rise. Sometimes, though, she returned to her husband's bed, and it was on those nights the parody of our lives knifed me.

"You have a mole here," she said to me one night, tracing a pattern on my back with her finger. "Did you know that?"

"If I did, I've forgotten." I was gazing out the window, feeling her heat behind me, her tiny fingers, the sharp points of her fingernails.

"A few moles, actually. Or are they freckles?"

"I don't know what the difference is."

"There probably isn't one," she said, and put her thin arms around my waist. It was amazing to me how transported I felt—how, with her, there was no ghetto, no war, no hunger, no children, no Emil, not even Kasia. I had everything I needed. Sala kissed my shoulder, and I rolled over to face her, to bury my head in her neck, to kiss her smooth, small nipples. She shuddered, and I licked the bony space between her breasts, and then her nipples again, and then down her stomach, concave and as hot as fire.

In the distance, the lights of the Ferris wheel rotated through space.

I told her that I loved her to try out what it sounded like, and once I said it, I couldn't stop saying it. I told her in Yiddish, in Polish, in French, in Portuguese, in Latin, in my pidgin Spanish. I told her in Mandarin, in Cantonese. I told her in Russian. But my favorite, of course, was to tell her in English: three simple syllables, subject, verb, object. I (Adam Paskow) love (with my whole heart) you (Sala Wiskoff).

Love sounded best in English. I said it again and again.

"I love you," Sala whispered back to me one night. "That means what I think it means?"

She didn't know English, and I had never thought to teach her. "Yes," I said.

"Ah," she said. "Is that true?"

"Yes," I said, having never been as sure before as I was at that moment.

"Ah," she said again. She did not say it back, but I didn't really mind. I loved the words for the sound they made, for the cleanness of expression, for the solidity of what they meant: I loved Sala, and therefore I had a reason to keep living. I kissed the warm soft back of her neck, which tasted like dust and salt.

TWENTY-THREE

In class, I decided to veer away from poetry, because, despite my best efforts, I was starting to forget some of the poetry I had memorized over the years, and there were only so many times I could attempt to teach them "If."

From my sparse selection of English books, I could have picked *Huckleberry Finn*, but I wasn't always sure how to pronounce the words, and I didn't want to teach my students the wrong thing. So I settled on *Moby Dick*, which I had always liked better anyway. I picked a few passages, the ones that were most like poetry. I copied the paragraphs out by hand on some of my journal paper and passed them around the class so that we could read, together, in English:

"'Some years ago—never mind how long precisely—having little or no money in my purse, and nothing particular to interest me on shore, I thought I would sail about a little and see the watery part of the world.'"

"Does everyone understand?"

Blank, hungry faces. We read the passage again.

"Is 'the watery part of the world' the ocean?" Rafel asked in Yiddish, which I allowed.

"It is."

"Ah," said Rafel. It was February, dark and cold. "I would like to see the ocean."

"You did see it once," Arkady told his brother, "when we went to Danzig. When we were little."

"No, that was just the Baltic Sea," said Rafel. "I mean the ocean. Like the Atlantic or the Pacific. An ocean that separates continents."

Arkady, usually quick to put his brother down for his silly ideas, agreed. "If we got to the Atlantic, we could keep going," he said. "We could go all the way to New York. It's just on the other side."

"After the war, we could go," Rafel said.

"After the war, we won't need to," Arkady said.

"Will there be 'after the war'?" asked Jakub Joseph.

"Of course there will," I said, surprised at the sharpness in my voice.

To all of our surprise, two more children bumped their ways downstairs for class. It amazed me, the consistency and the dedication of these kids, or of the kids' parents who sent them here to learn English. Five of them, in a circle: Arkady, Rafel, Charlotte, Roman, and Jakub, bundled up in their coats and gloves, their breath puffing out in white clouds. They were lovely children. I loved them all. I sat down in their circle, which was not normal; usually, I took a command position leaning against the back of my overturned barrel.

"Now that everyone's here, let's recite again."

"'I thought I would sail about a little and see the watery part of the world.'"

I wished I had some food with me, something to share, but save for the necklace, my satchel was empty. Since Filip's death, I had stopped asking the children to trade for things, so I, too, had been reduced to nothing but my ration coupons and the few zloty I earned every week. What was I eating? Bread flavored with sawdust, watered-down powdered milk. A few mornings before, I had walked into the kitchen and imagined Mariam Lescovec there, frying the skin from chicken feet; I was certain I saw her, even said hello, then I realized I was dreaming.

The children were yawning. *Moby Dick* was going to be a stretch. "Are you doing all right?" I asked, which was a question I tried not to ask.

"It's gotten harder," said Charlotte. Her brother nudged her. She wasn't supposed to complain.

"You know, if you haven't used your ration coupons yet today, there's rye bread in the Aid Society kitchens," I said. "Real rye bread. And potato porridge."

The children nodded. They had almost certainly used their ration coupons already; they knew the meager Aid Society offerings, and there was no way for me to make them sound more tempting than they were.

"Do you think they'll have eggs again?"

"I can try to find out," I said, even though I knew the answer was no. They looked at each other, at their fingers. I would have given anything I had for a few biscuits to hand out. "So what else shall we talk about today?"

They were quiet. Then Jakub said, "A poem about war."

"Okay," I said. "Let me think of one . . ."

"A poem about revenge," he said, but he said this quieter, in Yiddish.

"I don't know any poems about revenge," I said.

"Nothing?"

I racked my brain. "I'm sorry. And the ones I know about war are very long. Too long to recite." I sighed. "War is long."

"Teach us a poem of food!" Roman said, in his wonderful clumsy English.

"No! No, I can't listen to a poem about food," Charlotte said, but she was smiling. "I am too hungry!"

"Food! That gives me an idea. Wait a minute." I picked up *Moby Dick*. "There's a passage here that is sure to remove your appetite— listen." I flipped through the pages until I found it.

"'In the case of a small Sperm Whale the brains are accounted a fine dish. The casket of the skull is broken into with an axe, and the two plump, whitish lobes being withdrawn (precisely resembling two large puddings), they are then mixed with flour, and cooked into a most delectable mess, in flavor somewhat resembling calves' head, which is quite a dish among some epicures.'"

They all stared at me, so I repeated the passage in Polish.

"Brains? They're eating *whale brains*?"

"What is an 'epicure'?" asked Charlotte.

"Say it in English."

"An epicure."

"Someone who loves fancy food," I said.

"Epicures eat *whale brains*?"

"Oh God, I think I did lose my appetite," Charlotte said, grimacing dramatically in the way of twelve-year-old girls. "For the first time in a year, I'm not the slightest bit hungry."

"You want to hear more?"

Like kids listening to a horror story, of course they wanted to hear more.

"Okay, here we go: 'In Henry the Eighth's time, a certain cook of the court obtained a handsome reward for inventing an admirable sauce to be eaten with barbecued porpoises, which, you remember, are a species of whale. Porpoises, indeed, are to this day considered fine eating. The meat is made into balls about the size of billiard balls, and being well seasoned and spiced might be taken for turtle-balls or veal balls. The old monks of Dunfermline were very fond of them.'"

"Turtle balls?" squeaked Roman.

"Barbecued porpoises?"

"What is a 'porpoise'?" asked Rafel.

"It's like a dolphin."

"What's a 'dolphin'?"

"It's a small whale," Arkady said.

"How small? Like a fish?"

"Like a big fish. Well, bigger than a fish. Smaller than a whale."

"When we went to Danzig, we saw them," Arkady said quietly.

"We did?" Rafel looked at his big brother.

"Yes," he said. "Abba was picking up a delivery at the import office, so Eema took us to the beach for a picnic—"

"No!" Charlotte squealed. "Don't mention food!"

"And we sat on the sand. We had a blanket. You were scared, because you'd never seen that much sand before."

The kids, finding themselves in a mood of hysteria, began laughing at the idea that anyone would be scared of sand, although really at this point they would have laughed at anything, they would fall apart at the slightest provocation.

"And Eema pointed at the ocean, and there were all of these black humps rising and falling out of the water, with their fins up in the air. There seemed to be a line of them, or maybe they were the same ones going back and forth. I don't know. You were scared, of course"—more laughter from the assemblage—"because you thought they were sharks. But Eema said they weren't sharks, she didn't know what they were, perhaps they were whales. But they were small, and there were so many of them. We asked someone else who was on the beach, and he said they were porpoises, and that they were very rare in the Baltic Sea, and seeing them like this was almost impossible—they never got this close to the shore. But it was Eema's birthday, which is why we were all on vacation together. So we decided the porpoises were visiting for her birthday."

"And then what happened?"

"We watched them for so long we were late to meet Abba. And he was annoyed, but then we told him we saw porpoises, and he wasn't mad anymore. He said porpoises were so unusual that it was practically a miracle to see them. They'd been fished almost to extinction. He said it was good luck that we'd seen them. Eema was really happy."

Sala on the beach with her boys, watching a line of porpoises leap out of the sea. If I closed my eyes, I knew I would be able to see, would be transported there, so I didn't close my eyes; I needed to stay with the children.

"Then what happened?" Rafel asked.

"I don't remember," said Arkady. "It was a long time ago."

"Did you ever eat porpoise, Pan Paskow?"

"Try asking in English, Jakub."

"Do you eat porpoise?"

"I have not," I said.

"Is it kosher?" asked Charlotte.

"No scales," said Roman, in English. "Not kosher."

"Okay, so here's a question," said Rafel. "If someone came down these stairs and said, 'Hey, everyone, I have a plate of fried whale brains. It's not kosher. It's definitely whale,' would you eat it?"

"You're asking am I hungry enough to eat whale brains?" Charlotte asked.

"Yes," said Rafel. "Would you do it?"

"Fried whale brains," mused Arkady, in English.

"I would do it," said Jakub. "I would eat anything right now."

"Eww!" squealed Charlotte.

"I would eat anything," Jakub repeated.

"So would I," said Roman."

"Uch, I wouldn't. I'd rather starve," said Charlotte. "And I know what it feels like to starve, and I'd *still* rather starve than eat fried whale brains."

"I mean, if we're willing to eat, say, the shin muscle of a cow, then why wouldn't we eat the brain of a whale?" Arkady asked, philosophically. "Isn't it all basically the same thing?"

"A brain is not the same as a muscle! A brain is not a muscle! A brain is . . . eww, a brain!"

They were off and running in Polish, but I didn't stop them. Strangely, talking about food did not make me feel hungry or even wistful. It felt like talking about a fantasy, a line of dolphins rising and falling off the coast.

We ended class at three thirty, before the skies could grow too dark, and said our goodbyes at the top of the basement stairs. Charlotte and Roman headed off in one direction, and Arkady, Rafel, Jakub, and I headed in the other. The clouds were lowering. It was going to snow again, which was, all things considered, a good thing: we put tubs on the windowsill for the snow to collect and ate it out of cups. Meanwhile, the trees shivered in the wind, and the boys pulled their collars up against their necks.

On the corner of Nowolipki and Smocza, we saw a light beaming in the window of the old Nowolipki Street Café, which hadn't been open in many months. We were drawn to the light like moths; even though none of us had much money, we wanted to see if there was food being served, and what that food might be. We wanted to see waiters, with white aprons around their waists and trays on their arms, deliver steaming platters. We wanted to see food that required a fork and a knife. We wanted to see a wineglass, maybe, or a brown bottle of ale. We wanted to look at a dream.

We peered in the window.

In the middle of the room was a single table. On the single table was a red-patterned tablecloth, a fork, a knife, a white napkin, a crystal glass, a plate filled with rich-looking food. Bigos, maybe—if someone had been able to procure so many different cuts of meat. Or maybe it was a different sort of stew. And there was a basket of bread and a small dish of something white beside it. Could it have possibly been butter? How long since any of us had seen butter?

And, at the table: a blond woman eating alone.

"Jakub," whispered Rafel, "isn't that your sister?"

Jakub didn't answer. But, yes, it was indeed his sister, eating in small, thoughtful bites. Her camel coat was hung in the corner of the room, on a coatrack. In another corner, a waiter stood, expectantly, ready to attend to whatever her needs might be. He refilled her crystal glass with water poured from a silver pitcher. He brought her more bread.

"Are you going to go in there and get her?" Rafel asked Jakub.

"I can't," he said. "She'd kill me."

Of course, we weren't the only ones drawn to the mysterious light of the Nowolipki Street Café, and soon a small crowd had gathered with us at the windows, watching Szifra Joseph eat her luxurious meal in rapt silence. How was it possible to gather the ingredients for something like this? Where could any baker find white flour? Two loaves for one person? I hoped to God she was planning on bringing some home to her brothers.

"Who is that whore?" whispered an old woman standing next to me.

"Shh," said someone else, a murmur of discontent rippling through the assembly by the window. We wanted to watch her in peace, to imagine eating alongside her, savor the butter with her. Digest.

"Truly, who is that? Does anyone know?"

"It's my sister."

"You, kid? That's really your sister?"

"Yeah."

"Now how in the devil's name did she arrange something like this?"

"I don't know," Jakub said. "She's always been good at getting what she wants."

"If that were really your sister, you'd go in and have dinner with her." Jakub shook his head. "I can't."

"What's that she's eating? Is that bigos?"

"Oh my God, how many years has it been since I've tasted bigos?"

"Could that be sausage in there?"

"Not kosher."

"I've seen that girl around, you know. She's always making nice at some Nazi."

"She is *not*," Jakub mumbled. "Making nice."

"That's how you get food around here. Have good looks, make nice to a Nazi."

"She is *not*," said Jakub.

"She's a whore," said someone.

"She is *not*."

"Shh, Jakub, it's okay."

"Whore!"

"Stop it."

"I call it like I see it."

"I said, *stop it.*"

Together, we watched Szifra wipe her lips, then take another bite of whatever was in her bowl. Together, we watched her signal the waiter for more water in her crystal glass. If she noticed us, she did not pay us any mind. The waiter cleared her plates. A few minutes later, he brought out a slice of cake. Black and pink. What could it have been? Chocolate and raspberry? Alongside a bowl of whipped cream.

We watched her eat with a stone in our stomachs and another in our hearts. And only when it seemed that she was done with her meal did we disperse, too cowardly to confront her, to ask her the question we knew the answer to: How do you get a meal like this in the ghetto?

By being beautiful, by being shameless. *Have good looks, make nice to a Nazi.* "Whore," spat an old woman as she walked away.

"That's my sister," said Jakub again, to the window.

Name: Jakub Joseph
Date: February 20, 1942
Age: 10
Height: Maybe 139 cm?
Weight: I have no idea. Szifra
might know.

J.J. So what do you want to talk to me about, anyway? Is this for English school?

A.P. No, it's not for school.

J.J. Good! I was afraid you wanted me to talk in English the whole time.

A.P. Well, you're welcome to if you'd like.

J.J. No, thanks! That language is crazy. No offense.

A.P. None taken.

(Jakub and I are speaking at the Aid Society soup kitchen. I had not planned to conduct this interview, but he sat down next to me as I was taking my break and I realized I had an opportunity to take some notes for the archive. Moreover, it is sometimes easier to interview someone than it is to just make polite conversation.)

J.J. So then what is this about?

A.P. Well, my project is to talk to different people in the ghetto and find out their stories, what their daily lives are like. So that we have a record of what it was really like after the war, before we start to lose our memories.

J.J. Oh. I don't have memories.

A.P. What do you mean? Everyone has memories.

J.J. Not me. I don't remember things at all. Like the other day, in your class, when you asked us about our first friends at school, I never would have remembered that. I don't remember the day before yesterday. My sister thinks I have some kind of problem.

A.P. But that's not true. You remember your English lessons.

J.J. Lessons, yes. And I can remember addresses and telephone extensions and how to add and subtract and that sort of thing. But events? Things that happened? I don't remember any of it. Like when my mother died, Eli said we had to wait for the rabbi on the sidewalk for hours, but I don't remember any of it. I don't even remember finding her dead.

A.P. You were the one that found her?

J.J. I guess. Honestly. I don't remember.

A.P. So Eli told you you found her?

J.J. Yes, but I really don't know. I'm sorry.

A.P. No, don't be sorry. Is your soup okay? You're not eating all of it.

J.J. Oh, I will. I try to eat slowly. It makes me full for longer. And also . . .

A.P.

J.J. Well, Szifra's brought more food for us. She's getting it from . . . She has a source for food. So I'm not really as hungry as I used to be.

A.P. That's good, Jakub.

J.J. I guess. I mean, I feel sort of bad, because I know there are so many people here who would do anything for more food, and here I am eating this potato mush *and* I'm eating bread and cheese at home.

A.P. No, Jakub. No. That's never how you should look at it. You need to survive here. If Szifra is able to help you survive, don't think twice about it. Eat the food she brings you, okay? Eat all of it. Every bite.

J.J. Yeah, well, it's a lot better than this slop.

A.P. I'm sure it is.

(Like all of the children, Jakub has grown taller during his year in the ghetto, and his face has started to change. He has slightly overlapping teeth. He has gray eyes and light-brown hair. Outside the walls, he would have grown up to be a handsome kid, better-looking than his brother, and kinder too.)

J.J. She brought us ptasie mleczko last week. I couldn't believe it. I didn't even think they made it anymore! But she had two bars of it, and you know what was funny? I almost threw up! Or I felt like I was going to throw up. Because I didn't think I could handle that much sugar—there's a lot of sugar in chocolate and marshmallow.

A.P. Did you?

J.J. No way! Because Szifra said after everything she had to do to get us that candy if I threw it up she was going to make me clean up the throw-up and eat it again.

A.P. She said that?

J.J. She's got a bad temper these days. Or else she's just nervous. Or sad. I think she's sad about our eema, even though she would never admit it.

A.P. It's hard to lose your mother.

J.J. Is your mother alive?

A.P. She is. She lives in Palestine.

J.J. And she didn't take you?

A.P. Well, I was an adult when she left. She tried, though. She wanted me to come.

J.J. My parents never wanted to leave. I remember
they talked about it once—I wasn't supposed to overhear—
and they were just laughing about all the cowards who were
running away to Canada or Palestine or wherever. And Szifra
overheard too, and she just looked worried. I mean, I think Szifra
knew what was going to happen before anyone else did. She
told us once. She said that it was going to be bad, but not to
worry, she would handle it. And so far she has! I mean, ptasie
mleczko!

A.P. Did she tell you how she got it?

J.J. Nah. She doesn't give details. Do you want the rest of my
soup? It's kind of . . .

A.P.

J.J. Really, you should eat it.

A.P. (Holding on to my last bare shred of dignity) No, Jakub.
Eat it yourself. It's important you get enough calories.

J.J. (Shrugging but taking another spoonful of soup) That's
what Szifra says. We need to eat to have as much strength as
possible for our journey. And we have to be extra-nice to her all
the time because she's saving our lives.

A.P. She says that?

J.J. Yeah. She's not always that nice, though.

A.P. She's doing her best.

J.J. I guess. Sometimes she says we're just a burden, though,
and it would be a lot easier if she could go without us. Did
you know that? She's going to go, and she's going to take us
too. Even though she doesn't want to. Or she doesn't think we
deserve her good graces.

A.P. She said that?

J.J. I told you she wasn't always that nice.

A.P. She wouldn't leave you, Jakub.

J.J. I hope not. If she did, there's no way we'd ever get out of this dump.

A.P. I'm certain she won't leave you.

J.J. Yeah, probably not. I guess. I'm just counting the days until we can go. You're sure you don't want this soup? I really don't think I can finish it.

A.P. Finish it, Jakub. You never know where your next meal is coming from.

J.J. But—

A.P. Please. Do it for me.

(A good boy, Jakub does.)

TWENTY-FOUR

O nce upon a time, I woke up in the morning in a comfortable bed in a sunny two-bedroom apartment in the Mokotów District of Warsaw, the capital of the newly reunified country of Poland, a country my family had lived in since the beginning of time.

If it was a weekday morning, my alarm would ring; I would open my eyes, turn my head, and see my sleepy wife, Kasia, drowsing beside me. She had to wake up too, to go to her job at the Ministry of Foreign Affairs, where she translated important documents from Polish into English and back again, but she was slow to rise and loved to eke out a few extra minutes in bed while I showered and dressed.

We had a bathroom with a tub and a shower. There was always hot water. There was always enough water. I washed my body with soap and washed my hair with shampoo. I dried myself off with clean cotton towels.

I brushed my teeth with a toothbrush and with toothpaste we purchased at the pharmacy on the corner, the one that always had enough medicines, soaps, syrups, ointments, salves, and bandages, the pharmacy that never had a reason to turn me away.

In the mornings, as I dressed, Kasia would sometimes go down to the newsstand to buy the morning papers. Sometimes she would stop at the bakery and buy some bread or kolachki. Sometimes she would simply make coffee in the small silver percolator that rested on the stovetop.

We bought our coffee at the general store on Mokotów Street—the nicer one—the one that always had enough sugar, salt, flour, paper, pens, ink, cotton balls, shoe polish, table polish, needles, thread, envelopes, and nail scissors. The one that had a telephone hanging on the wall that anyone could use at any time, providing he or she had five groszy. A store that never had a reason to turn me away.

We would drink our coffee and eat our breakfast together and talk about what we expected from the day, or whether Gruby was looking particularly fat, or whether Kasia's father was taking her to lunch. We talked about a new book one of us was reading or a theater production or a concert one of us wanted to see. We talked about a vacation in the Carpathian Mountains, and whether or not I would ever learn to ski. We talked about where she was in her cycle, and whether I should get home soon after work so that we could try, again, to have a baby.

On some days, my wife would clean the breakfast dishes, and on other days, I would.

At seven fifteen, we would leave the house and walk to the tram station on Wiktorska Street. Kasia would take the trolley north, to the government district. I would take the trolley west, to the Centralny Lyceum. Most mornings, during my commute, I would see Weiss, who monitored Warsaw transportation, sitting up near the conductor. If he wasn't too busy making notes in his small red notebook, he and I would chat for a minute or two about the news of the day. Weiss was a small man with a thick, curled mustache that he fiddled with when he spoke. He had two small daughters who also loved trams and trolleys. On Sundays, after a week of riding Warsaw public transportation, he would take his daughters on trolley rides for fun.

I would arrive at the Lyceum at seven forty-five.

I taught five classes every day: three English, one Latin, one German.

In between classes, I advised teachers who were having problems with their students.

I talked to the principal about new ideas for our language program.

I ate lunch in the large faculty cafeteria.

Nobody ever had a reason to turn me away.

I would stay late some days to provide extra tutoring for the students who needed it, who liked working with me, and on other days I would hurry home.

In the evenings, Kasia would cook dinner. She liked to experiment with different kinds of foods: French, Italian, even American. For this reason, I would sometimes arrive home to a dinner of a lumpy gray patty on a piece of bread. "It's a hamburger," my wife would say. "It is very popular in America."

I was sure that this was not exactly what they ate in America, but I knew better than to protest. We would eat the lumpy patties with mustard and potatoes on the side and drink lots of beer the way we imagined they did in America and thought, *You know, these are actually not so terrible.* But were they good? Maybe they weren't that good. So then we would eat apple dumplings or share a slice of cake from the bakery, which tasted to us the way food should taste.

In the evenings, we would read, we would listen to music, we would listen to the radio, we would take a walk, we would drink a glass of wine or beer at the café on the corner. We would make gentle plans about the future. Occasionally, we would see my mother or her father, but not too frequently.

Twice a week, a Polish girl from the suburbs came in to the house to clean and take care of the laundry. She had one eye that drifted lazily to the left, and would speak only to Kasia, never me. Around me, she would scowl and keep a distance. She did good work, though, and she charged affordable rates, and at night sometimes Kasia and I would laugh at her provincial anti-Semitism.

At night, we would get in our bed, the one the Polish girl had made up with clean sheets.

In summer, we went to the seashore, we went to the mountains, we went to the lakes. Sometimes Kasia's father would entice us to visit his country chalet, and we would see Kasia's nieces and nephews and take a ride in her father's convertible car. We would play tennis. We would dine at the family's absurdly long table. Even if they wanted to turn me away, they wouldn't. They didn't.

For many years, as my life plodded along full of ordinary joys I was too stupid to notice, I complained about the ordinary things: A colleague wasn't teaching according to the agreed-upon curriculum. A student's parents were angry that I failed a child who had cheated on an exam. I was putting on a little weight in my belly, and my pants were getting tight. The general store stopped stocking the razors I liked.

Kasia listened to my complaints and took them seriously. When it was her turn, she complained about runs in her new stockings, a friend saying something catty, a lonely feeling as she passed children playing at Mokotów Park.

For a while, we thought that not being able to have a baby was the worst thing that could happen to us.

Then, after the accident, when it was clear she wouldn't recover, I thought: *How could there be any greater tragedy than the death of a beautiful woman—young and beloved, strong and smart, funny and spoiled, eager and curious, sharp and energetic—cut down by a bewildering accident in her fourth decade? With so much to offer, not just to me, but to her friends, to her colleagues, to perhaps, even, to future children. To the newly unified nation-state of Poland. To her cranky, arthritic mother and three splenetic sisters. To our neighborhood, to our home. How could someone so vital simply stop existing? And could there be any greater tragedy than that?*

If you had said to me, when Kasia died: "Yes, there is a greater tragedy than that, and that tragedy is the deaths of thousands. Not just one, not just your wife—even though, of course, she was *your* wife, so we can see how her death might seem particularly tragic to *you*. But on a world level, a world-altering level, the deaths of *thousands* will always surpass the death of one." If you had told me that, I might have countered that each one of those thousands is, in fact, no more and no less than an individual tragedy. In fact, the deaths of thousands is not at all a tragedy: it is just an abstraction that becomes clear only when you focus the abstraction down to each individual loss. To each individual person gone from this earth.

But I would have conceded your point: of all the individual losses ever suffered in this brutal world, only one has ever really mattered to me.

In a sunny apartment in Mokotów four years ago, I woke up without my wife, but in many ways she was with me when I wanted her. Except for the few things of hers that I had packed up and given away, I still had all her belongings: her books, her records, her boots, her clothes. I could touch them any time I wanted to. Nobody turned me away.

I had her jewelry in a blanket in our bedroom. I didn't think about it much.

Whenever I really missed her, I took out one of the photo albums and looked at the pictures of us soon after we met in university: Kasia in her tight, colorful sweaters, me with that ridiculous haircut.

Sometimes I liked to give an entire night over to my grief and sit out on my safe balcony and look out at my lovely neighborhood and think, *Nobody's life has ever been as sorrowful as mine. Nobody's, never.* And even if I knew in my heart I was being a little bit melodramatic, I also knew in my heart I was right.

TWENTY-FIVE

April 1942: The winter had receded the way many Polish winters receded, terrifically slowly and then all at once. It was difficult to tell from the radio reports how the war was moving, although what we did learn never sounded good. U-boats were sinking ships in the Gulf of Mexico. American troops were starving in Bataan. ("Where is Bataan?" "They're fighting *there*?") Ringelblum reported on more massacres to the east, and that a German soldier, Anton Schmid, who had saved hundreds of Jews in Lithuania, had been executed by his fellow Germans upon discovery. Ringelblum had known of Schmid's heroism for several months and asked us to say Kaddish for the man. It felt surreal, saying Kaddish for a German soldier, but life underwater being what it was, we did as he asked.

Jakub and Eli kept showing up in my English classes long after I expected them to disappear, although Szifra never came and I never saw her outside the classroom either. I was curious how she was spending her time, but her brothers didn't seem to know. They looked fed, though, or at least they weren't starving, and their clothing seemed intact, which meant that someone must have been looking out for them. They said they had moved to a slightly nicer apartment, on Gęsia Street, which had been abandoned by a missing family. They liked this apartment better; the hallway toilet flushed.

In the middle of April, a German guard was killed just outside the ghetto walls. Who killed him? Could one of us have possibly shown such bravery? We doubted it, really, but no matter; on a Friday night, the ghetto asleep under the protection of the Sabbath, Nazi guards swarmed through our apartments and hauled possible perpetrators out of bed. (The right ones? The wrong ones? Did anyone care?) They lined them up in the streets, above the screaming of wives and children and neighbors, and shot them in pulses of machine-gun fire. One of the dead was Menachem Linder, a member of our Oneg Shabbat group.

We said Kaddish for him, as we had for the Nazi.

We began piling furniture in front of our doors at night, the furniture we hadn't yet burned for heat. We did not think it would stop the Nazis from barging into our apartment, but perhaps it would slow them down enough to give one or more of us time to make our escape.

In May, the dandelions started pushing up through the cracks in the crumbling sidewalks. According to Lieberman, our resident ornithologist, a pair of sparrow hawks had made a nest near the spire of Saint Augustine's, which he could see over the wall with his contraband binoculars. This was interesting, he said, as nesting hawks rarely set up in urban areas, but he imagined that the increased number of rats running around the streets made excellent pickings for a pair of birds of prey.

It was now generally understood, at least among those of us in the Oneg Shabbat group, that Jews from the East were being rounded up en masse and deported to camps even farther east. We did not understand the logic behind the deportations—which Jews went, which Jews stayed—but we assumed that any Jewish community with the misfortune to stand in the German army's way was doomed to liquidation. As for ourselves, the Germans seemed to be over and done with us; they'd taken Poland, they'd rounded us up, they kept us penned like animals, then they seemed to lose interest. What would the use be in rounding us up and deporting us, anyway? We stood in nobody's way; we asked for nothing.

In May, we celebrated Arkady's thirteenth birthday. Rafel gave him two pairs of socks he'd traded for on the outside. Sala and Emil wrote him a poem that rhymed, and he blushed throughout its recital. They would have a Bar Mitzvah for him another year.

In May, we received a surprise delivery of margarine and saccharin at the Aid Society, and for a few weeks all the soup tasted strangely sweet and oily.

In May, Sala came to my room eight nights in a row. I told her I loved her. I tried to learn new languages in which to tell her. Sometimes I made up my own languages. Sometimes she whispered back, "Ton nit haltn." *Don't stop.*

"I won't stop. I love you."

"It is so silly, the things you say."

"You don't believe me?"

She was on top of me, my palms on her bony hips. She had lost so much weight that her body almost looked like a child's: tiny breasts, straight, flat stomach, collarbones like knives. Her eyes were closed. I closed mine too, felt her move up and down and heard her whimper.

"I love you," I told her in English.

"I know," she said in Yiddish. "Ikh veys."

In June, we had a small heat wave and found ourselves seeking fresh air up on the roof, away from the grime of the street. Rafel and I picked through the remains of Filip's small shed and all his wondrous animals. "These are pretty amazing," Rafel said, picking them up and turning them around. Filip had refined his technique over the months of confinement, finding small colorful stones and gluing them, somehow, to the places his figurines should have eyes and mouths. He had carved delicate scales down the backs of his snakes and dinosaurs and dragons, had used the natural curve and coloration of the wood he found to amplify the characteristics of each beast he created.

And in the back of his shed was still his small jar of sucking candies. Rafel and I shared them, lying on our backs on that roof, anticipating each time a fresh breeze blew the sweat from our faces. How wonderful was the taste of blackberry in our mouths, of licorice, of raspberry, of lime.

In July, I came home from the Aid Society to find Emil sitting in the kitchen with a look on his face I had never seen before. Sala was across from him, looking down at the table.

He had discovered us. Of course he had; we'd been waiting for it.

"Paskow," he said, "sit down."

Well, I thought, *I would confess it all, but I wouldn't apologize. I loved his wife. I was in love with his wife. It wasn't right, of course, and I was sorry for any hurt I caused, but I was not sorry that, in these desperate circumstances, I had found love.* I found my gut clenching. I would not have the courage to say these things out loud. I would pack my things and skitter away, homeless until I found somewhere new to squat, missing Sala, missing the desperate pathetic nature of my old life.

"Paskow," Emil said sharply. I sat, kept my eyes on my lap. "Deportations are coming."

"Excuse me?" I looked up at him then.

"The Judenrat has been asked to make lists of Jews here in the ghetto to be deported east."

"I don't understand," I said, although I did.

"Jews will be gathered and taken to the train station on Strawki Street. From there, they will be transported to some sort of relocation camp in eastern Poland."

"And what then?"

Emil looked at me bleakly.

"What will happen, Emil?" Sala asked.

"We don't expect them to survive," he said.

"Why not?" she asked. "Where do they go?"

Emil was silent, as he could not bear to tell her.

Finally, I spoke. "They go to execution chambers," I said. "Where they are gassed."

"What?"

"Yes," I said. "As soon as they get off the trains."

"This can't be right. Emil? Is this right?"

"Yes," he said. "It is."

"I don't believe that. It doesn't make sense," she said. "Why can't they just shoot people? Why take them somewhere?"

"Efficiency, I suppose," Emil said. "It's easier to kill many people at once in the execution chambers. Or maybe it's something else. Who knows what's in these monsters' minds?"

"But it doesn't make sense."

"Of course it doesn't."

"And you're supposed to make a list?"

"Well," Emil said, "really they want Czerniaków to make the list, but he has asked a few of us to help figure out what to do. How to respond. It's rather impossible."

"Well, just don't," Sala said. "Don't cooperate."

"If we don't give them names, they will shoot us and our families." He looked away from her face, out the window.

The cold stone in my gut split apart into a thousand sharp pieces.

"*Nein,*" Sala said, and the echoes of Mariam Lescovec's no rang in my head, the no of every mother in the ghetto.

But who were we to say no? Or, rather, we could say yes, or no, or nothing, and none of it would matter. All this language, all this talking, years of talking under the pretense that somebody cared enough to listen.

Emil lifted himself, heavily, out of his seat. He went to the window. "For now, they are sparing workers, members of the council, Jewish police," he said. "So we have some time."

"But only if you turn in your neighbors," I said.

"Correct," Emil said.

"*Nein,*" Sala whispered.

"Czerniaków has a day to comply. He has already pled for the lives of several residents—the spouses of factory workers, the sanitation workers. Some of the medical staff. The Germans have agreed to spare them. For now."

"What about children?"

"They are showing no mercy to the children," Emil said. "They want to include the orphanages in the first deportation."

"The orphanages! But why? What harm are these orphans to anybody?"

"It's not that they're a harm, Sala. It's that they're Jewish."

"Yes, but—"

"Please stop looking for logic where there isn't any."

How could we have been such fools not to know this was coming? Even now, even after all that we had lived through, how could we have not known?

"I just don't understand why they would do this. Why are they doing this?"

"Stop asking me questions, I beg you," Emil said. "Please. This is horrific enough without your stupid questions."

At this, she started to sob, and Emil just looked at her, disgusted, and it was all I could do not to take her in my arms, but of course I couldn't take her in my arms in front of her husband. I touched her heaving back, once, and she shook me off. I retreated to my room then, took the necklace from the floorboards, put it back in my satchel.

NOWAK WAS AT his station at the Twarda Street gate. He was smoking a foul brand of cigarette, smoke pluming around his face. He laughed as I winced.

"You can't get Chesterfields anymore, friend," he said. "These are the best they have."

"Is it true they're planning on sending us east to be killed?" I asked.

"What?" He scratched the back of his neck with his free hand. He had a dumb, thoughtful look on his doughy face. "I haven't heard that. Of course, I have no particular inside information. I put on a uniform,

I stand here all day, I go home. I don't know more than what they tell me."

"You haven't heard anything?"

"That they're planning on killing all of you? No," he said. "I hope they don't do it. I need this job."

"I need papers," I said, and reached inside my satchel with trembling fingers. I would do this. I would trust Nowak with the only thing of value I had left. With my life.

"If you've come to try to bribe Duda, you're a little late."

I removed my hand without the necklace in it.

"Your friend was shot for double dealing two days ago," he said.

"Henryk?"

"Yes, indeed," Nowak said, squinting through cigarette smoke. "Playing both sides," he said. "It's not a good idea." He dropped the cigarette to the ground, blunted it out with his shoe. Gave me a knowing half smile. The weight of his pistol made his belt sag under his belly. In a different life, he would have been the guy who wouldn't stop talking at the tram stop.

Henryk was dead.

"What happened?" I asked.

"So on the one hand," Nowak said, grinning, glad to be the guy with the inside information, "he secured all these apartments for Germans. Nice ones for the important people, small ones like yours for the more minor functionaries. You know, he fixed things between the German bigwigs and the Polish civilians. Bribed them, of course, so that he could stay in his own place."

"I didn't realize—"

"Why do you think he wanted you out of your place?"

"I didn't think about it too much," I said.

"He needed as much real estate as he could get to stay one step ahead of them. He brokered apartments, country houses, estates. Everything. First he took them from Jews. Then he took them from Poles killed on the front."

"Why didn't the Germans find their own places to live?"

"They don't like dealing with most Polish people."

"So Nazis live in my apartment."

"Sure," Nowak said. "What did you think?"

Thinking about my couch, my bed, my books, a Nazi kicking off his big boots on my rug, fixing himself dinner in my kitchen, on my plates, washing himself in my bathroom . . .

"You're going to vomit?"

"No."

"You look like you're going to vomit," Nowak said.

"I'm not," I said. "What happened to Henryk?"

"Well," he said, pausing to light another cigarette. "The same time he was acting as a fixer for the Nazis, he was passing on information to the Polish Home Army. You know, who lived where, who was planning what—whatever information he could gather. Papers when he could get them. Which is how he got caught. Some Nazi found him with papers in his briefcase."

"He was caught."

"You always get caught," Nowak said. "They shot him and his whole family at the gate by his house. Grandkids, all of them. Even the dog."

"Jesus," I said. His foul wife. All the children. They must have gotten another Doberman—they always got the same kind of dog.

"The neighbors came out and watched," he said.

"Of course they did."

"Anyway, sorry to share this sad news," he said, but he didn't look particularly sorry, and to tell the truth, neither was I.

Grief? Could I feel grief for them? I did notice that my heart was beating faster, but I thought that was probably just fear.

"That's why I try to keep my head down, you know?" Nowak said. "Just keep my head down and try not to get noticed."

"So you can't get me papers." Well, it had all been a daydream anyway, to escape. You couldn't run when you lived underwater.

"Who says I can't get you papers?"

"I thought you just said—"

"Duda can't get you papers, that's true. But if you've got the money. I can figure something out for you."

"I thought you said you kept your head down."

Nowak blew smoke directly toward my face. "How much money do you have?"

I coughed, reached back into the satchel. The children had, for the most part, stopped paying me for English lessons. Ringelblum hadn't distributed stipends in many months. I had my small salary from the Aid Society, but that was barely enough for a few extra potatoes each week, a tube of toothpaste. I had already traded away almost everything I had of value: What was left now were my tattered clothes, my shoes, the blanket on the bed that I slept on. And this necklace. Which meant nothing to me, really—my wife never even wore it—but might still mean something to the outside world.

I looped the necklace chain around my fist so that Nowak couldn't grab it and showed him the nice fat pearl surrounded by diamonds.

"Huh," he said, looking at my hand. "So that's it, huh?"

"It's worth about twelve thousand zloty." We both stood there, breathing. "You can keep the change," I finally said.

"Of course I'm going to keep the change," he said, stretching out his palm.

"Are you going to help me?"

"I'll get you the papers."

"I need more than papers," I said. "I need transport. I need people on the other side who can get us to Sweden."

"Twelve thousand zloty can get a lot done."

"It's enough to save my life."

"Perhaps," he said, slipping the necklace into a pocket inside his coat. Watching it disappear, I felt dread bloom in me once more: in my heart, I knew I'd never see him or it again, nor papers.

How could I have given it all away so quickly?

What other choice did I have?

"Meet me here the Thursday after next," he said. "I'll have a kennkarte."

"I don't trust you," I said.

"You can trust me or not," Nowak said. "It doesn't matter. I'll be here Thursday. You don't want the papers, someone else will buy them."

"This is my life," I said again.

Nowak shrugged, stomped out his cigarette, lit a new one.

WALKING HOME WITHOUT the necklace, I felt surprisingly light. What was this lightness? It didn't make sense.

And then I realized: I had given it away. I had given everything away. This was the lightness that came with the freedom from hope. I practically floated all the way home.

TWENTY-SIX

"P̲an Paskow!"

"Szifra, is that you? Where have you been?"

She was in front of our building at dawn. In the weeks since I'd seen her, she seemed to have aged ten years. She had circles under her bright-blue eyes and cracked maroon lips. "Busy, busy. Trying to arrange everything so we can go. But every time I think we're ready, there's one more detail."

"Are you safe, Szifra?"

She snorted, and I felt myself turn red, embarrassed to have asked such a stupid question. I noticed she smelled different than she used to—she had once worn a flowery fragrance that smelled expensive. Now she radiated a sort of musky sweatiness, and perhaps even the rankness of alcohol.

"I need you to tell me how to say something. And not to ask questions. I just need to know how to say it in German."

"Of course, Szifra. What?"

For a second, she looked abashed. Thin early sunlight filtered down over the grimy rooftops and disappeared onto the street. The day was still cool, and Szifra wore her camel coat. She dug her hands deep into her pockets.

"How do you say 'I am a virgin'?"

"A virgin?"

"Yes, I need to—"

"But why?"

She scratched her elbow, looked away.

"Szifra?"

She tilted her face up at me so I could look directly into her eyes, crisscrossed with blood vessels, and her pale, tired face.

"Ich bin eine Jungfrau."

"Right, of course," she said, quietly. "Like the Jungfrau Maria."

The Virgin Mary.

"Are you okay, Szifra?"

"The people that are helping me"—she dug her hands deeper into her pockets—"they like virgins."

I would not think about what I saw in my basement classroom. I would not imagine Szifra being passed from Nazi to Nazi like a worn-out doll.

A pale, funny rash had spread across her cheeks. I hadn't noticed it before. "I do it for my brothers, you know," she said, chin tilted up.

"Szifra, please, I'm sure you don't—"

"If it weren't for them—I already have what I need. But I must secure their papers."

"Isn't there another way?"

She gave me that old imperious look. "Of course there is not."

And for a moment we were both quiet. Then she said, "thank you, *Pan* Paskow."

I couldn't let her do this to herself, although I had no idea what to say to make her stay. "Szifra, you don't have to—"

"Thank you, Pan Paskow."

"But Szifra—"

"Danke, Herr Paskow," she said, turning her face from mine and then, after a moment's hesitation, heading down Sienna Street. The smell of her lingered for several seconds after she disappeared.

TWENTY-SEVEN

My brother and I found out that my father had died via a telegram delivered by the neighborhood grocer on a Monday in April 1915. Our father, Leopold Paskow, age thirty-three, was killed somewhere on the front in Russia. Szimon received the telegram at the front door and held it in his hands for a minute or two while the grocer stood there, awkwardly mumbling apologies. It was a beautiful spring afternoon, and the cherry trees were blooming. "Shall we find your mother?" he finally asked.

"Not yet," Szimon said.

"I'm awfully sorry," said the grocer, a nice old man who extended credit to the soldiers' wives in the neighborhood and passed the local kids a free candy every so often from the bowl by the register. "You'll be okay?"

"We'll be okay," Szimon said. He was thirteen then, a sweet kid. He found me in the tiny room we shared, but I had been listening to the conversation—our house was so small that it was easy to hear what was happening at the front door even from our bedroom. I had stopped doing my math sums and was just blinking at the numbers in front of me as they slowly turned illegible.

"You heard?" Szimon asked. I was sixteen but still thin, not yet having grown into myself. I had no hair on my face. I had no Adam's apple. My skin was as smooth as a baby's. And now I was the man of the house.

"I heard."

"How do we tell Eema?" Szimon asked.

"We don't," I said.

Our mother worked as a laundress at the commercial laundry in the middle of Bródno, our small Warsaw suburb. When she came home, her feet ached, her fingers ached, and her cheeks were red from steam. It was my job to have supper prepared. It was Szimon's job to make sure the house was tidy and the mail had been picked up from the post office.

"She'll find out eventually," Szimon said.

"Okay," I said. "But it doesn't have to be today."

So we went about our afternoon chores: I prepared cutlets for dinner while Szimon swept up, then washed the cooking pots as I finished with them. We were quiet, although at some point Szimon said, "I think there's a widow's pension," and I agreed that I thought there was.

Our mother came home at six o'clock, as always, rosy-cheeked and sore. She had frizzy brownish-blondish hair, the same as Szimon and me, and green-brown eyes. It was easy to see how she could have been pretty once, how she was the same woman who had posed, seventeen years earlier, as a lace-covered bride next to her tall mustachioed husband. It was easy to see what had brought them together: they were both attractive then, both optimistic. Although people tended not to smile in wedding photos back then, you could see pleasure in their straightforward stares.

She took off her coat, took off her shoes, kissed us both on the tops of the heads, and thanked us, as she always did, for doing our chores. "Mmm, kotlety. How wonderful. And is there any mail, Szimon?" Meaning, is there any mail from your father?

"Nothing today, Emma."

"Ah, too bad. But then we'll probably hear from him tomorrow. Something to look forward to."

And then we ate our dinner together and cleaned up and read for a bit and went to sleep. Szimon and I avoided each other's eyes.

The next day proceeded the way days usually proceeded: Szimon and I rose before the sun, washed up, and headed to school while our mother, whose shift didn't start until nine, sat with her coffee and the newspaper. We were a bit worried leaving her at home—what if the grocer came by with a condolence delivery?—but there was nothing to be done about it except hope it didn't happen and be glad to be away from her oblivious presence.

That afternoon, when Szimon got the mail, there was an envelope from our father. It enclosed two letters, as it always did: a jolly one for us and a sentimental one for our mother.

"I don't want to read it," Szimon said.

"I will," I said, and saw that it was full of all the usual platitudes and admonishments, to do our schoolwork, help our mother, be brave like the good little soldiers we were.

"Jesus Christ," said Szimon.

My father had gotten his first taste of fighting against the Russians in 1905, went back for more in 1907, and joined up again earlier that year to fight alongside the French and British. He left with the sort of enthusiasm with which children went to the amusement park, despite my mother's crying, her pleading, her literal shredding of the blouse she was wearing.

"You must stop this, Regina," he had said to her. "You must stop." We were at the train station; he was wearing his uniform and his pistol, and she sat next to him, shredding her blouse.

My mother's tragedy: she couldn't see that our father loved war even more than he loved her or his children (which was a reasonable amount, certainly—it was his love for war that was unreasonable). In the years there were no wars to fight, he tried to bide his time in other arenas: he was an able-enough mechanic (but put off by the ceaseless anti-Semitism of his coworkers) and, believe it or not, a decent cook. But only in his uniform did he really feel like himself. Whenever there was a call to battle, he was the first in his armament to respond.

Our mother came home that day, saw there was a letter from our father, and hummed happily to herself throughout dinner. She always saved his letters to read to herself in bed; they were her reward for getting through another day.

The rest of the week went on similarly: Wednesday, Thursday, Friday. When we went to pick up supplies early Friday afternoon, before Shabbos, the grocer asked us how our mother was doing, and we told him, truthfully, that she was well. He put a bottle of cherry liqueur in our grocery bag, on the house.

We lit candles that night, ate the challah our mother had baked early that morning, before her shortened Friday shift. Saturday it rained; we stayed inside. Sunday was six days since we had heard the news about our father, and we needed candles, soap, and flour. The grocer opened for a few hours after church on Sundays for the convenience of his Jewish customers.

"I'll go for you, Eema."

"Oh, I could use the walk," she said. "Besides, you two have been such good kids all week. Go find your friends at the park."

"No, really. I'll . . ."

But she had her coat already; she was walking down our dusty street. Szimon and I looked at each other and the door closing behind her. We gave her seven minutes, then followed her down the street, keeping a careful distance, past the stumpy houses that lined our unpaved road, a right past the football field, a left past the grammar school, and the pond, and the church. We stood behind the ornamental cross on the church's lawn, where we had a view of the grocer's door. We watched her go in. We waited. For what felt like the entirety of our lives, we waited.

And then we saw her come out, collapse on the sidewalk, sobbing a sort of mute sob, and we rushed to her, and we held her, and we told her we were sorry, and none of us were ever the same.

Name: Adam Paskow
Date: July 23, 1942
Age: 43
Time: 2:00 p.m.

I find myself hiding from today's events by scribbling in this notebook. This is cowardly, I know, the hiding, and perhaps I shouldn't write any of it down for posterity. Perhaps I should pretend I spent the day distributing false working papers or hiding children in attics or shoving as many people as possible under holes in the walls to imaginary safety on the outside. But I have done none of these things. I have simply sat here at the kitchen table, pretending that what is happening outside isn't happening.

Yesterday we saw the posters: We were to report to the Umschlagplatz for resettlement to the East. Those who reported voluntarily would be rewarded with two kilos of bread and a kilo of jam.

Those who didn't comply voluntarily would be forcibly removed.

And this morning, people started lining up! Not because they were fools, but because the promise of two kilos of bread, to a starving person, is more powerful than the fear of death.

Still, there were not enough volunteers, and so, as I write, the Germans are dragging away the most miserable among us: the starving on the sidewalks, the homeless, the clearly crazy. It is easy for the Nazis to fill their rolls from among the destitute, many of whom put up no resistance whatsoever. I have even seen Nazis be surprisingly gentle, lifting a woman up by the arm, helping a faltering old man stand. Of course, they are also more than willing to club anyone who resists.

And off they march.

Meanwhile, the rest of us—those whose names have escaped notice, for whatever reason—are left to go about our business. I need something to do to keep my hands and mind busy, as I have no shift at the soup kitchen today, nor am I scheduled to teach any classes. And, to be honest, even if I were, I wouldn't be able to do a decent job. How would the students learn with the begging and screaming on the streets above our basement classroom? How could we talk about poetry, about anything, with the German shouting, and the gunshots, and the trucks rattling our streets and our buildings? And then the terrifying quiet.

It is said that once at the Umschlagplatz, deportees are lined up, counted, and counted again before the trains pull in. Their names are checked against lists. Why? What makes one Meyer Huffberg, one Shlomo Brach, one Isaak Nurenbaum different from any other? Are we nameless herds, or are we being specifically selected for murder? Who do we matter to, exactly?

The Germans call this the Grossaktion. In English, the grand action. In Yiddish, the groys kamf.

Frankly, I do not know why any of it is surprising to me—I had more warning than most—yet I find myself shocked each time I raise my head and look out the window. The streams of trucks plowing down our dented roads. The lines of smartly uniformed gendarmes. The people being dragged by the armpits. The people walking slowly next to their Nazi captors. The people wailing, begging, shoving employment cards in the gendarmes' faces to prove their worth. There are 6,000 of us going today. I assume the same will happen tomorrow.

6,000 people is a lot of people, more than used to live in many of our small towns and villages. 6,000 people is hours and hours of work to move. 6,000 people is enough to support a rabbi and a synagogue, a few schools, a grocer, a milkman, a confectioner, a dentist, a clinic, a clothing store, a funeral home. A small planet.

This morning, as I walked through the ghetto for my pail of soup, I saw the Nazis cordoning off a building on Chłodna Street. On my way back, they were removing its inhabitants at gunpoint, forcing their hands behind their necks. Even the children. The ones who stumbled were shot. The mothers who wailed were shot.

Sala Wiskoff, my housemate, asked me what I had seen outside, and I told her nothing, because it was too difficult to find the words.

(I still have some soup in my pail; for the first time in quite some time, I have lost my appetite.)

At two in the afternoon, the streets here are emptier than they have been the entire year and a half we've lived here, emptier than they were on Yom Kippur or Rosh Hashanah, emptier than at the height of the typhoid epidemic. Those who have a house to hide in are hiding in their houses. Those who do not are in the public buildings, the basements, squirreled away in attics or on rooftops.

I will admit that as I have collected testimonies for this archive, I have not always understood what the point of the archive was, or I have seen it in the mildest of terms: that the Oneg Shabbat group has been creating a collective portrait of Polish Jews at this peculiar moment in our history so that we remember what really happened, inscribing the truth of what we went through so that liberation wouldn't erase our memories.

But now I realize that we are creating a portrait of Polish

Jews at the end of our history—not one peculiar moment, but the very last moment.

It is yet another surprise that it has taken me so long to understand that. When this is over, there will be no more of us. Even among the survivors, should there be any survivors, there will be no more of us.

Does it matter if I write of our thousand-year history on this land? If I write of the culture we have created? The literature, the theater, the science, the economies, the mutual aid societies, the customs, the friendships, the discoveries, the paintings, the newspapers, the cemeteries? It will all be gone, ground into the dust. I am watching it now, out my window, being ground to dust under the wheels of the Nazis' trucks.

And as I watch, I find myself thinking, of all things, about language.

Although it has roots as a West Germanic language, English has stolen words and spellings and grammatical constructs from so many languages from around the world. Pajama from Hindi. Alcohol from Arabic. What was once a minor language spoken on a remote island is now the language of the most powerful nation in the world, with a vocabulary to suit: bayonet, blockade, bulwark. I love English for this reason, for its mutability, its ability to change and survive. I love it for its forward momentum. I love it for its willingness to compromise and be stronger for it.

And, of course, I love Polish, the language I started learning as a child, the language in which I conducted the day-to-day business of my happy life. This was the language my father used to speak with me, the language of the country he died for. Polish is the language in which I earned my money and paid my taxes and slept with my wife.

But I want to tell you that the first language I ever heard was Yiddish. Whispered in endearments from my mother: bubbeleh, sheffeleh, meyn neshama. When we were babies, when we were very young boys, Yiddish was the only language in the world, and it was entirely a language of sweetness and home.

My thoughts, rid of any ability to imagine my fellow man, now turn only toward Yiddish as I watch the German trucks crush our streets and our people under their wheels.

If I somehow manage to leave this place, I will conduct the rest of my life in English or in Polish (or in French, or in Hebrew, or even, God forbid, in German). And if I die, my Yiddish will die with me. Will anyone miss it or remember it? Will anyone miss or remember me?

Nein, nein, nein.

Date: July 23, 1942
Time: 11:30 p.m.

I am continuing this diary entry to report that the five inhabitants of this apartment have returned at the end of a busy and miserable day to their respective spaces here: Emil and Sala Wiskoff are huddling in the living room, which is where they sleep, and their boys are in the large bedroom. Tonight, Sala has forced them to bathe as best as possible and eat some of the bread she has been squirreling away: she felt it was important for them to have some sense of normalcy. However, as soon as they were dispatched to their room, Emil Wiskoff, an adviser to the Judenrat, told us that Adam Czerniaków, the lead politician of the ghetto, unable to save the orphans of Śliska Street from deportation, killed himself with a cyanide tablet and left his body for the Nazis to find.

TWENTY-EIGHT

And yet . . .

Each of my regular students survived the first Grossaktion. In fact, six of them showed up the next day, strangely unmoved by the deportations surrounding them; their parents had assured them that they weren't going to be affected, and that was that, as they still trusted what their parents told them. Further Grossaktions would be taking place every day, but right now the Nazis were concentrating on anyone they suspected of political scheming, plus the everyday vagrants and the homeless. My students, children of the once-upon-a-time elite, guarded by work papers and some sort of civil authority, were cushioned by whatever luck their old life had afforded them or whatever their families could still do for them. I looked at their wizened faces—Charlotte, Roman, Eli, Jakub, Rafel, Arkady—and felt an almost smothering love for all of them, even if I should have resented them for their blithe privilege. They weren't innocent; they knew what was happening all around them. But they were not insensitive to their fortune, and they were going to use it to learn English. Or solidarity, or whatever I could offer.

(I could offer them only the best of what I had, as a teacher and a person.)

And so we spent that day memorizing a favorite silly poem of mine, "The Owl and the Pussy-Cat," which had absolutely no relation to war or death or health or luck, but only love and dancing and music.

"What is a 'runcible spoon'?" Charlotte asked, tripping over the pronunciation.

"I have no idea," I said. "I don't think 'runcible' is a real word. The poet—his name was Edward Lear—he liked to make things up."

"It is a real word," said Rafel. "It means 'made of diamonds.'" He was leaning back on his hands on the basement floor, the way that Szifra used to.

"I don't think that's right," I said. "Where did you learn that?"

"I just know," Rafel said. "I'm certain. 'Made of diamonds.'"

"Horsecrap," Arkady said, but Rafel was steadfast.

"That's what it means," he said, and his face was almost frighteningly still and changeless, and so I decided that that is what *runcible* means: "made of diamonds."

"I think I learned it when I was a baby."

"Horsecrap," Arkady said again, in Yiddish, and then, admirably, in English.

"Think what you want."

"I will."

"You do that."

"Enough! Time to work."

Together we recited:

"'Dear Pig, are you willing to sell for one shilling
Your ring?' Said the Piggy, 'I will.'
So they took it away, and were married next day
By the Turkey who lives on the hill.
They dined on mince, and slices of quince,
Which they ate with a runcible spoon;
And hand in hand, on the edge of the sand,

They danced by the light of the moon,
The moon,
The moon,
They danced by the light of the moon.'"

"Children, isn't that fun to say out loud?"

The students looked at me as though I were a bit pathetic, as four of them were teenagers now and far too mature for silly poetry like this, but also they didn't want to hurt my feelings.

"Come on, everyone. Didn't you like that?"

"Pan Paskow, what is 'quince'?" Charlotte asked, sparing me by changing the subject.

"It's like an apple," I said. "I think. I've never had one."

"Are they red?"

"Yes," I said, though really I had no idea.

"Do they eat them in England?" she asked in Polish.

"English."

"In England?"

"I imagine they do."

She looked wistful, England being a place she knew out of fairy tales and the poetry I had been teaching her for months.

"Our father says that England's going to surrender soon," said Roman casually, biting the corner of a fingernail.

"Why would he say that?" I asked.

"It's just his intuition."

"Then your father's a moron," said Eli, who had been fatherless for almost two years.

Roman shrugged. "He reads a lot of newspapers."

"Do the newspapers give actual military updates?" Eli asked. "Do they predict the future? Or are they full of propaganda and lies?"

Roman shrugged again.

"Propaganda," Eli said. "And lies."

"It doesn't matter anyway," Roman said. "We're going to escape here soon. My father's trying to get us papers."

"We already *have* papers," Jakub said.

"Shush, idiot, " Eli said.

"If you have papers, why are you still here?"

"We don't actually have them have them," Jakub said. "Szifra's picking them up tomorrow, I think. Or the next day. She has a connection."

"Jesus, Jakub, shut up!" Eli was apoplectic.

"What does it matter?" Jakub said, petulant. "We're leaving in two days."

"Jakub, *shut up.*"

"Really?" Arkady asked. "You're leaving?"

"What," Eli said, now turning his glare on his classmate. "You're going to miss us?"

"No, I just—"

"Jealous?"

Arkady shrugged.

"Ha, you're jealous."

"I could leave if I wanted," Arkady said.

Rafel looked at him. "You wouldn't," he whispered.

"You have papers?" Eli said.

"I could get some."

"Liar."

"All right, everyone," I said. "Enough with all that. There's no need for papers, because, no offense to your father, Roman, but the tide is turning in the war and Germany in fact will be surrendering soon. Not England. I read the papers too. The English papers. So I know what's going on." (I had never been such a good liar before the war.) "So why don't we try reciting our poem again one more time?"

The kids just blinked at me.

"That's what the English papers say?" said Arkady.

"Which English papers do you read?"

"The *Times*," I said, trying to remember English newspaper names. "The *Herald*."

"How do you get them?" Eli was suspicious.

"I have my ways."

"And that's really what they say?"

"Yes," I said. "A German surrender soon. Are you ready to recite the poem?"

"What are your ways?"

"Class?" I said. "The poem."

"What are your ways, Pan Paskow?"

"Connections. Znajomości," I said. "Let's go."

"Connections from where?"

I started: "'The Owl and the Pussy-cat went to sea in a beautiful pea-green boat . . .'"

Silence.

I repeated: "'The Owl and the Pussy-cat went to sea in a beautiful pea-green boat . . .'"

Silence.

"Children? If you please. Class isn't over."

"What are your connections, Pan Paskow?"

I looked away from their anxious expressions. "A secret. I'll get in terrible trouble if I tell you. So let's just recite our poem."

"But—"

"Truly. I wish I could tell you, children. I do. But I can't risk it."

So finally, wearily, they chimed in, first Charlotte, then Rafel, then the rest:

> "'They took some honey, and plenty of money
> Wrapped up in a five pound note.'"

And as the owl and the pussycat decided to marry, and found the pig who would sell them the ring, the children recited a bit more energetically, their words a half beat after my own. (For, of course, they were only repeating what I said, having neither the skill nor the will to memorize a nonsense poem in an hour's time.)

"Shall we do it again?" I asked, and they agreed, so once more we took the owl and the pussycat on their journey across the ocean. It was amusing, or at the very least distracting.

"No offense," said Eli, "but that's not a very good poem."

"It's neither good nor bad," I said. "It just is. A poem, I mean. It's supposed to make you smile."

"Why do you have to be so rotten all the time, Eli?" Charlotte said.

"Why do you have to be such a princess?"

"Doesn't it matter to you that nobody likes you?" Charlotte said.

"Children, enough."

"What," Charlotte said to me. "Do you want me to repeat myself in English?"

I tried to remember what would happen at the Lyceum in the face of this sort of insurrection, but I could think of nothing beyond my mother trying to broker an ineffectual peace between my brother and me when we were small. "Charlotte, apologize to Eli."

She shook her head primly.

"It doesn't matter anyway," Eli said. "I never have to see any of you people again." He grabbed his brother's hand. "Come on, Jakub. We're going."

"Now?"

"Now."

Jakub shrugged. "Goodbye," he said to us in English, and we watched them head toward the stairs. I did not try to stop them.

"Goodbye," Rafel said to the empty space where they'd been sitting.

For several seconds, we were quiet.

"Pan Paskow," said Charlotte, who seemed satisfied. "Could we say the poem one more time?"

"Really?"

"Yes," Charlotte said.

As we began reciting the poem again, we heard the boys pound up the stairs, reach the door at the top, heard it open heavily and then shut. For a moment, the noise of the street penetrated our classroom. Would I ever see Eli and Jakub again? Would I remember them? I hoped I would not; I knew I would.

"Are you going to get papers, Pan Paskow? Are you going to leave?"

I thought of my runcible necklace. "No," I said.

AFTER CLASS, IT struck me like a stone to the eye that I had met their parents once, at a school function to celebrate the Lyceum's one-hundredth anniversary. The father, tall and imperious. The mother, blond and thin. A fur coat. A fancy ring. *Hello, hello, how do you do? Ah, yes, you're the English teacher. Our daughter, Szifra, says so many nice things about you. Yes, she's a lovely girl. Yes, yes, very bright.* No way to look at them and think these people could be Jews. A slight German accent, even, in the mother's Polish. A beaded handbag. A silk cravat. Long, thin hands that barely brushed mine when I reached to shake. The father, drinking vodka in a small crystal glass. Around the mother's neck, a necklace, runcible.

TWENTY-NINE

There was a homemade sleep remedy making the rounds of the ghetto, sold by an underground pharmacist who refused to divulge his ingredients but promised that everything he used was to the highest standards and that, anyway, anybody who asked questions didn't deserve his magic medicine. The stuff was sold in small jars and smelled like rotting pears, but according to those brave enough to try it, it really did knock a person out for a few hours, and in these troubled times a few hours of rest seemed worth the possibility of inadvertent poisoning. Emil, who was now advising the new head of the Judenrat, Marc Lichtenbaum, had taken to slugging down a jar of the potion most nights around ten, and was snoring by ten thirty. Sala would find me then, sometimes in bed and sometimes, now that it was hot, on the roof, where we would curl up in the remnants of Filip's shed.

"I cannot believe I am naked in public."

"We're hardly in public," I said, although the ghetto did spread out below us, and above us were birds and fighter planes.

"I don't even care anymore," she said, sitting on top of me, straddling me, and anyone could have found us, and nobody ever did. I brought her face to mine and kissed her and felt great relief that I was never too weary to want her.

Meanwhile, early in the morning and again in the afternoon, Germans rounded people up in their apartments or in the streets. It was less and less clear why some were taken and others weren't; according to Ringelblum, the Nazis' goal was to remove everyone who couldn't demonstrably provide some service. But what was service? That, too, felt unclear—service was feeding the hungry or working in the German factories, or guarding the prisons, except that a few of the prison guards were hauled off without any explanation, and one of the women who had helped organize shifts at the Aid Society was removed in the middle of the lunch rush. Service was certainly the Judenrat, which meant that Emil and Sala were safe, but for how long? When would the Nazis decide the Judenrat knew too much?

Early in the morning, in the narrow bed in the maid's room, Sala and I tried to figure out what to do next. We went over and over the possibilities: We could try to wait out the Grossaktion—or at least Sala and Emil could, with the boys—and perhaps in the meantime I could find a more secure job at a factory. Or maybe I could apply to be a member of the Jewish police. But that was insane; I was no more a policeman than I was a housewife. Emil could possibly get me a job with the Judenrat, but I had no qualifications; I wasn't a lawyer or a bureaucrat. Perhaps, I mused, I could try to sneak out of the ghetto altogether.

"You would leave me?" Sala asked.

"I would never—"

"I'm sorry, that's selfish. Of course you should leave me."

I hadn't told her about the necklace, mostly out of shame—shame that I had owned something so precious, shame that I had so carelessly gambled with it.

"I would never leave you, Sala."

"Are you kidding? Of course you would," she said. "If there was a chance for you to get out of here and survive—"

"But there isn't."

"You'd make it on the outside, wouldn't you? You're kind of blond."

"Barely," I said.

She perched on top of me, ran her fingers through my hair.

"I think you're kind of blond." She buried her face in my hair, kissing my scalp.

"Come with me," I said.

She laughed dryly, kissed me on the mouth. Both of our mouths tasted permanently sour, and I had learned to love Sala's sour taste.

"I'm not kidding," I said.

"I can't run away with you."

"Why not?"

"My husband."

"Forget about him."

She sighed, rolled over so that she was next to me instead of on top of me. I preferred her on top of me. "My children," she said.

"We'll take them."

"Oh, Adam," she said. "No matter what other kind of miserable woman I am, I'm not the kind of woman who runs away with her lover and her children and leaves her husband to die."

"You make it sound so sinister," I said.

"What else would you call it?" she said, and kissed me again with her sour mouth.

"What if something happens to him. Then would you go?"

"Adam!" she said, sounding halfway outraged, and I knew I should change tacks, but it was hard to stop the fantasizing now that I had allowed myself to start: Sala and me, somewhere on the outside (Stockholm, Palestine, New York City, the moon), together, doing things that normal people did, the things I remembered normal people doing. Lying together like this every night. Clean sheets, clean bodies.

"I'm just saying that bad things happen to people here all the time," I said.

She smacked me on my side. "Stop."

"I don't want to."

"I love my husband," she said, but she said it while she was naked next to me, so it didn't sting.

"Okay," I said, putting her finger in my mouth.

"Enough," she said, and rolled away.

So I put it out of my mind: Sala in a clean dress, neat shoes, a bedroom with a bed big enough for two people, a record on the record player, a nice stew on the stove, outside the sounds of birds chirping, no Germans, no Emil, brushed teeth. But I stored the image before I put it away so that I could close my eyes and return to it any time I wanted.

"I can't hurt my children," she said.

We were quiet for a while. The ghetto had become noisier at night— people wandered the streets, wailing, like figures out of some biblical story. Curfew didn't seem to matter anymore. They wailed so loudly it was as though they were inside the room with us. But if we closed a window, the room became unbearably hot.

"I honestly don't care what happens to me, but I will do whatever it takes to save my kids," she said. "I will bribe whoever I need to bribe. I will hurt whoever I need to hurt," she said. "They will not get on that train."

"I know," I said.

"You don't," she said. "You're not a parent. I don't mean to be cruel, but there's no way you could know."

"But I do know."

She propped herself up on an elbow. "I will dig holes in this earth and hide them underground until this is over. I will smuggle them in cargo ships to England. I will do anything. I will kill anyone who tries to take them. With my bare hands."

"The English newspapers say the war will end soon," I blurted, repeating what I had told my students, what had made them stop talking.

"What are you talking about?"

"The English newspapers," I said. "The *Times*, the *Herald*."

"That's not what Emil says," she said.

Ashamed, I went quiet.

"Adam . . ."

"I'll help you," I said.

"How?"

"I'll get them out of here," I said. "It's possible." And even though I was still ashamed, I told her, "I had a necklace. It was valuable. I bribed one of the guards." And immediately, I was overcome: That necklace might have been worth enough for papers for Sala, for her children, even for Emil, and I had used it all for myself, just given it away. If I had been savvier about it, if I had been a consummate trader, like Filip . . .

Rotten. I was rotten.

"You bribed a guard for passage out of here?"

"For papers," I said.

"Is he trustworthy?"

"I have no idea," I said. "Probably not."

"It doesn't matter," she said. "I mean, for you it matters, but my children don't have papers. You couldn't get them out of here anyway."

"Maybe we could find a forger."

"We're out of money," she said. She closed her eyes. The moon was bright through the narrow window in the maid's room, shining on her thin face. Her eyebrows were sparse, her nose was narrow, and her lips were cracked. Small veins had appeared and broken across her nose. I didn't know why she was so beautiful to me.

"We'll find you money."

"Do you have any more necklaces?"

"We'll find you money. Somehow. I promise."

"Stop," she said.

I kissed her shoulder. Outside, the wailing seemed to grow louder.

"Are you going to go?" she asked, her eyes closed. "I want you to go."

For some reason, that did sting.

"I wouldn't leave without you."

"That's insane," she said. "If you have papers, you have to go."

"I wouldn't."

"Promise me you'd go."

I didn't say anything.

"If I had papers," she said, "I would pack my children up and go, and I wouldn't look back."

"Really?" I asked.

"Really," she said. "I would never look back."

How awful it was to be left by the only two women I had ever loved in my life. Even though Sala's leaving me was only theoretical. Even though it seemed quite clear, with her husband and children tied around her neck like weights, that she would never leave.

"I love you," I said, in English.

She was crying now. I wiped a tear from under her eyes.

"I love you," I said again, still in English. Then, in Polish: "I love you."

She shrugged her shoulders. She stopped crying. "I love you too," she said in Yiddish. "But if you have the chance to get out of here, promise me you'll take it and run."

THIRTY

Although the ghetto's population was decreasing by six thousand souls a day, the streets seemed busier than ever: people trading the last of their possessions, smuggling themselves out of the gates, finding forgers to create working papers or false Polish kennkartes. (Never particularly useful on the Aryan side, but maybe, maybe, enough to get you through the gates.) More posters kept appearing—the reward for resettlement was now three kilos of bread—and that was enough for the people who would not believe that the rumors were true of what actually awaited them in the East. There were lines at the Umschlagplatz every day.

In our house, meanwhile, we were starting to fray. Emil looked more and more wan, his hefty body bent with the pressure of negotiating a new list of deportees every day. His face had broken out in a strange rash, and he was short with his wife and children. He smelled, always, like rotten pears. Sometimes I heard him calling for his mother, not even in his sleep, but just sitting at the table: "Bitte, Mamma, helf mikh, bitte." His mother had been hit on the head twice in front of his eyes, had fallen down dead in front of him; still he could never imagine what the Nazis had in store for the rest of us. Which was not his fault, but simply a failure of his imagination. (Who among us could have ever imagined?)

Shipments of wheat and cabbage and potatoes and oil still came into the ghetto on trucks; Ringelblum still begged his associates in New York to send whatever supplies they could. And now, with the draining population, there was, for the rest of us, a little more to eat: Two slices of bread each, sometimes margarine. Cabbage stew. Onion soup. Did we feel guilty that we were less hungry because our brethren were dead? I didn't know about everyone else, but for me, I ate my bread with gusto.

In the hours between Grossaktion movements, I finished my shift at the Aid Society and headed to my classroom an hour early; it was a startlingly warm afternoon, and I looked forward to the coolness of the basement. I was wearing what was left of my decent clothing: a worn white shirt with the sleeves rolled up, gray pants that had gone shiny at the knees. My shoes had holes in the toes, and I felt the grime of the ghetto street push up against my socks. The sun beat down on my head. I felt derelict, disgusting. I understood why someone would give it all up for a few loaves of bread.

The door to the basement felt heavier than usual. I pushed it against my shoulder and was met with a foul smell—a dead-animal smell, like a rat or perhaps a dog. How would a dog get down there? I pulled my shirt up against my nose and walked down the stairs thinking, *God, why now?* Class started in an hour. I would never be able to hold class in this stink.

The light had burned out, and it took me a moment to adjust to the dimness, but then the moment passed and I saw something on the floor. It was a form, a form of a body, a woman's body. A woman I knew. I stepped back, almost screamed, bit my tongue in time.

She was barefoot, wearing torn stockings. She was wearing her beautiful camel coat. Her blue eyes were open, her neck bent at an unnatural angle, her chin jutting up toward the ceiling. Her blond hair perfectly curled. How long had she been down here? The smell was wretched.

Across her clear, pale forehead, someone had scrawled, in black ink, in Yiddish: ZOYNE.

Across her beautiful coat, someone had scrawled the same thing in Polish: DZIWKA. To make the point perfectly clear.

Slut. Slut.

A slow chill started at my fingers and spread from my hands up my back and neck. Poor tough, stupid girl. Poor Szifra. She had been my student a million years ago at the Lyceum, showed up every day in her neat blue uniform. I had known her since she was twelve years old.

Keeping my shirt pulled up over my nose, I bent down next to her, put my finger to her neck, even though it was ridiculous. I had seen, by now, enough dead people to know. But still I put my finger to her neck and waited. Her neck was cold and still.

(Szifra, walking down the street, casually, with her Nazi. Szifra eating a torte with whipped cream and drinking water out of a crystal glass. She should have known nobody gets away with such treason for so long.)

Why was she wearing her camel coat? It was the middle of summer.

Holding my breath, I unbuttoned the coat and reached inside to where I thought there might be a pocket. There was indeed a pocket right there, in the satin lining. And in that pocket, as I thought there might be, as though I dreaded there might be, were two perfectly authentic gray Polish kennkartes for two boys, Jan and Piotr Krasinski, ages ten and thirteen. Birthdays, places of birth, region, religion. And, where the photos of Jan and Piotr should have been, small square photos of Jakub and Eli, Szifra's brothers.

Carefully, I rebuttoned her coat. I sat back on my heels. I did not think. I instructed myself: *Don't think.* I put the kennkartes in my satchel and hurried up the stairs.

I did not think to stop to say Kaddish, even though I had said it for a Nazi and for Jews I barely knew.

On the street, as the Germans were beginning their afternoon deportation rounds, I found a member of the Jewish police and quickly explained what I had discovered in my classroom. He listened calmly, unsurprised and probably unable to be surprised. "You're sure she's dead?"

"I am."

"Then what would you like me to do?" he asked.

"Well, isn't there . . . ?"

He waited. "Yes?"

I suppose I'd expected an investigation, or at least a feint at an investigation. But, of course, who would have the resources to investigate? Besides, Szifra could have been killed by any one of us, anyone who had seen her eat her meal, drink her water, look down at the rest of us imperiously. How could you search for a killer when everyone in the entire ghetto could be a suspect? Besides, everyone in the entire ghetto would eventually face punishment—if not for this crime, then for anything else they'd done since the moment they were conceived.

"Well?" the policeman asked.

I sighed. The policeman looked at me expectantly. "Can you get someone to remove the body?"

"The hearses will make the rounds this afternoon," he said.

"Is it possible to ask one to stop?"

"If I see one," the policeman said. "They're rather busy these days."

I returned to my classroom and waited outside the door to tell the students there had been an emergency, that class was canceled. I tried not to think of Szifra downstairs, her broken neck, her sullied face. Her wide-open eyes.

I did not know what I would say when Jakub and Eli showed up, but fortunately, I never had to say anything, as the two boys never appeared, and after a while the hearse cart came, with the driver. I pointed him down the stairs, told him what he'd find, and took the long way home.

IT WOULD BE a lie to say I didn't know where they lived. I could have found them if I had wanted to. I knew where they were squatting. I could have found them.

But what would they have done without Szifra? They never could have gotten out of the ghetto without her. Would they have had the wit to lie their way past the guards? Would they have remembered their Catholic names? I mean, Eli, maybe, but dumb, sweet Jakub? How long until he stumbled right into the arms of the Gestapo? And then it would have been straight to the trains with them. And then what would have been the point, after all, of their sister's sacrifice?

If here, in the ghetto, one life was as worthless as any other's . . .

If here, in the ghetto, one boy was essentially the same as any other . . .

I showed Sala the kennkartes that night, in the kitchen, after everyone else was asleep. Silently, without looking at me, she found Filip's old whittling knife in my satchel and carefully removed the photos of Eli and Jakub from the identification pages. Then she took her boys' Jewish papers, removed their pictures, and attached them to where the pictures of Eli and Jakub had been.

Like magic, there they were, her sons: Jan and Piotr Krasinski, Roman Catholic boys from the Warszawa region of Poland. As free as water.

Still without looking at me, Sala put the Krasinski kennkartes in the pocket of her housedress and went to the room where she slept with her husband. I heard the creak of the bed as she got in. I heard Emil murmur as she rolled over. As for me, I could not move, staring down at the kitchen table at the tiny, dislocated photographs of Eli and Jakub Joseph, their faces looking back at me, as blank as the sky.

THIRTY-ONE

I, Adam Paskow, oldest son of a decorated sergeant in the Polish army, graduate of the University of Warsaw, teacher, brother, Jew, married government translator Kasia Agata Duda on a brilliant spring day in May 1930. This really did happen. Even though everything in my past has become hazy, my mind gone soft with hunger and fear, I know that this happened. I no longer have the photographs, but I know it happened.

I have memories.

Kasia wore a pale-blue dress that hit just below the knee and a matching hat with a sprig of lace at the front. Her father had given her a pearl necklace, the pearl surrounded in diamonds that glowed against her dress. It rested just below her throat. Meanwhile, I wore my nicest—my only—dark suit, and in my pocket I held her wedding band. I had asked her what kind of ring she wanted, and she said she didn't care, that whatever I wanted was what she wanted too. So I found a thin gold ring at the jeweler's on Mokotów Street and had our initials inscribed. It cost me five weeks' pay.

We met in front of the registry office at the courthouse and went inside together, holding hands. We were a modern couple, and we were happy to be doing things in this modern way. I told her she looked beautiful. She told me I looked handsome. In my parents' wedding photograph, my mother sat in a white dress while my father stood behind her, stiff and mustachioed, in his soldier's uniform. They looked young and happy and nervous. In Kasia's parents' wedding portrait, framed in the parlor of their house, her mother was draped in so much white lace you could not even see her face.

But here we were, in the bright new year of 1930, modern beyond reason, beyond white dresses, beyond religion, beyond even guests at the wedding ceremony. (We would use whoever the registrar's office provided to serve as our witness.) It was just the two of us, and afterward a luncheon (Kasia's father wanted to throw us a gala affair, but we resisted, knowing that such a party would be for him, not for us) at Honoratka, the old place on Miodowa Street. We had invited our parents to this, of course, her sisters, my brother, a few friends from university.

In truth I don't remember much of the ceremony itself, but I do remember small images and feelings from the morning. For instance, I remember the nerves. I remember being terrified for a moment when I couldn't find the ring in my pocket. I remember the kind face of the city registrar, and the mildly disapproving one of the witness he provided: "Paskow," he said, looking at my identity card. *Paskow.* I remember my hand shook a little when I signed the paperwork. I remember Kasia saying her new name to me—"Kasia Paskow"—and my feeling sorry that I had replaced her proud Polish name with my Jewish one. And then thinking, *Oh, who cares.*

I remember thinking Kasia was so lovely, but it's hard for me to draw a picture, in my mind, of exactly what her face looked like. Much of what she looked like in her youth has been swallowed by what she looked like seven years later, bruised and bandaged after the accident. When I try to remember her now, I see only small flashes. I wonder if Kasia would blame me for this, or if she would understand all that had happened in my life since she died and forgive me for what has happened to my memory.

But even after everything that's happened, sometimes I think: *How could she not be here?* And sometimes I blame her for not being here.

I think: *If she had lived through the invasion and the aftermath, she would have moved us once and for all to England.* She would have read the writing on the wall; she was far more sophisticated than I was. We would have joined the Home Army abroad, in London, would have worked for Polish liberation on the Allied side of the line. She would have done it out of righteousness and a sense of adventure. I would have done it because she had convinced me to.

But without her, I lost my radar, my map to the world. I lost my ability to see what was what, to see what might happen next. In fact, I had entirely given up and let her father shuffle me off to this place, this ghetto, where I lived like an animal, scrounging enough day to day, not thinking when it didn't do me any good to think.

What would she think now of the man she had married? I wanted to argue with her: *If you hadn't left me, this never would have happened.* In my mind, in my softened mind, I spent too much time arguing with a dead woman.

At the wedding lunch in the garden of Honoratka, my mother and brother sat at one table, pinch-faced and silent. My mother, who ostentatiously never drank alcohol, kept stirring more sugar into her cup of tea. My brother drank glass after glass of vodka and grew more and more morose; when it was time for someone from my family to give a speech, he stood, raised his glass, said "Congratulations to the mighty couple!" and slumped back down to his chair. My mother and brother behaved this way because they were upset, not that I was marrying a Pole, but that I was marrying someone so above my rank that they could no longer treat me miserably and hope that I would care. What would I need them for anymore, now that I was married to Kasia? What would it matter if my mother hectored me or bemoaned my small salary or implored me to write letters to the government on behalf of a war veteran's wife and then yelled at me when the letters did not result in whatever result she'd been hoping for? What would it matter now if my brother got drunk at a tavern and came home to tell me that I wasn't too good for him no matter how many degrees I earned?

Because I *was* too good for him now, clearly. Look who had agreed to marry me.

Kasia's father's speech was long-winded and lavished inordinate praise upon me, the intellectual, the son of a patriot, the care with which I took of his daughter, and the purpose of the speech was to convince everyone in attendance that just because I was a Jew didn't mean I wasn't also a decent enough kind of guy. Kasia nudged me in the side, and we both laughed and applauded and kissed when Henryk shouted, "Twoje zdrowie!"

As we were about to be sent off in a car full of wedding gifts, Kasia's mother pulled me to the side. It was the first time she had ever spoken to me without anyone else around, and I imagined that the revelry of the afternoon might have softened her stance toward me, might have even caused her to embrace me. But then I saw the withering look on her face.

"I curse you for doing this to us," she said, in a crone's whisper. "I will be pleasant to you, because my husband has asked me to be pleasant, but I want you to know that I curse you in my heart."

I was a little bit drunk and very happy, and it took all I had not to laugh.

She shook a finger in my eye, the crone, and turned away.

Kasia and I got in the car, surrounded by wedding presents: pewter plates and china bowls and picture frames and envelopes full of zloty. We went straight to our new flat in Mokotów, and I didn't tell her what her mother had said. Not because I thought it would upset her—she knew her mother was a spoiled old crone—but because quickly we got up to other business, and soon enough I had forgotten that the conversation ever happened. A curse! She cursed me! Pani Duda, like a figure from an old German fairy tale, spreading around curses, brewing up witchy potions, eating children for breakfast.

My mind, as I said, has gone soft from hunger and fear, and it is possible that I am only imagining that Pani Duda cursed me, but I think this memory is right, I think this really happened. I am almost certain it happened. And the more I ponder it, I think it's possible that Pani Duda was a crone of such enormous and terrible power that, in cursing me, she accidentally ended up cursing her own family, her own country, her youngest daughter—all to die awful deaths. Henryk Duda was married to a terrible sorceress. Perhaps he knew it. Perhaps it was from her that his power really stemmed. Is such a thing possible? Had she bewitched Henryk as well?

Of all of them, I was the only one left alive.

Perhaps that, in the end, was the true nature of the curse.

THIRTY-TWO

Thursday afternoon, I dragged myself to the corner to stand in honor of my foolish hope. And it was that very foolish hope that kept me standing and waiting for what felt like eight million years. I had arrived at the corner at four in the afternoon; the deportations for the day had concluded, and slowly life was returning to the streets: trading Jews, smuggling children, begging mothers holding their babies. As with everything in the ghetto, everything in our lives, we had become used to our new daily horror, and didn't let even the deportations of our friends and neighbors keep us from the rituals of our ridiculous days. Therefore I watched, in amazement, as a child in a doorway across the street from me, no more than seven years old, traded a potato for a clean pair of men's socks, for paper and pencils, for a bag of bright red candy.

I had learned to tell the time by the activity in the streets: four o'clock became four thirty became five. I stood there, even though I knew he wouldn't come; standing and feeling like an idiot was my punishment for having given up Kasia's necklace so foolishly.

"You! Why are you loitering?" And I'd pretend to look busy, tying a shoe, sneezing. Every so often, I had to duck into a storefront to keep from catching the attention of a passing guard, and around six thirty a gendarme approached me, demanded my papers, slapped me on the cheek when I didn't present them fast enough. The slap on the cheek felt appropriate; in my addled state, I was happy to be a martyr.

"You work?" he asked, in German.

"At the Aid Society," I responded, also in German, which was a trick, I knew, for escaping punishment. (Germans looked slightly more kindly on those of us who could speak their language.) The gendarme nodded at me curtly, slapped me again, and walked away.

And out of the corner of my eye, in his usual spot by the gate at Twarda Street, I saw him. Nowak. I walked directly to him, almost tripped, chilly with panic and a sudden and unwelcome sense of hope. He met me under the archway near the old haberdasher.

"You let him hit you?" Fat Nowak was jiggling with laughter.

"Where have you been? You said to meet you four o'clock."

"Admit it," Nowak said, still laughing. "You didn't expect me to come at all."

"Do you have the papers?" I hated the squeaky desperation in my voice, but there was nothing I could do about it.

"You never thought you'd see me again," Nowak said, still laughing. If he hadn't had my life in his hands, I would have put my hands around his fat neck and throttled him.

"Do you have the papers.?

"Do I?"

"Nowak, if you don't, please just tell me and let me go."

"That was a very valuable necklace," Nowak said. "It was smart of you not to give that necklace to Duda. I doubt he would have gotten you papers with it," he said, and now my hope and fear turned into a sort of nauseated miasma that surrounded me, the air around me. Whatever had happened to my necklace it had not magically turned into a Polish kennkarte. "Especially because he probably could have used it to stave off the Germans for another week. Did you know it came from La France Diamante?"

I had never heard of La France Diamante. "Nowak. Please. Just tell me."

He was still chuckling, but as he chuckled he put his hand on the holster of the gun that hung low on his belt.

He was going to kill me.

Jesus. What an idiot I was. I deserved this death for being an idiot. I was too ashamed even to run.

But then he reached underneath the holster and removed, from some secret compartment there, an envelope, tightly rolled. "Do not open this until you get somewhere safe." All trace of joviality was gone from his voice.

"What?"

"Put this in your bag. Do it now." I nodded and trembled as I put the envelope inside my satchel.

"You must leave on Saturday morning, eight thirty, through the Chłodna Street gate. Head directly for the chemistry building at the University of Warsaw, and ask the woman behind the desk for the assistant secretary."

"Who is the assistant secretary?"

"If you ever want to leave this place, you must go Saturday."

"But what is . . . Are you sure?"

And then his face changed, his voice changed completely. "Jew! Get home, and stop pestering me! Go! I have no news of your children. Stop asking!"

And then he turned around quickly and returned to his post by the gate, his face set in a bureaucratic frown.

"But what do I . . . ?"

He did not look at me.

I stood there for just a moment, looking at his fat figure, his hands resting on his belt. It occurred to me that perhaps I had been saved. I hurried away.

I made it to the apartment with my heart still racing, the miasma of nausea running through my veins. Emil was sitting in the kitchen, in his undershirt, his head in his hands. He did not look up at me; I hurried past him and into my small maid's room, and opened the tightly rolled envelope.

A gray, slightly worn-looking Polish kennkarte for a man named Adam Pasternak, age forty-three, my height, my weight, from Warsaw. Light-brown hair, blue eyes. Roman Catholic.

Ten tram tickets.

Ten ration cards.

Eight hundred zloty in crisp hundred-zloty notes.

Leave Saturday morning, eight thirty. Head directly for the chemistry building at the University of Warsaw. Ask for the assistant secretary.

Who on earth was the assistant secretary? Did it matter? I had no currency left but these eight hundred zloty and trust.

I sat on my bed, now empty of everything but a bare pillow and a single stained sheet. I had no more books, no more of Kasia's things. I had nothing left in the world, really. No plans on how I could continue to survive here.

I hid the papers under the floorboards and just sat for a while. Then I went out to the kitchen to see if there was any food, or even some water. Emil was still sitting there in much the same position that he'd been before. The strange rash now covered his face; his eyelids were red and puffy, and his cheeks were a mottled purple under his scraggly beard. Behind him, Sala was finely chopping a boiled potato.

"We have another potato if you're hungry," she said. "The boys traded for some this morning."

"What did they trade?" I asked. My voice sounded creaky.

"They didn't tell me," she said, and sat down next to her husband, put her hand on his arm, and slid the potato, on a plate, in front of where he sat. "You have to eat," she said to him. And it was suddenly clear to me that we were now on different sides of the only divide there ever was: those who would survive and those who would not.

"I can get them out," I said.

She raised her face from the table. I saw that she had the rash too, but more faintly—what was it? Small raised reddish bumps on her cheeks. The rest of her skin looked dry and white. She blinked at me.

"I have papers," I said. "A Polish kennkarte."

She bit her lip. Emil, senselessly, picked at his potato. "They have taken everything from us," he said. "They have taken everything, everything."

"Emil, hush," Sala said. "Is it authentic?"

"Yes," I said. "I have a bit of money now too, and a place to go."

"For the necklace?"

I nodded. "The guard turned out to be . . . noble, I suppose. He might be part of the Home Army. I don't know. I didn't have time to ask him questions."

"Can he get more papers?"

"For his safety," I said, telling her the truth, "I doubt he'll ever talk to me again."

Again, she bit her thin chapped lip. The lone white potato sat on the cracked white plate. Emil took a chunk of it with his finger and placed it in his mouth, chewed widely, with his mouth open.

"You'll take the boys," Sala said.

"Yes."

"When?"

"Saturday," I said. "Through the Chłodna Street gate, at eight thirty in the morning."

"That's the day after tomorrow," she said.

"Yes."

She pinched the bridge of her nose. "Where will you go?"

"There's someone, or maybe a group, I guess, at the University of Warsaw," I said. "They're expecting me."

"You'll take them," she said. "You'll take the boys."

"I will."

"You'll keep my boys safe," she said.

"Yes."

"You swear it," she said.

How could I swear to such a thing? "I do," I said.

"Swear with everything you have."

"I do," I said. "I swear with everything I have."

She looked away from me, out the window.

Emil was gazing down at his chunks of potato, and I did not know if he was listening to us, if he had lost his ability to hear, if it mattered anymore.

"Come with us," I said to Sala.

"I can't," she said. "I just . . . It would put everyone in danger. And my husband is here. I don't look Catholic, even a little. And I don't have papers. If I went . . . I don't know what would happen."

"Please," I said.

Emil suddenly spoke up, his voice hoarse. "She's my wife," he said. "She will not go with you. She's my *wife*."

"Emil . . . ," Sala said.

"She is my wife," he said, now looking at me with his bloodshot eyes.

Sala buried her face in his neck. "Honey, please. Please. I would never leave you."

I could spend my eight hundred zloty on forged papers for her—it was possibly enough money. I could get her out of here. I could rescue her. I could take her away with me. Eight hundred zloty was enough to get us somewhere.

He turned to her, put her thin face between his palms. "Don't go. Please, Sala. They've taken everything, everything. Please. They cannot take you too."

"I won't leave you," she said, and she kissed his forehead. "I won't leave you. I promise."

"Don't leave me," he said.

"I promise, my love. I won't."

And then, unbearably, this big man, this counselor to the Judenrat, my lover's husband, started to cry. Sala kept her lips pressed to his forehead. She did not look at me as I left the room.

THIRTY-THREE

When I say that I had nothing, I don't mean that I truly had nothing, only that I had nothing left that could conceivably have any value. Nothing that anybody would trade for. But I still had a few of my brother's old postcards, with his address written in his sloppy hand in the corner. A town called Reḥovot. I had never heard of it before, but I imagined it was big enough to be found, should I make it to Palestine.

What else did I have? My satchel. A faded watercolor on my wall. One spare pair of underwear, one spare pair of socks. I spent a few of my precious zloty on a new pair of shoes so that I wouldn't look quite so sorrowful on the outside; I didn't want to look pathetic enough to draw suspicion. The shoes were too big and I felt a bit like a clown, but their soles were intact and I could walk in them more or less comfortably.

I paid the barber five zloty for a haircut and a shave.

I went to the street where Charlotte and Roman lived and asked around until I found their apartment. The hallways smelled like burned oil and human filth, but the apartment, when I got to the top of the stairs, seemed all right. Their mother was a stout woman who looked so much like Mariam Lescovec that when I saw her I felt a tiny bit faint.

She took a look at me. "You're the English teacher?"

"I am," I said. "How did you know?"

"My children talk about you all the time," she said, in mellifluous Yiddish. "They like you very much." She smiled a gap-toothed smile, wiped her hands on her apron. The apartment smelled like soup—soup with maybe some meat in it—and I thought perhaps these children would be okay. The foyer where we stood had framed photographs hanging on the walls, and the murmur, in the background, of a radio. I remembered that this woman had already lost one child to South Africa and the arms of a Polish man. But she smiled generously and betrayed no loss.

"Unfortunately, the children aren't here now. They're out somewhere running around. They'll be back by sundown." She looked at me. "Do you have somewhere to go for Shabbos, Pan . . . I'm sorry, you know what? I don't know your name. In our house, we just call you the English teacher."

"I'm Adam Paskow."

She smiled again. "Do you have somewhere to go for Shabbos, Pan Paskow?"

"Oh, that's all right. I'm just here to—"

"Really, you should stay. We have food. Enough to share." And for maybe half a second, I wanted to. I wanted to stay right there, even though it wouldn't be safe forever, but at least it would be safe that night. I wanted to say the blessings I barely knew and speak Yiddish and be with my students and their families and their history and future.

(This is what they meant when they called it Oneg Shabbat. A feeling of comfort and joy that I knew I would find very hard to replace. That perhaps I would never replace.)

I could not stay. "That's very kind of you, Pani Grosstayn. I'm grateful for the invitation, but unfortunately I must decline. I'm just here to let your children know that, sadly, I will no longer be conducting English lessons."

"Oh dear," she said. "Are you sure?"

"Sadly."

"They'll be sorry to hear that. They really enjoyed learning all the poetry. What was the last one? 'The Owl and the Pussy-Cat'?" In Yiddish: "Di Aul aun di Pusikat."

"Yes," I said.

"Oh, they liked that one very much. They kept laughing about it when they got home."

"I'm glad," I said. I was. "Please tell them . . . Please tell them it was an honor to meet them. Please tell them I hope they continue to study. They're very bright, you know. I think they have wonderful futures ahead of them."

She looked at me critically. I felt myself grow less steady under her gaze.

"Pan Paskow, forgive me for speaking out of turn, but I hope you're not planning to go on a train. Please tell me . . . You know those trains aren't really for resettlement."

"I know."

"No matter what," she said, maternal warning in her voice. "Don't get on one of those trains."

"I know, Pani Grosstayn. I know."

She nodded at me, wiped her hands on her apron again. "Okay, then. Well . . ."

"Well . . ." And we stood there, smiling dumbly at each other.

"You will be missed."

"Thank you, Pani Grosstayn."

"God bless you," she said, "and good Shabbos." And I hurried back down the apartment building's stairs.

AT HOME, SALA had her boys lined up by the sink. "Look what I found," she said to me as I walked in the door. It was a box of hair dye. Blond.

Which, I had been told, one could not find for love or money anywhere in the ghetto. She was mixing the dye in a bowl on the table.

She wasn't wearing her wedding ring. It was the first time I had ever seen her without it. And there was a small book on the table, a tiny togbuch, black leather. Sala saw me looking at it. "It's from Emil's mother," she said. "It's a history of the family. The births and deaths, more or less. I was reading them the names."

"Ah."

"Pan Paskow, what's going on?" Rafel had a suspicious look on his face: Hair dye? Family names?

"'Beila Batan,'" Arkady said. "She was our great-grandmother. 'Natalia Wiskoff. Avraham Wiskoff. Feige Levin.'" He leaned forward to flip through the book.

"Be still," said Sala. "The box says twenty minutes."

"You don't want them to look too different from the photographs on the kennkartes," I said.

"'Ettel Blon,'" Rafel said. "See? I can still read Yiddish. 'Lana Murmisky.'"

"They won't," she said. "This is just to make sure they look as—as good as possible, so nobody even checks them."

Rafel put down the togbuch. He and Arkady looked at me curiously. "What kennkartes, Pan Paskow?"

Sala met my eyes.

"You'll need to discuss this with your mother," I said, and went to the maid's room and closed the door. But through the flimsy door, I heard Sala speaking in low tones to the boys, and I heard the boys, one of them, start to cry, and say no, and Sala firmly say yes, and then she changed from Polish to Yiddish and told them that as soon as the war was over, they would meet again in Saska Kępa. And that was it. End of discussion. They were going with me.

And one of the boys said, "But what if the war doesn't ever end?"

And Sala said, "All wars end."

"But what if the Germans win?"

"Oh, no," she said. "That's not what the English newspapers are saying. The *Times* and the *Herald*. Everyone thinks the war will be over quite soon."

"So then why can't we stay with you?"

"We'll find each other again soon, meyn neshama. This is just for now."

I put my head under the pillow then to keep from listening anymore.

Later, that night, they sat down together as a family for a Shabbos meal. I was hungry. I had some bread in the kitchen, and I wanted to get it. But I did not dare go out and interrupt them; instead, I stayed in my room and listened to them pray together, as a family, the Shabbos prayers.

THIRTY-FOUR

═══════════

S aturday at dawn, I left the apartment and went to Ringelblum's building. I had my white notebook with me, and a letter thanking Ringelblum for the chance to be part of this work. I rang the bell, ashamed to be bothering the family so early in the morning, and on Shabbos, no less, but when Yehudit answered she was already dressed and her hair was smartly arranged. She invited me in, but I told her I couldn't stay.

I gave her the notebook in its entirety, minus one interview of about seven pages.

"You are resigning from the project?" she asked.

"I am leaving the ghetto," I said. It felt shocking to say it out loud.

She raised an elegant eyebrow. "Ah," she said.

My throat was pulsing with nerves for what the day would bring. "Please tell Pan Ringelblum that it was a great honor to be part of Oneg Shabbat, and that I wish him and the rest of the archivists well. I hope that . . . I hope that history will take note of what he has done for us."

She smiled gently. "You were an intrinsic part of it, Pan Paskow."

"Oh, I don't know about that. But I'm grateful I had the chance. Let him know I'm grateful."

"I will do that, Pan Paskow," she said.

"I have great faith that this project will tell the world our history. Will tell the world our story. It will not have been in vain."

"That is the prayer, Pan Paskow."

"I don't know how he found me, but I'm very glad he did."

She smiled. "Emanuel knew who you were from the beginning," she said. "He knew you were a wonderful English teacher, and very brave."

"Oh." I laughed. "Really, I'm not so sure."

"You're leaving, aren't you?"

"I'm a nervous wreck."

"Well, that's natural. But still, you're leaving."

"Yes," I said. "I suppose I am."

What else was there to say? There was nothing. Still, it was hard to move and say goodbye.

"Good luck, Pan Paskow."

I had been dismissed. I nodded at her and walked back to the apartment, where the boys were waiting, dressed in their neatest clothes, looking infinitely younger and more scared than I had ever seen them.

They were my boys now. Jan and Piotr. My boys. My responsibility. My promise to their mother.

"All right," Sala said. "Is everyone ready?"

Arkady and Rafel had nothing with them. I had their kennkartes in my satchel. Whatever else they needed we would purchase on the outside.

"Remember," Sala said, as we stood together in the doorway. "This is your uncle. Your father is fighting in the war. Your mother is ill at home. So you are staying with him."

Ordinarily, this might have been met with an eye roll and *We know*, but instead Arkady said, meekly, "Yes, Eema." Rafel said nothing.

"Tell me your names," Sala said.

"Jan Krasinski," said Rafel.

"Piotr Krasinski," said Arkady.

"Tell me again," she said, and the boys repeated their new names.

There was nothing else to do. I wanted to tell Sala goodbye, and that I loved her, and that I would miss her, but she knew all that already and it was all beside the point.

"Come here," she said, and drew her boys to her, and said to them, with her hands on their heads: "Baruch atah Adonai elohanu melech haolam, ha tov v'ha meiteev."

Blessed is the Lord, king of the Universe, who is good and who brings us good.

Then she drew them into her and whispered something I could not hear. And then she pushed them away.

"Go now," she said. "Go."

"Sala . . ."

"Go," she said, her eyes spilling over, her hands shaking. "Please. You promised me you'd keep them safe. You swore it. Keep your promise to me."

"I love you, Sala."

"If you love me, keep your promise."

"I will," I said.

"Go," she said. "Go now."

So we did, walking down the five flights to the street, stronger than Lot's wife: we never once looked back. The boys and I crossed the horrid ghetto streets, full of the usual begging and wailing—the deportations were beginning for the day—dodging gendarmes and familiar faces.

At eight thirty, I presented us and our kennkartes at the Chłodna Street gate. The Polish guard looked me up and down. "Pasternak?" he said.

My heart was beating so fast I thought that I might die right there, but I managed a loud-enough "Yes."

"And what is your name?" he said, turning to Rafel.

With the frightening stare I'd seen once before, frighteningly still and changeless: "Jan Krasinski."

The guard relaxed. "Very good," he said. He'd been expecting us. He said, "Go ahead." And then, as though it were nothing, as though it were any other day and we were any other people, he opened the Chłodna Street gate.

ONE DAY, I would give these boys the words of their mother, the remembrances of their mother. How she gave birth to each of them in their old house in Saska Kępa under the light of the all-seeing moon, and how she felt that each of them gave her purpose in life. How she loved her children so much that, like Moses's mother, she gave them away.

But for now, they were mine: my charge, my responsibility, my promise to Sala, a woman I had loved. I held their hands as we walked through the Chłodna Street gate. It was strange and immediate how the air outside the ghetto was cooler, cleaner. The noises on the street were of automobile traffic and bicycle bells. The boys' faces were impassive and still.

Together, we crossed the street toward the spires of Saint Augustine's Church, where the tram stop was.

"We'll never see them again," Rafel said, but he said it to himself, and there was no need to answer. I didn't answer. "We'll never see any of them again."

Neither Arkady nor I said anything. We didn't look at one another. Instead, we sat down on the bench across from the Chłodna Street gate, new people, born anew, the ghetto walls blocking our old lives from view, as we waited, invisibly, for the tram.

AFTERWORD AND ACKNOWLEDGMENTS

While this book is fiction, it is based on historical events, and real people make cameo appearances. Today, one can visit the Oneg Shabbat Archive at 3/5 Tłomackie Street in Warsaw and see actual diary entries, sketches, and other paraphernalia collected by the archivists. The Archive also displays one of the giant milk cans in which the trove was buried before the Warsaw Ghetto's destruction in 1943.

I would not have learned about the Oneg Shabbat Archive had my sister, Jessie Kennedy, not taken me to Poland in the summer of 2019. I am thankful to her and to all the Kennedys and Grodsteins for their constant encouragement, good humor, and willingness to schlep. And of course I am grateful to Ben, Nate, and Penny, the best company a writer could ask for at home or abroad.

Aleksandra Makuch and the Taube Center for Jewish Life and Learning, based in Warsaw, were wonderful sources of information as I wrote this book. The Rutgers Research Council provided funding for me to continue my work.

Samuel Kassow's *Who Will Write Our History?*, Yehuda Bauer's *Rethinking the Holocaust*, and Emanuel Ringelblum's own journal, *Notes from the Warsaw Ghetto*, offered crucial context about the destruction of Polish Jewry during World War II.

Kathy Pories edited this manuscript with her usual mix of brilliance and cheer. I cannot believe how lucky I am to work with her and with all the wonderful people at Algonquin. And I can't imagine where or who I'd be without Julie Barer, an incredible agent and an even better friend.

My great-grandparents fled Warsaw approximately twenty years before the war. In all likelihood, I would not be here had they stayed. I wrote this book humbled by that knowledge and by the desire to honor those who remained, who died, and who left us their words. Although separated by language, continents, and decades, I did my best to hear, and to share, what they could not shout out to the world.